Shades
of Blue

Books by Bill Moody

Solo Hand
Death of a Tenor Man
Sound of the Trumpet
Bird Lives!
Looking for Chet Baker

*For Richard Gigi —
all the best!*

Shades
of Blue

Bill Moody

Bill Moody

Poisoned Pen Press

Copyright © 2008 by Bill Moody

First Edition 2008

10 9 8 7 6 5 4 3 2 1

Library of Congress Catalog Card Number: 2007935721

ISBN: 978-1-59058-485-9 Hardcover

Poisoned Pen Press
6962 E. First Ave., Ste. 103
Scottsdale, AZ 85251
www.poisonedpenpress.com
info@poisonedpenpress.com

Printed in the United States of America

*For Sarah and
Teresa Moody 1958-2005*

Introduction

Nobody is really listening, so nobody notices the drummer misses my count for the tempo on the opening tune. For a few seconds, "On Green Dolphin Street" is a traffic jam as he and the bass player—I'd only met them both a half hour before the gig—scramble for the beat, but by the second eight bars, we settle into a loping, relaxed two beat rhythm that feels comfortable and starts to swing.

We're not quite wallpaper, as musicians sometimes call these gigs, but, up here, we're kind of the no name trio, providing background jazz for the party. For our trouble, we get to partake of the buffet, some Napa Valley red wine, and two hundred bucks each.

The loud conversation surrounding us is distraction enough, but when I glance back over my shoulder at the drummer, I see there's more. He shrugs and sheepishly smiles, nodding toward a woman standing close by in a low cut black dress that clings to her body like the material is wet. One arm across her body, cradling her elbow, she holds a long stemmed glass of red wine. She takes a sip, tilts her head slightly, smiles at me briefly, then glides away and up a few steps where there is a lavish, hot buffet being served by waiters in white shirts and maroon bow ties.

The host for this gathering is a multimillionaire who designed guitar amplifiers that are used and endorsed by every major rock star and band on the scene. This is his annual party for a hundred or so of his close friends, so I was told when I got the call. His home is a Tuscany style villa on top of a mountain, about an hour north of the Golden Gate Bridge.

After a fifteen-minute climb up the twisting mountain road, I had to punch in a code for the electronic gate, drive another mile or so, and park alongside of the house by a large man-made pond with huge lily pads floating and the occasional fish breaking the still water's surface. The small parking lot was already crowded with Mercedes sedans, BMWs, expensive SUVs, and even a couple of sports cars that must have been in the hundred-thousand-dollar range.

I get a brief tour, courtesy of the bass player, Terry, who's done this gig a number of times. I lose count of the many rooms and levels. The indoor swimming pool, the game room, the expansive office, equipped with all the latest computer gear, and of course, the grand piano in the ballroom sized living room I'm playing now. Yes, rock does pay better than jazz.

I've landed here virtually by accident. The bassist, Terry Henry, a wiry guy with an RAF mustache and an infectious laugh, is a friend of a friend who'd called and offered me the gig when he heard I'd moved to northern California. Why not, I thought. I'm a long way from Amsterdam, or Los Angeles for that matter, and getting into the Bay Area scene means taking gigs as they come. That's how it happens when you're starting over in a new town.

We play for about an hour, then Terry calls a break. We sample the food out on an enclosed patio area, then wander outside for a smoke.

"So, Evan, what do you think?" Terry asks me. He paces around as he talks. He has a kind of perpetual squint and smile, like he knows something I don't. "Like to do some more of these gigs? I can set you up."

"Tell him about the deli," the drummer chimes in.

"Yeah, man," Terry says. "Every Sunday night. House trio, guys come by and sit in. Very cool scene."

"A deli?"

I hesitate for a moment, gazing out over the pond. The perimeter is lit by evenly spaced small lamps, and a sandy path veers off and seems to disappear into the woods. I've played a lot of gigs in a lot of strange places but never in a delicatessen. Well, why not. Andie was on assignment and I am, as they say, available.

"Okay, I'll give it a shot. It's a jam session kind of thing huh?"

"Yeah, been happening for a few years now. Good exposure. Might catch some gigs out of it. It's in Crockett, near Vallejo."

I sigh. Vallejo is in the East Bay and must be more than an hour and a half drive from Monte Rio and my new digs. I'm barely moved in but I've gotten to like it so well I hate to leave the area. Still, if I'm going to work, get established here, I have to be out there and show my face.

"Okay, you're on," I tell Terry.

"Cool," Terry says. "First exit over the Carquinez Bridge on I-80, then turn left and go down the hill. You can't miss it." He looks around, sees our host peeking outside, waving his flute at us. Terry nods to him. "Guess we're on."

The host, since it's his house, gets a chance to dig out his flute and join us on a couple of tunes. He may have made his money in rock but he's a jazzer at heart. More people gather around as he joins us and finds his way through a few standards. But he tires quickly, shrugs at his rustiness, and lays his flute on the piano before retiring to host duties and mingles with his guests.

We play two more sets. It's all very low key, no pressure, and the evening goes by quickly. A few people actually do listen, especially a tall thirty-something guy in a blazer and slacks with dirty blonde unkempt hair, who I see now is with the girl in the black dress I'd seen earlier. As the party starts to break up, he comes over.

"Evan Horne, right?" He has a friendly smile and puts out his hand. "Cameron Brody. I saw you a couple of years ago at the Jazz Bakery in Los Angeles. You were subbing for Monty Alexander."

"Yeah, that's right. I hope it was a good night." We shake hands.

"Oh definitely." He pauses for a moment, not quite knowing how to say what I know is on his mind. "So, what are you doing here?"

"I've been in Europe, decided to give the Bay Area a try. You live around here yourself?"

"Yeah, Berkeley. I do some work for Fantasy, Concord Records." I see the girl tug lightly on his arm. "Look, I have to go but let me know where you're playing." He reaches in his coat pocket and hands me a card. It has his number and e-mail address and ASCAP Representative printed in the center of the card. "Good to see you again," he says, and walks off with the girl.

"Sure, you too."

On the long drive home, I'm pleasantly tired with a little of that wired, after-gig feeling, and still enjoying the newness of my car. I'd found it parked alongside River Road with a For Sale sign, an almost new VW Beetle with all the extras—sun roof, CD player, five speed. Some guy had bought it for his wife and she'd decided she didn't like shifting, so it was a good deal for me.

Guerneville is pretty much shut down as I cruise through and continue on to Monte Rio. I cross the small bridge over the Russian River and turn onto Bohemian Avenue, pull in and park in the driveway.

My place is on the top floor of a duplex with the front door at ground level. Walking up the short flight of stairs into the entry hall still gives me a charge as much as it did the first day I looked at the place. As soon as I looked down that hallway and saw the wood floors, wood paneling waist high, and glass all around, even a couple of sky lights in the high ceiling, I knew I was home.

The laconic owner leaned against the wall, checked his watch, and studied me as I looked around. "At least you're on time," he said.

There was a small kitchenette, a wood stove, built in bookcase on one wall, fairly large bedroom, and a deck off the living room.

"Loft up there." The owner pointed to a door off the living room. Small but again surrounded by glass. I slid one of the windows open a few inches and smelled the redwoods. One was so close I could almost touch it. I wondered how hard it would be to get a piano up there.

Less than two blocks from the Russian River and virtually around the corner from Margo Highland, who was now back in Amsterdam with Fletcher Paige, the expatriate saxophonist who I'd done a solid three months with in Amsterdam at the Baby Grand. Now it was Monte Rio. Peaceful, quiet, probably two hours from San Francisco, but I like to drive.

By then I was itchy to see Andie more and get back home. Fletcher had some jazz festival commitments so it was time to part and go our separate ways, but we both knew there'd be other times, other gigs. Being here would help a lot.

Coming back down from the loft, I smiled at the owner. "Really nice," I said, and stuck out my hand. "Evan Horne."

"Hayden Clay," he said, scowling. "What do you do?"

He'd been like that since I'd arrived, like he was annoyed that he even had to show the place and didn't care whether I liked it or not.

"Musician. I play piano." I waited but his expression didn't change a bit. "What do you need from me? References, deposit? I'd like to take this. I really like it." I got the feeling he was just going through the motions.

"What I need is somebody that's not a deadbeat. Somebody who doesn't bounce checks and pays the rent on time."

I nodded, thinking I understood. People don't always like to rent to musicians. "Had some trouble?"

"Don't get me started," Clay said. "I had to evict the last tenant. I've been in court six months trying to get my money and this place has been vacant ever since." He frowned at me. "What makes you different?"

I spent the next fifteen minutes making a case for myself as the ideal tenant. I was prepared to fill out a long application, which seemed to be the custom up here, and so different than L.A.

Clay paced around, listening to me, nodding, mulling it over. Finally, he turned and said, "I go on my gut mostly. I guess I have to take a chance on somebody." He looked me right in the eye. "Tell you what. Give me five hundred to hold it and it's yours."

Ten minutes later we'd negotiated the rent and security deposit. I made out a check, and Hayden Clay left me to look around on my own. "Soon as this clears I give you the keys," he said. "Close the door on your way out. It locks by itself." Halfway down the stairs he stopped and turned. "What kind of music you play?"

"Jazz."

"Dixieland or like that Bird guy stuff, Charlie Parker."

"Bird." He smiled then and so did I.

Now, most of my stuff is in and I'd managed to get four guys to help me get a small spinet piano I'd found in Santa Rosa up the stairs to the loft. I've only been here two weeks but it feels like I've always lived here.

I turn on some lights, grab a Henry Weinhard from the fridge, and step out on the deck, Miles playing "So What," from *Kind of Blue* with the volume way down.

As always, I'd initiated the place with it. I love the music and no matter how many times I play it, I hear something new. Miles, Coltrane, Cannonball, Bill Evans, Paul Chambers, and Jimmy Cobb. But there was something else about *Kind of Blue*, as if I'd heard this music before I'd even become aware of it. It had sounded familiar the first time I'd listened.

I smoke a cigarette and listen to a light rain starting to pepper the windows and just before I turn in, the phone rings.

"Hello."

"Hi Babe, what's doing in the hinterlands?"

"Hey, Andie. You back already?"

"Yeah, just got in, on a late flight. Want to venture into the big city tomorrow or must I trek out to the boondocks? I'm off I think."

So far, Andie Lawrence and I were keeping our own places. She'd balked at me renting in Monte Rio but hadn't pushed it. "I'll come in. Got some place to go. Might be a connection for a gig."

"Good, I don't feel like that long drive. Oh, there's a couple of phone messages for you. Roy Haynes and some lawyer in L.A., Roger Scott. You want the numbers?"

"Roy Haynes the drummer?"

"He didn't say what instrument," Andie says. "I guess he figured you'd know."

"Yeah, I know." I didn't know of any other Roy Haynes.

The lawyer was equally puzzling. I had nothing legal pending as far as I knew, and I wondered how he'd tracked me down. Since I'd come back from Europe, I hadn't talked to anybody but Danny Cooper and a couple of musicians. "No, I'll get the numbers when I come in. He won't be in his office tomorrow. Anything else on the message?"

"No, just his number and said it's urgent."

Urgent. That part I don't like. "Okay, I'll be in before noon."

"Don't you want to know what I'm wearing?" Her voice takes on a low throaty sound.

"You're awfully naughty for an FBI agent."

"You should know."

"That I do. Get some sleep. Let me think about it."

"I'll be here."

Before I turn in, I go through my CDs, find the one I want, and put it in the player. Chick Corea, Miroslav Vitous—and Roy Haynes, who must be in his seventies now. He'd played with everybody from Bird to the Brecker Brothers and from what I've read, is playing better than ever.

I listen to the trio do a tune called "Matrix," something by Corea, thinking how unlikely it was that Roy Haynes had called me.

I also can't resist looking up matrix. Webster's calls it, "an impression from which a large number of phonograph records can be duplicated."

Chapter One

"Hey, sleepy," Andie says, as I wander out of the bedroom. She's at a small desk working on her laptop computer, legs crossed, still in her short robe.

"Catching some bad guys?"

"Not really, just answering some e-mails."

I nod, pour myself some coffee, and look at the messages again Andie had written down for me. Roy Haynes and a lawyer. No contest on who to call first.

"Hang on a sec," Andie says. "Let me shut down here so you can call."

"Take your time." I take my coffee and a cigarette out on the small balcony. The sun feels warm on my face as I sit down in one of the chairs and think about last night.

Terry had been right. Niki's Deli was a good scene, kind of like Cheers with jazz. Apparently, there was a group of regulars who came every week and everybody did seem to know everybody's name.

During the first set, Andie and I had one of the best sandwiches either of us had ever had while we listened to Terry play piano. He was even better on piano than on bass. I sat in during the second set while Terry played trumpet—his first instrument he told me—and later, a couple of other horn players had come by to play and both had taken my number. Let the games begin. I knew that Niki's Deli would be a regular haunt for me.

Andie joins me outside with the phone and the messages. "Here you go, babe," she says, handing me the phone. I take a deep breath and dial the first number.

"Blue Jay Productions," a woman's voice says.

"Hi, this is Evan Horne, returning your call. The message was from Roy Haynes."

"Oh yes, just a minute," the woman says. "I'll connect you." While I wait, I glance at Andie. She's leaning over the rail of the balcony and the robe is creeping up her thighs and...

"Evan Horne. Larry Klein. I manage Roy's bookings. Thanks for getting back. I'm sure you know all about Roy."

"Of course."

"Well, he's planning a new project, a recording with several different pianists and bass players, kind of his favorites over the years, some he's worked with, some he just likes."

"Sounds like an interesting idea," I say. I light a cigarette and start to get excited. Klein has a loud, booming voice and talks fast.

"Oh yeah," Klein says. "Killer concept given Roy's history. Anyway, your name came up." He pauses for a moment. "Roy would like you to do one, maybe two of the tracks."

I hold the phone for a moment, too stunned to speak. "You're kidding."

"I never kid," Klein says. "Got a pen?"

I motion to Andie for a pen and paper. "Yeah."

Klein gives me a New York number. "That's Roy's home phone. He'd like you to call him and let him know you'd be interested."

As I scribble down the number, my mind is swirling. "When should I call?"

"Sooner the better. He's done two tracks already. Benny Green, and Chick, of course. Herbie Hancock is scheduled next."

Of course. "Okay, well thanks. I'll call right away."

"Outstanding," Klein says. "Later."

I punch the off button on the phone. Andie looks at me. "Well?"

"The drummer Roy Haynes. He's doing a CD with a bunch of piano players and wants me to be one of them."

"I know I should be impressed," Andie says, "and I would be if I knew who Roy Haynes is."

I laugh. Andie wasn't quite up on her jazz history yet but she was improving. "Bird, Miles, Coltrane, Monk, practically everybody who is anybody from the fifties to now. He's played with them all. He must be on over a thousand recordings."

"Okay, now I'm impressed. He must have heard you play somewhere or on a record, right?"

"Yeah, I guess." But how or when escapes me. I had that one recording I'd done years before and the new one as well, but it hadn't got much air play or decent sales. "Guess I'm going to find out."

I dial Haynes' home number and check my watch. It's two in the afternoon in New York.

"Hello."

"Roy Haynes?"

"Last time I checked."

"Hey, it's Evan Horne. I got your message and just talked to Larry Klein."

"Oh yeah, man, how ya doing?" His voice is suddenly full of warmth.

"Fine."

"Larry tell you about the project?"

"Yeah, sounds pretty interesting."

"I got the record company to get behind this and with the cats I can get they're up for it." He pauses for a moment. "Bet you wondering how I heard about you, huh?"

"Well, yeah I am, frankly."

Haynes laughs. "I just got back from a European tour, met up with my old pal Fletcher Paige. He told me all about you and said if I didn't include you on this he'd start telling stories on me."

"How is Fletch?"

"He's doing fine, playing his ass off as usual. Anyway, I checked you out, got a copy of your CD. Man, you should be with a major label. I liked what I heard, so if you're up for it, I want you to do one, maybe two tracks. We're doing it in New York."

"I don't know what to say."

"Easy man, just say yes."

"Yes."

"Cool. Larry will be in touch with the details. Think about a ballad and something up tempo, okay?"

"Sure. Hey thanks, man, I appreciate this. It will be a privilege."

"Talk at you soon then. Bye."

"Bye." I lean back and expel a big breath. Once in awhile, you're in the right place at the right time under the right circumstances. If I hadn't gone to Europe, met Fletcher Paige…My mind reels off the chain of events that cause Roy Haynes, one of the premier drummers in jazz, to call me and offer a record date. What a way to start the week.

I have another cigarette and try to calm down before calling the lawyer.

"Law offices," a woman's voice says.

"Yes, this is Evan Horne, returning Mr. Scott's call."

"One moment." There's a couple of clicks then a man's voice.

"Mr. Horne. This is Roger Scott. I had a devil of a time tracking you down. If it weren't for your friend Lieutenant Cooper, I don't know if I would have found you."

I tense a little. This kind of call always makes me apprehensive. "Yes, well I've been out of the country and in the Bay Area since I came back. What's this about, Mr. Scott?"

There's a slight pause before Scott continues. "I'm afraid I have some bad news. You are acquainted with Calvin Hughes. Is that correct?"

I grip the phone tighter. Cal Hughes and I were more than acquainted. He'd been a kind of mentor to me and at one time took me on as a student. Our relationship had been good but sporadic. The last time I'd seen Cal was during the Gillian Payne business, and after that nightmare was over, Cal had looked in on my recording session.

"Mr. Horne? Are you there?"

"Yes. Sorry. What about him?" But I already knew. Cal had been sick for a long time, living on borrowed time and too stubborn to have anything much to do with doctors.

"I'm sorry to tell you, Mr. Hughes died last week."

I stand up and glance at Andie. She looks at me questioningly.

"There's already been a funeral I take it."

"Well," Scott says. "Mr. Hughes was a member of one of those societies. He'd made arrangements to be cremated." Scott pauses and clears his throat. "This is rather awkward on the phone. I'm sorry Mr. Horne. I only knew him briefly, just taking care of a couple of legal things for him, his will, the house in Hollywood."

That Cal even had a will much less a lawyer surprises me, and makes me realize how little I really knew about him. Except for Milton, his Basset Hound, he had kept to himself as far as I knew, and had few visitors. He'd never talked about any family and I'd never pressed it.

"Which brings me to more pleasant news," Scott continues. "Mr. Hughes has named you as sole beneficiary to his estate, minus taxes and fees of course."

"His estate?"

Cal lived in a tiny bungalow in the Hollywood Hills, wedged between two much larger homes. I had no idea what it would be worth, but he had told me developers had been after him to sell several times.

"Yes," Scott goes on. "And it's considerable, all things being equal. The will has been authenticated and the title to the house cleared. What I need is for you to come to Los Angeles and well, accept your inheritance. Would that be possible? I could mail the papers I suppose but someone needs to go through his possessions at the house and you—"

"No, I understand. I'll come down there. When?" Andie is standing by me now, her hand on my shoulder.

"Well, the sooner the better," Scott says. "I'm going out of town myself and I'd like to clear my desk on this."

"Fine," I say. "I'll try to get a flight for tomorrow."

"Perfect," Scott says. He gives me the address and I write it down. "See you then, Mr. Horne. I look forward to meeting you. Mr. Hughes spoke very highly of you. It's a shame really."

"What's that?"

"He seems to have had no one but you. Goodbye."

"Bye." I press the off button on the phone, sit down numbly, and turn to look at Andie. "Remember Cal Hughes? He died last week and left his house to me and some other stuff."

"Oh God, I'm sorry," Andie says. I catch a flicker of something in her eyes before she turns away.

When I'd become a kind of go between for the FBI and a serial killer, I'd been checked out thoroughly by the bureau and that included friends and acquaintances. Cal Hughes was one. Andie and I had one battle about her checking Cal's background.

"You were pretty close to him weren't you," Andie says.

"Yeah, I was." Maybe more so than I thought. I was never sure about Cal. He could be so damn cantankerous, but on the other hand I'd always felt some strange connection to him. I could never exactly figure it out, but it was there nonetheless.

"Are you okay?"

"Yeah, just, well hit me harder than I thought it would," I reply, even though I knew this was coming. "I should have seen him when I came through L.A."

"Oh don't do that, Evan. Don't beat yourself up. You couldn't have known."

Andie is right, but I'm floored with regret. I get up and let her hug me. "I think I'm going for a walk."

She studies me. "You want some company?"

"No, I don't think so. I'll be back soon."

"Okay, I'll get some lunch going but I've got a stakeout tonight. Guy we've been keeping under surveillance is about to move, we think."

One of the hazards of living with an FBI agent is that the bad guys never sleep. She looks at her watch. "Damn, I've got to go by the bureau too and—"

"Hey, don't worry I'll get something."

"Are you sure?"

"Yeah, I'm fine, Andie, really."

But I was anything but fine.

At Oakland Airport, there's a long line to clear security and as my luck would have it, something sets off the beeper. Not only do they check my bag closely but I have the electronic wand waved over me and I'm told to take off my shoes. By the time I get to the gate, I just make it. As I board the shuttle flight to Los Angeles, regret and remorse continue—classic case of I wish I had done this or that, said something, visited, seen Cal one last time.

He'd come to the recording session, even brought along Milton. He'd listened to the playback for two tunes, nodded and said, "You don't need me here."

But I had and I wanted his approval. I'd called him just before I left for Europe. All he'd said about that was, "Good move."

I wished there'd been more, or that I'd stopped in when I hit California, but I couldn't now. Calvin Hughes was dead and gone.

The landing announcement takes me by surprise. It doesn't seem possible we're already descending into L.A. I have a seat near the front so I'm one of the first off. I'm surprised to see Danny Cooper waiting by the gate. I'd called him when I was coming down but expected him at the street exit.

"Hey, sport," he says. He's dressed casually in jeans, sport shirt, and a light jacket. "Good to see you." He gives me a hug and steps back to look at me. "I think San Francisco agrees with you."

"Damn good to see you too, Coop. How'd you get in here?" Then I stop and laugh as he rolls his eyes.

"Official police business. I flashed my badge, said I had a lead on a fugitive who'd been in Amsterdam."

I laugh again as we start down the corridor toward the street. "I bet you're parked at the curb too, right?"

"Where else? Got a security guy watching my car."

"Ah, the abuse of police power."

"Always a plus."

A security guard in a yellow jacket is leaning on Coop's car as we come up. He looks at me, checking for handcuffs I suppose. "This the guy?" he says.

"No, but a material witness," Coop tells him. "I appreciate your cooperation."

The guard straightens up and almost salutes Coop. "Glad to be of help." He tips his hat and walks off. I try to keep from laughing as we get in Coop's car and drive away.

"Sorry to hear about your friend." Coop maneuvers out of LAX and heads up Lincoln Boulevard. "The attorney that called me said Hughes told him if anything happened to call you or me. I guess Cal remembered me from our fun and games with the FBI."

"Yeah, well he'd been sick for a long time, but it's still kind of a shock, almost as much as what this lawyer told me about his estate." I look over at Coop. "By the way, thanks for putting him in touch with me."

Coop nods and turns onto the Santa Monica Freeway. "Thought I'd drop you at the lawyer's first. I'm sure you want to get that out of the way. Then maybe we can have lunch. I'm off today."

"Great. I'd like that. Thanks for picking me up."

I give him the address and he exits and heads north to Wilshire Boulevard and an office complex in Westwood.

"I got a couple of things to do. An hour be enough?"

"Should be."

"If it's longer I'll be in there." He points to a coffee shop across the street.

"Cool," I say, getting out of the car. "See you there."

Roger Scott's office is in a small building shared by other attorneys and business types. I find his name on the directory in the lobby and jog up some stairs to the second floor. The office is small with a tiny waiting room and a secretary-receptionist manning a desk and phone. I give her my name. I'd already left a message about my flight.

"Oh yes," she says. "He's expecting you. Just a minute. I'll tell him you're here."

She comes back in a minute and directs me into Scott's office.

"Mr. Horne," Scott says, rising from his desk.

Scott is a small compact man, probably early sixties with graying hair and rimless glasses. He's wearing a smartly cut dark suit and floral tie. We shake hands and I sit down opposite him.

"I appreciate your coming so soon," Scott says. "I'm trying to wind up things. The wife and I have a short vacation planned."

"No problem," I say.

Scott opens a file folder on his desk and goes through some papers. "Well, this is fairly straightforward. As I said, the house is yours as are the contents for you to dispose of as you see fit. Mr. Hughes was very definite about that."

"What about Milton?"

"Milton?" Scott looks puzzled for moment. "Oh, the dog. Well there's a girl, I believe, a student at UCLA who was helping with that. I assume she has him."

He shuffles through some of the papers. "Yes, here it is. Dana Trent. Her number is in here. She lives nearby and the last few months has been taking the dog for walks. Mr. Hughes was having trouble getting around near the end." He looks away for a moment before continuing.

"There are also some moneys, some accounts. Mr. Hughes lived a fairly frugal life. He named you as beneficiary of those as well." He hands over some checkbooks and papers from a savings and loan.

I take them and glance through noting the amounts, then look back at Scott in surprise.

Scott smiles. "Yes they are correct. I was surprised myself."

I spend the next half hour going over paperwork, signing a sheaf of papers. I give Scott my address and phone number. He verifies my identification, makes a photo copy of my driver's license, and finally calls in his secretary to witness my signature. He then gives me a small envelope with the house keys.

"Well," Scott says. "That about does it I believe, except for one thing." Scott looks suddenly uncomfortable.

"What's that?"

"Mr. Hughes' remains, his ah, ashes as it were. I believe I mentioned he had stipulated cremation."

I close my eyes for a moment. I hadn't even thought of that. "How does that work?"

"Well the society picks up the body and performs the cremation and holds the remains for"—Scott searches for the right word—"release." He hands me a folder from the society. "This is the address. They're in West Los Angeles."

I take the folder and glance at it. "Do I just go over there and—"

"Yes," Scott says. "I've given them your name. They hold the remains for I believe it's sixty days."

I nod, lost in thought for a moment, as Scott busies himself straightening things on his desk. After a couple of minutes he breaks the silence.

"Do you have any other questions?"

One thing does occur to me. I'd never heard Cal mention a lawyer. "Do you know how Cal came to choose you as his attorney? I'm just curious."

Scott smiles. "Funny you should mention that. I wondered myself. He never said, but I had the feeling he just picked me out of the yellow pages."

That would be so like Cal. I smile and shake my head. "Well, I can't think of anything else. Oh, was there a letter, an envelope, anything like that?"

"No, nothing like that," Scott says. "I'm sorry. Were you expecting something?"

I shrug. "No, I suppose not."

"Well, I'll get these papers filed this afternoon." He hands me a card. "If you have any questions or if there's anything I can do, please call me. I'll be back in a week or so."

We both stand up and shake hands again. "I am sorry for your loss, Mr. Horne."

"Thank you."

Scott hesitates a bit, as if he was going to tell me something.

"What?"

"Oh nothing really. I just had the feeling that Mr. Hughes didn't quite tell me everything. It's just me I guess. I can usually tell about these things."

"I know what you mean."

Coop is already in a booth at the coffee shop, nursing a Bloody Mary when I come in. "That looks good." I order one for myself. We both settle on sandwiches and I realize how hungry I am.

"So, everything go okay?" Coop asks.

"Yeah, I'm amazed. I now own a house in the Hollywood hills and came into a few bucks, well more than a few. Just really doesn't make sense, Coop. I mean I didn't see Cal all that much. We had our moments and he taught me a lot about piano but…" I shrug. "It never occurred to me he'd do this."

"Well, I guess there was no other family and he must have thought a lot of you."

"Yeah, makes me feel guilty I didn't come to see him when I got back from Amsterdam. We always had this kind of connection. It's hard to describe."

"Nothing you can do about it now," Coop says. "What are you going to do with the house? Sell it, rent it?"

Good question. "I don't know. I certainly don't want to move back here. I like the Bay Area a lot. But Cal always held off the developers that wanted it, so I'm not sure what to do yet. I have to go out there and see it, go through his stuff and decide what to keep. I'm not looking forward to that."

"Yeah," Coop says. "Not a fun job. Well, best to get it over with quickly."

"There's also his remains." I tell Coop about the cremation. "I have to pick them up sometime."

Coop looks at me. "What are you going to do with the ashes?"

"No idea."

"He didn't leave any instructions, last wishes?"

"Evidently not."

"Well, you'll know what to do when it's time."

I nod as our order comes. We eat and I catch Coop up on my adventures in Amsterdam, my move to northern California, and Andie.

"I can see you got it bad," Coop says, smirking. "How does she like it up there?"

"Seems to like it fine. She's on bank robbery detail now, and I'm just playing it by ear." I tell him about the place in Monte Rio. "You'll have to come up some weekend, get away from the smog and traffic and crime."

I also tell him about the Roy Haynes offer although Coop knows less about jazz than Andie and has no idea who Roy Haynes is.

"Think about it as if I were a struggling country n' western singer and Garth Brooks wanted me to be a guest on his next record."

Coop smiles. "Now that would be impressive." He nods and picks up the check, then hands it to me. "Hey, you're an heir now. You can take care of this."

We go back out to Coop's car and I light a cigarette, feeling a little overwhelmed with everything, thinking how quickly your life can change.

"What do you want to do?" Coop asks. "I could drop you at the house then pick you up later. You can crash with me."

"Yeah I guess that's the best plan. I don't think I want to stay there. At least not tonight anyway."

We head up Sunset then at La Brea, turn north to Franklin. At Beachwood Drive, I tell Coop to turn north again and we wind up into the hills a few blocks. When we pull up in front of the house, Coop keeps the motor running. "I won't go in," he says.

"Thanks, Coop. I'll give you a call later."

He leans over and looks up at the house. "Damn it's a tiny place, and all those steps. Don't trip."

"Yeah, Cal called it his built-in stair master."

Chapter Two

It's been a long time since I've seen the house. Even longer in daylight. For one reason or other, I'd usually visited with Cal at night. I trudge up the steep steps to the little bungalow, feeling the sun on my back, and take out the envelope with the keys. It feels strange to unlock, open the door, and go inside with Cal not there. The two large houses on either side block most of the sun but I open the musty curtains and look around.

Cal's chair and padded ottoman are where they always were, almost in the center of the room facing the tiny fireplace that as far as I knew, had never worked. On the table beside the chair sits the perennial stack of books. Cal had been a voracious reader, mostly mysteries. A television on a rolling cart, the old upright piano in the corner, and a small love seat leave little room for anything else.

I stand still for a few moments, listening. I can still feel Cal here, his voice echoing in my mind.

I shake off the feeling and stroll around, just glancing here and there, coming to terms with what I have to do. In the bedroom there's just the bed, a small dresser, and a night stand stacked with more books, and a small lamp. I'd never been in here but over the dresser I notice a framed photo of Miles Davis standing next to—yes, it was Cal—and another man I don't recognize. I shake my head. In all the time I'd known Cal he'd never once mentioned or showed it to me.

Nothing in the bathroom but an old robe hanging on a hook on the door, some towels draped over the shower curtain rod. I open a small mirrored cabinet over the sink and see several plastic bottles of medications. Some have never been opened. They have the label with the pharmacy and the prescribing doctor's name typed on them.

The kitchen is sparse, a few things in the refrigerator, pantry, and a half full bottle of Scotch. I walk back in the living room and open the door to the small balcony and look out with a narrow view of Hollywood below. There's a stereo with maybe fifty LPs. I flip through them quickly. Most are pretty old. There are also a few compact disks, and an inexpensive CD player. This was a new addition. Cal didn't like the sound of CDs. Too clean, too perfect and sterile, he'd said.

I finally stop at the old scarred piano and wonder how he'd got it up all those steps. I run my hand over the keyboard, feel the layer of dust, and play a few notes. The Mingus tune written for Lester Young, "Goodbye Porkpie Hat," runs through my mind. I sit down and start playing it, the way Cal might have. When I finish I lean forward, my head on my hands. This is harder than I thought it would be. I hadn't seen Cal much over the years but I'm going to miss him.

"That was beautiful."

I whirl around and see a young girl peering in the screen door. She opens it and comes in. "Sorry, I didn't want to disturb you." Milton, Cal's Basset Hound, is at the end of the leash she holds. The dog sees me, wags his tail and lumbers over to me. He nudges my hand for me to scratch his ears.

The girl is maybe mid twenties, athletic body with shoulder length dark hair and a very pretty face. "You must be—"

"Dana. Dana Trent. I helped Cal out a little before he…before he died."

"Oh right, okay. I'm…"

"I know who you are. Evan Horne. Cal talked about you a lot."

"All good I hope."

She smiles. "Oh yes, all good."

"Well come in, sit down."

"Thanks." She sits on the ottoman. She's wearing shorts, a UCLA t-shirt, and running shoes.

"Nice to meet you, Dana. Were you here when…"

"I found him," she says, looking away. "I came up to walk Milton. That was kind of one of my jobs. Cal was just sitting there in his chair, a book open on his lap, like he was asleep, a record playing. I knew he was gone but I called 911." She looks back at me. "He was a very nice man."

I nod. "That was not fun I imagine. How did you meet?"

She shrugs. "By accident really. I was walking by. He had Milton with him but he was having trouble getting up the steps. I asked if he wanted some help." She laughs remembering. "He said, 'No, just an old trick to get next to good looking young girls.'"

"Yeah, that was Cal."

"He invited me in. We had coffee. Well I did, Cal had Scotch. We talked awhile, he asked me a lot about my courses. I'm working on a Masters in English." She shrugs. "Then he offered me a job. I live just a few doors down. He wanted me to walk Milton, go to the store for him, that kind of thing, you know."

"Yeah, well that was good of you to do it."

"Oh he paid me, way more than he should have. I'm living with my aunt and on a couple of scholarships so money is tight."

"Uh huh." I look at Milton laying near her feet. "How does your aunt feel about Milton?"

She shrugs. "It's okay. I told her it's temporary." She reaches down and scratches Milton's head. He looks up at her adoringly. "Anyway, I was walking by and thought I saw the door open." She looks at me. "I guess you know he was cremated."

"Yeah, I just found out yesterday. Cal's attorney called me. I've been in Europe and San Francisco for a few months."

Dana nods. "I wrote an obituary for the L.A. Times," she says. "I really didn't know what to do. I hope that was okay. There was nobody to call that I knew of."

"Sure. Thanks for doing that."

She smiles. "I've got the paper at home if you want it."

"Thanks I'd like that."

"Two men who said they knew Cal from a long time ago called and left messages. They were musicians I think. I didn't know what to tell them but I've got their numbers too."

"Well, I'm glad you were there." I stand up. "Can I get you something to drink?" I glance at my watch. "Or how about some dinner or something. I'd like to hear more about your time with Cal."

She hesitates. "Well I've got some reading to do and…"

Suddenly I want to spend more time with Dana Trent, hear more about Cal's last days and she's the only link. "Come on. Just an hour or so. I'm buying. I'd kind of like to talk to you about Cal and since you were the last one to see him I—"

She shrugs. "Okay, sure, why not?"

"Oh wait, I don't have a car. My friend dropped me off."

"We can go in mine," she says. "Let me run home and change. I'll be right back."

I watch her go down the stairs two at a time. I turn to Milton. He looks puzzled to see Dana go.

"Okay guy, you're in charge." I lock the door and jog down the steps to wait for Dana.

We drive to a small place on Sunset, a Chinese place Dana recommends. Once we're seated and put in our order, I go in the back near the restrooms and call Coop.

"How's it going, Sport?"

"Kind of rough, you know, being there and him gone."

"Yeah I can imagine. So you ready to be picked up?"

"Not quite. I'm having an early dinner with this girl who worked for Cal, walked his dog, helped out. She's catching me up."

"I bet," Coop says, unable to keep the smirk out of his voice.

"Settle down. She's about twenty-five, a grad student at UCLA."

"Uh huh, and thick glasses, short stumpy body, straggly hair, right?"

"I'll tell you all about it later and you can see for yourself."

"I can hardly wait."

"Let's say eight. The White Dragon on Sunset, near La Brea."

"Got it."

I hang up the phone, still smiling as I walk back to our table.

"Everything all right," Dana says.

"Yeah my friend is going to pick me up here. Save you a trip."

She shrugs. "I wouldn't have minded."

I nod at her. "I can see why you would get along with Cal."

She looks away, remembering. "Yes, he was easy to be with."

The waiter brings our order. Kung Pao chicken and steamed rice for Dana; Mongolian beef and fried rice for me. I unwrap the chopsticks and start picking out the peas, making a small mound on the edge of my plate.

Dana laughs. "What are you doing?"

"I just don't like peas."

"Who are you?" She laughs. "I've seen Cal do the same thing."

"Long story. So what did you do with Cal?"

She takes a mouthful of her chicken. "Mmm, this is so good. Well, mostly just walked Milton at first, then went to the store for him, you know, whatever he needed, although he wasn't very demanding."

"No, Cal just liked to be left alone."

"I know. I used to worry about him when I wasn't there. He just read and watched TV. The last month or so he hardly got out at all. I tried to get him to see a doctor, but…"

"Yeah I know." We finish eating and I order some coffee. "Only so much of this green tea I can stand."

"He talked about you a lot," Dana says. "He was gruff at times but I could tell he really liked you. He said you were a great pianist and I don't think Cal gave out that kind of praise much."

"Thanks, and no, he didn't. I was his student some years back. He taught me a lot. Did he ever play for you?"

"Never. I asked him too but he just brushed it off and I didn't push. I did become something of a jazz fan though. He played a lot of records for me, pointed out things I had no idea were going on. You know, I'm an old rocker, but I liked a lot of it."

She studies me for a minute. "So what are you going to do now? With the house I mean."

I'd already been thinking about that. "I'm not sure. I live in the Bay area now. I don't want the house, but I don't know if I want to give it up yet. The house isn't worth much but I'm sure somebody would pay for the property."

"Oh yeah, it's prime area and Cal said he'd had a lot of offers."

We finish our coffee and I pay the check. "You mind if we take a walk. I'm dying for a cigarette. I want to run something by you."

"Sure."

We go outside and stroll down La Brea toward Santa Monica Boulevard. I get a cigarette going and ask her how much longer she's got at UCLA.

"Probably another year and then my thesis. Why?"

"And the arrangement you have with your aunt is temporary, right?"

"I'm supposed to be looking but I haven't been trying very hard and money is tight and…"

"Exactly. I've got a proposition for you. How about if I rent you the house. I'll pay the utilities, charge you reasonable rent and in exchange you watch the house and continue taking care of Milton."

She walks, head down studying the sidewalk. "Thanks but I could never afford it. You know what places rent for around here these days?"

"Let's say, oh, five hundred a month?"

She stops and looks at me. "Are you crazy? You could get more than three times that."

"I know but I want somebody there I know, somebody who knew Cal. I don't know what I'd do with Milton and it would also give me a place to crash if I come down to L.A. for something, you know a gig or recording maybe." I quickly add. "Of course if you had plans, a boyfriend or something, I'd always check with you first." She blinks, her face lit up by oncoming traffic. "There's no boyfriend."

She stops again and puts one hand on her throat. "God, I don't know what to say."

"Say yes." We turn and start heading back toward the restaurant.

"Are you sure? I can handle five hundred and I would take good care of the place and Milton."

I smile at her. "I know you would. So is it a deal?"

She gives me a big grin. "Hell, yes!"

"Great. I'll be around for a few days. I have to go through Cal's things. Might be some books you can use, so I'll get everything boxed up I want to keep and you can take whatever you want."

She seems kind of dazed by it all.

Coop's car is parked at the curb when I get back. He gets out and comes over. "Dana, say hello to Lieutenant Danny Cooper, Santa Monica Police. Coop, Dana Trent. She's been taking care of Cal's dog."

Coop gives her a big smile and shakes hands. "My pleasure, Miss Trent."

"Dana," she says.

Coop nods and glances a me. "Dana it is."

"Be right with you Coop. C'mon, Dana I'll walk you to your car." She waves to Coop and gets in and rolls down the window. I lean in. "Come by tomorrow and we'll work out all the details. I'd like to talk to you some more about Cal."

"Okay. I've got a seminar in the morning but I should be back by four."

"Whenever. Thanks, Dana."

She smiles and I stand for a moment, watching her drive away.

I go back and get into Coop's car. That smirk is on his face as he pulls away. "Uh huh," he says.

"Shut up."

"Better not let Andie see her, I mean especially the way she fits in those jeans."

"Shut up, Coop."

The next morning, I have Coop drop me at a car rental on his way to work. I'm not sure how long I'm going to be around and I can't keep having him drive me everywhere. "I'll call you later," I say as I get out of the car.

"Okay. Say hi to Dana for me." He laughs and drives off.

I rent a little hatchback and drive back to Hollywood, stopping off at a supermarket to pick up some heavy duty trash bags and talk the produce clerk out of some discarded boxes.

A light drizzle starts by the time I get to the house and I have to make several trips up the steps with my purchases and the boxes. Inside, the house seems so dark and deserted. This is not going to be fun, but I turn on a couple of lamps and get started.

Cal's record collection is pretty predictable. Mostly straight ahead jazz, some that goes back to the 40's. There's some big band stuff, Miles, Coltrane, several piano trios, including my own first recording. Some I think collectors would like to have. There are also two with Cal listed in the liner notes. I box them up, decide to keep them and remember I need some tape and a marker pen for labeling.

I take a break, get my cell phone out of my bag, and call the power company to change over the name. Then I call the phone company. Surprisingly, I have a dial tone in twenty minutes.

The piano, I decide will have to be hauled out of here. I hate to imagine getting it down all those steps. Maybe I can donate it someplace. In the bench I find some sheet music—old Broadway show tunes and some penciled music paper with untitled tunes.

I look at the first one. It's all yellowed now but the chords are readable as is the melody. I hear it in my head then sit down and play it out. "Boplicity," from the Miles Davis *Birth of the Cool* recording in 1949. There are two others, also penciled in Cal's scrawl, and both are from *Kind of Blue*, also by Miles, done ten years later.

Was Cal just transcribing the record, learning the tunes and the changes? I set them aside and go though the other music and find a copy of *Downbeat* magazine dated 1949, with a story on the *Birth of the Cool* band.

I feel the hair on the back of my neck prickle. In all the times I talked with Cal, I don't remember a single one where we talked about either of these recordings.

Birth of the Cool was just that. Ushering in the cool school of jazz. Gerry Mulligan and Gil Evans wrote a lot of the arrangements. Mulligan's partnership with Chet Baker was still three years down the line. *Kind of Blue* was another landmark in jazz history when Miles began to explore modal jazz and discovered a young quiet pianist named Bill Evans. It's all kind of spooky. I don't know what to make of it. I gather up the sheets and put them together.

In the bedroom I go through Cal's meager wardrobe. There's not much. Some slacks, a few sport coats, and a half dozen shirts on hangers. I decide to bundle everything from the closet into a couple of the big trash bags, maybe for Goodwill or the Salvation Army. Some I just toss.

The small dresser was more of the same. One drawer for socks and underwear, another for t-shirts, another for sweaters. The bottom drawer is stuck. I have to move and wiggle it get it open. It's full of papers. Digging through it, I find canceled checks, bills, receipts, an old pocket watch on a chain, a program from the Newport Jazz Festival, and a lot of other junk I don't feel like going through. In the end I just dump the contents of the drawer upside down on the bed.

I stop then, frozen to the spot.

Taped to the bottom of the drawer is a small manila envelope. I stare at it for a moment, knowing whatever is in it is somehow going to change everything for me.

I sit down on the bed and light a cigarette, just thinking for a couple of minutes. There were no missing legal papers from the lot the lawyer Scott had given me so this is something else entirely. Cal never struck me as a secretive man, so why this? I put out the cigarette and tear off the envelope.

Inside, is a note and another smaller business size envelope.

Evan,
    I know what you're thinking. A cliché from a detective novel, a clue taped to a drawer but I'm not thinking creatively these days. Somehow I know you'll be the one to find it. As for the other envelope, it's up to you whether to open it or not. Might be better to just tear it up and throw it away. I'm sorry we didn't spend more time together, but what time we did have was good, at least for me. I'm sorry things went down the way they did. Hope you don't think too badly of me.

I read and reread the note, puzzling over it, wondering how long it had been here. The masking tape looks fairly fresh, so maybe just a few weeks, a few days? I put the note aside and reach for the other envelope turning it in my hands.

Tear it up and throw it away? Cal, you knew me better than that. Inside is a grainy black and white photograph of a very young Calvin Hughes, standing next to a baby carriage, smiling at the camera. All very uncharacteristic for Cal. In the background there's a view of a building and part of a sign I can hardly make out. OTEL. Hotel but the name isn't visible if there is one.

A clue? What does he mean? A clue for what? Don't think too badly of him? About what?

"Evan? You in here?"

"Dana? Yeah in the bedroom." She comes in carrying a plastic bucket filled with cleaning material supplies and some rags.

"Thought I'd give this place a going over." She sees me holding the photo and the note from Cal. "What have you got there?"

I hand them both to her. "What do you make of these?"

She reads the note and studies the photo. "Where were they? Hey, that's Cal isn't it? He was a good looking dude."

I show her the drawer. "They were taped to the bottom of this drawer."

She reads the note again. "God, that's weird. I don't know, but he wanted you to find it that's for sure. Oh my God," she says, "do you think Cal had a baby?" She studies the photo again.

"Cal? I don't think he was ever married." She gives me a look. "Okay, he could still have a child, but what am I supposed to do?"

"You'll figure it out," she says. She looks at me and smiles. "Sherlock. Hey you're a detective." She grabs the bucket. "I got cleaning to do."

I put the note and photo aside and finish the bedroom, boxing up the things I want to keep and putting all the old clothes in the trash bags. The drawer full of papers I put in a shoe box I find in the closet. I'll go over those later.

I grab my cell phone and go looking for Dana. She's in the kitchen scrubbing the sink and has trashed virtually everything from the refrigerator. "I'm done in the bedroom," I say. "How about a pizza? There's a place down on Franklin, I think."

"Manny's? Sure," she says. "I'm almost finished here."

I look around. "You don't have to do this you know."

"Yes I do. I'm going to live here and I want to keep my landlord happy. You go get the pizza. Everything on it, okay. The works."

"Coming up." I drag some of the trash bags downstairs and set them out for pickup and walk down to Franklin.

I order one of Manny's Deluxe to go and while I'm waiting, I step outside, light a cigarette and call Andie's pager. She calls back in five minutes.

"Hello."

"Evan? Where are you? How's it going?"

"I'm just waiting for a pizza. It's not fun. Just doesn't seem right Cal isn't here."

"I know it must be hard, but better to get it over with. Have you decided what to do about the house?"

"Yeah, this girl who's been helping Cal, walking the dog and all, I'm going to rent it to her for now. She's a grad student at UCLA."

"That's fast. How well do you know her?"

"I don't, but she worked for Cal and that's good enough for me."

"I suppose," Andie says but not very convincingly.

"Andie, I found something in the house." I tell her about the note and photo, how it was taped to the drawer. "Wrap your FBI mind around that."

There's a few moments of silence. "Jesus, I don't know. That's weird."

"When you guys were checking out Cal, was there anything about him being married, having a child."

More silence. "I don't remember," Andie says. "That was awhile ago. I've seen so many case files since then."

"Well could you check? There has to be a reason for him to have left this for me."

"I'll see what I can do. I don't think we dug that deep. We were just kind of vetting your friends." I sigh. I didn't like it then and I don't now. It was a subject neither of us had talked about.

I look through the window and see the pizza guy waving to me. "I gotta go, Andie. My pizza is ready. I'll call you but let me know if you come up with something, okay."

"I will but who knows, Evan, it may mean nothing."

"You don't really believe that."

"No, I guess not. Call me. I love you."

I walk back up the hill thinking about the note, the photo, and wondering most of all about one thing.

Who had been standing just out of the frame when that photo was taken?

Chapter Three

I get Coop to meet me at a small noisy diner in Santa Monica. It's close to police headquarters, the court house, and a favorite of cops. When I arrive Coop is already in a booth, reading a newspaper, a cup of coffee in front of him. There are several uniformed cops at the counter, others in plain clothes in booths, and a few suits who I guess to be assistant district attorneys. Public defenders probably have their own hangout.

Coop looks up as I approach the table. "Jesus, what happened to you?" I'd hardly slept the night before and I guess it shows. Dana and I had sat up talking about Cal till very late, and after the pizza and a few drinks, she got me to open up about my accident that had prevented me from playing, and to recount my previous stints as a reluctant detective. I hadn't talked as much to anyone since my sessions with the FBI psychologist after the Gillian Payne case. Not even to Andie. Dana is a good listener.

The memories came flooding back. Lying on the coast highway, my wrist shattered, the rehab, starting to play again, trying not to let things slip away. Starting over in a shopping mall in Las Vegas and helping my friend Ace Buffington dig into the past about Wardell Gray's murder in 1955. The only good thing to come out of that was meeting Natalie Beamer, but that had gone bad too eventually.

Then, just when things seemed to be going my way, getting a record contract, it was Danny Cooper who wanted my help. I became a conduit between the FBI and a deranged woman bent on some insane revenge for her brother's failures.

Andie Lawrence came out of that one, but Natalie was gone. Then escaping to Europe, playing again only to be side tracked by Ace's disappearance in Amsterdam and following in the ghostly footsteps of Chet Baker and sadly, discovering Ace was not quite who I thought he was. Do you really ever know anybody?

And here I am, many miles and murders further, coming home to find the one person, with the exception of Danny Cooper, I had some kind of real connection with, dead and gone but leaving me yet another mystery to solve.

I don't know how long I went on but when I had looked up at Dana, all she said was, "Well, your life certainly hasn't been boring." The rehash had left me edgy and restless. I found myself angry at the note and photo Cal had left. Angry at Cal, for dying, angry for knowing me well enough that I'd have to pursue this wherever it took me.

Coop grins at me as I slide in opposite him. "You and Dana get acquainted?"

"Oh fuck off, Coop. She's a kid."

"Yeah, way too young for an old guy like you," Coop's ever present smirk expanded to a grin.

A waitress, tall and blond with the hard look, I suppose, of too many sour experiences, comes over. "What'll it be boys?" She smiles at Coop and refills his coffee cup.

Coop grins. "How ya doin', Darlene? How's your boy?"

"He's great, finally doing well in school and—"

"Look, can I just get some fucking coffee? You two can stroll down memory lane some other time, okay?"

"Whoa, Sport," Coop says. They both stare at me. "I'll have the special and my rude friend will have some fucking coffee, I guess."

I shake my head and look at her. "I'm sorry," I say. "I'll have the special too, whatever it is."

"Sure," Darlene says, dismissing me curtly and walking away.

Coop continues to study me. "So what's going on with you?"

"This." I take out the note and photo from Cal, and slide them across the table. "I found those when I was going through Cal's things at the house yesterday. That is Cal's writing." Coop studies them both for a minute.

"Where did you find them?"

"Taped to the bottom of a dresser drawer."

Coop looks up to see if I'm joking, sees I'm not. "Well, that's original." He looks at the note. "That's what he means by not thinking creatively, huh?"

"I guess." I watch him study both items. "Well?"

Coop shrugs. "Well what? I don't know what to make of it but it's obviously something he wanted you to have, or..." He stops, looking away for a moment then back to the note. "It's like, he wanted you to find it but if you didn't, that would be okay too. You know what I mean?" Coop looks up at me then. "How about you. Any ideas?"

"I'm not sure." I watch Coop look, his face creasing into a frown. He's studied hundreds of crime scene photos and I'm hoping he sees something I don't.

"It's like a half-hearted confession about something. He knows he's dying, gets a conscience. Maybe somewhere along the line Cal had a child. I don't think this is just some girl he just met who happened to have a baby with her. Look how his hand is on the handle of the carriage." He leans over squinting at it and points to the photo.

I look again and realize I hadn't noticed it before.

"And he keeps it all these years. Why? Unless the baby in there is important." Coop looks up at me. "His baby?"

"Cal never mentioned being married, much less becoming a dad."

"Maybe he couldn't tell you." Coop suddenly sits up straight. "Jesus, maybe that's you. Maybe you're that baby in the carriage."

I shake my head. "Yeah right, and my mother is Lena Horne. Come on. My parents live outside of Boston. Richard and Susan Horne. You know them." But even as I say the words a tiny flicker of doubt seeps into some corner of my mind. Why? Where is that coming from? I brush it aside quickly. No, I know who my father is and it is not Calvin Hughes.

"But why not just leave it with the other papers, with the lawyer?"

"Good question. Maybe he wanted you to find it. In his mind, he gave it a try and you an option."

"C'mon, Coop. If you found something like that would you just tear it up and throw it away without looking ?"

Coop sighs. "No, but then I'm a cop. But Jesus, this could be anything."

"Okay, for the sake of argument, let's say he has a child somewhere. Maybe he was married, maybe he wasn't. He wants me to track her down, help her, give her money, whatever. Why wouldn't he leave more information, some place to start?"

Coop looks at me again, his voice is slow and measured. "Because he knows if you found this, you'd already know where to start. You just haven't figured it out yet."

"Thanks, Coop. That helps a lot."

Darlene brings our coffee then. She avoids looking at me but still has the big smile for Coop. "Be right back with your food," she says and hurries off again.

"I'd leave her a big tip if I were you," Coop says.

I add cream and sugar to my coffee and look at Coop. "When I got hauled into the FBI, they looked into Cal's background. Did you know anything about that?"

Coop takes a drink of coffee and shakes his head. "I wasn't really in the loop as far as the bureau goes. Why would they check on Cal?"

"Same reason they checked me and Natalie out? Andie told me about it but only when I asked her last night."

"You think something else is going on?" Coop asks. "What did she say?"

"She said she can't remember, that she's looked at hundreds of background files since then and it wasn't relevant anyway, just routine procedure."

Coop looks away for a moment, then asks the hard question. "Don't take this wrong, but do you trust Andie?"

Driving back to the house, Coop's question keeps pushing forward in my mind. Do I trust anybody? I think about what Coop said and at least part of it makes sense. I try to put myself in Cal's mind. Near death, doesn't know how long he has, and what he's been carrying around for who knows how long is eating at him. Somewhere out there is his child and now it's time to try to make some amends for all the loss. A dying man's last ditch attempt, however feeble, to make good on something that happened so long ago. So who does he pick? Me, the one person he's had any kind of close relationship with in years. Wasn't there any other family, and who was the mother?

In the photo, Cal can't be more than mid-twenties, thirty tops, so that baby is—if it's Cal's and depending on the year the photo was taken—would now be around forty something. Close to my age. That part of Coop's speculation is ridiculous. Because I'd already know where to start? No Cal, I'm sorry but I don't. Maybe Andie can help.

I weave through the traffic on Sunset, past the clubs, restaurants, shops of all kinds, and continue east to Vine Street. As I sit, tapping on the steering wheel, waiting to make the left turn, I suddenly remember there is someplace I can start.

When I get back to the house, I see Dana's car parked in front. Inside Milton is stretched out on the floor, and the sound of a vacuum cleaner comes from the bedroom. Milton manages to get to his feet and strolls over wagging his tail. I scratch behind the ears. He sighs and flops down again.

Looking around, I see everything has been transformed. Dana has done quite a job. In the living room books have been shelved, records stacked neatly by the stereo, and the piano even looks shiny.

The vacuum stops then. "Dana?" I walk back to find her wrapping the cord in her hand and looping it over the handle of the cleaner.

"Hey," she says. "How was lunch? I'm just about finished here."

The bed is made and my bag sits in the middle of it. "Those two boxes in the corner are books I'd like," she says. "You can go through them if you want. I put the stuff you set aside in the hall closet. If you want, I can drop off those bags of clothes at the Salvation Army. Might be better to get them out of here, huh?"

"Yeah I guess so." There were enough reminders of Cal already.

"Oh, I put the rest of the stuff from that drawer in that small box." She points to one in the corner.

"Thanks. I'll go through that later."

She turns and faces me. "When will it be okay for me to move in my stuff? My aunt is—"

"Whenever you want. I'm probably going to get out of here tomorrow or the next day, decide what else I can do about that note, see if I can figure things out."

"What did Cooper say about it?"

"Mostly speculation. He thinks it's Cal's baby in that carriage. I didn't notice it before but Cal's hand is on the handle. Coop thinks that means something."

"Can I see it again?"

I take it out of my pocket and show it to her, watch her study it. She nods. "So do I," she says. "And look at the way he's smiling."

I nod. "It's hard to know. Coop also made a wild stab at things."

"Oh?"

"He said, maybe that's me in the carriage." I force a laugh.

Dana doesn't laugh. "I didn't want to say anything but I think it's a possibility."

"But I told you my parents are still alive and live in Boston."

"I know but…oh well, I guess it is a crazy idea."

She glances at her watch. "I have to get out of here. I'm meeting with my advisor at three. If you want I'll come back and cook dinner tonight unless you have some other plans."

"No, that would be fine." I take out some money. "Here, get whatever you need."

"I do a pretty mean pasta and shrimp. That okay?"

"Sound great. See you then."

"Okay, I should be back around six or so. I thought I'd leave Milton here. He's getting a little disoriented going back and forth."

"Sure."

I watch her go then call Andie at her office. "Special agent Lawrence please," I tell the receptionist when she answers. "Evan Horne."

"One moment."

I listen to a few clicks then Andie comes on. "Evan, how's it going."

"Hi. I was going to ask you the same."

"I've been swamped, Evan. I haven't had time to do anything. When are you coming back?"

"Probably tomorrow or the next day. Things are mostly in control here." I pause for a moment. "Cal was cremated. I have to decide what to do about his ashes."

"God," Andie says. "I'm sorry, Evan. That's a rough one."

"Yeah, well at least I don't have to worry about the house or Milton. Dana is ready to move in and she got the place looking great."

Andie's voice is suddenly chilly. "How domestic of her."

"Andie."

"Okay, okay. I'm sorry, I'm just not ecstatic about you sharing that house with a hot coed. Did you talk to Coop about the note and the photo?"

"Yeah, had lunch with him today."

"And?"

"He's pretty intrigued and has some wild theories."

"Oh?" Is it my imagination or is her voice guarded? "He say anything else?"

"No. Like what?"

"I don't know. Nothing I guess. I gotta go, Evan. We're having a briefing in five minutes. Let me know when you're coming in. I miss you."

"Yeah, me too. Talk to you later."

I hang up and get the file from the lawyer, and look through the unopened mail. I look around again in the living room. Under the table on a small shelf are some magazines and two copies of the *International Federation of Musicians* newspaper. I flip quickly through both copies and I find what I want on the Notice to Members page.

I start for the door then turn back and go into the bedroom and take the photo of Cal with Miles Davis and the other man out of the frame and put it in the file. Milton looks up at me questioningly with those deep brown eyes.

"It's okay pal, I'll bring it back." I give him a pet and head for my car.

◇◇◇

Musicians Union Local #47 is not far from the house, on Vine Street just south of Santa Monica Boulevard. I pull the rental car into the parking lot and find a space easily so I know there's not much happening today, and it must not be studio musicians payday. Getting out of the car, I hear a big band from one of the rehearsal studios, and across the street, in front of the Professional Drum Shop, there are a lot of cars. Walking to the front entrance of the union, I think about dropping in over there. It's more than a drum shop, kind of a hangout for L.A. drummers. Maybe a good idea to show the photo of Miles and Cal.

"Hi," I say to the woman at the Directory booth in the lobby. She has a headset on. She glances at me and holds up one finger from the keyboard while she finishes with the phone.

"Yes?" She looks tired, as if she's seen and heard it all and hasn't been very impressed with any of it.

"Calvin Hughes, pianist. You have a listing for him?"

She taps some keys, the screen flickers and changes several times. She leans in closer. "Lapsed member. No wait, he caught up his dues a month ago and was reinstated. There's a listing for here in Hollywood."

"Uh huh. What about the life insurance? Who is the beneficiary?" Union membership comes with a small term life insurance policy at group rates. She looks at me as if to say, are you kidding? "He just died last week. I'm the executor of his estate."

Her expression changes to one of mild sympathy. "Sorry," she says, "but I still can't give out that information without authorization. The beneficiary will have to file a death certificate with the union. See one of the business agents. They can help you."

"I understand. Thanks." I start to turn away, then step back to the window. "Any of the business agents from way back. You know, 50s or 60s?"

She shrugs. "You might try Harvey Douglas." She nods toward the stairs.

"Thanks." I go up the stairs and turn down a hallway of offices for the business agents. Harvey Douglas is halfway down and on the phone. I tap on the open door. "Got a minute?"

Douglas crooks his finger at me "Be right with you." I take a seat opposite him and look around the office. It's not much. Small and most of the space taken up with Douglas' desk, file cabinets, couple of chairs, and a window facing Vine Street. A few photos hang on the wall.

"Look, let me get back to you on this. If there's no contract there's no way we can do anything." He rolls his eyes at me as he listens. "Okay. Yes, I promise I'll look into it." He hangs up the phone, shaking his head. "Some lady complaining about the band at her daughter's wedding. They didn't play all the right music she wanted."

He puts his hands flat on his desk and looks at me. "So, what can I do for you?" Douglas is wearing a short sleeved white shirt, dark knit tie, and black framed glasses. His thick hair is all white.

"My name is Evan Horne. I'm trying to track down some info on a former member, friend of mine. Calvin Hughes. I checked downstairs at directory. She said his membership lapsed but he caught up his dues and still has the life insurance."

"Was he a piano player," Douglas says. "I knew a Cal Hughes. We went way back. I always wondered what happened to him."

"You knew him? He's been living right here in Hollywood for over twenty years."

"No shit," Douglas says. "I was still playing trombone then." He jerks his thumb at one of the photos. "That's me with Les Browne. USO Tour." The photo is of a big band and Douglas is standing up in the trombone section. "We might have done some rehearsal bands together. That was a long time ago. Cal was a hell of a player if it's the same one. Nobody could figure out why he just kind of disappeared."

I take out the photo and show it to Douglas. He takes it, removes his glasses, and opens a desk drawer and takes out a magnifying glass. He studies the photo. "Yep, that's Cal all right."

"Do you know if he was married or had kids?"

He looks up at me. "Are you a relative?"

"No, just his friend, but he named me executor of his estate. He just died last week. I'm trying to find out who the beneficiary is for the life insurance."

"If Cal was married or had kids I never knew about it, but then we weren't close." Douglas hands me back the photo. "The beneficiary, whoever it is, will have to file a death certificate for payment."

"I understand." I show him the other photo from Cal's bedroom.

"Son of a bitch. Cal and Miles Davis. I didn't know about that either. When was that taken? Miles looks pretty young too."

"Do you know who the other man is?"

Douglas squints at the photo again. "No can't say I do, but…hang on a minute. I'll be right back."

While Douglas is gone I study the baby carriage photo, using the magnifying glass. Cal has his right hand on the handle of the carriage. His left hand is hidden behind the carriage. I move the glass all over the photo. The OTEL has to be hotel but there's no name, nothing to indicate where the photo was taken. I move the glass near the edge and then I see it. Part of another hand and a small band on the ring finger.

I lean back in the chair, trying to come up with some plausible scenarios. Maybe the woman is a married friend of Cal's and it's a congratulations photo taken by the husband. Or it's a girlfriend of Cal's who's married. But neither of those possibilities explain why Cal kept it all these years and left it for me to find. Coop and Dana are both right, I decide. That's Cal's baby.

Douglas comes back then. "Got it," he says. He lays the photo on the desk and taps his finger on it. "That's Barney Jackson, bass player. One of the other guys recognized him."

"Really? Is Jackson still around do you know?"

"Well it's easy to check." He punches three numbers on his phone. "Marge? Pull up Barney Jackson will you. Thanks." He holds his hand over the phone while he waits. "I'm sorry to hear about Cal." He takes his hand off the phone. "Yeah, Marge." He listens and writes down something on a pad in front of him. "Okay. Thanks, Marge. Wait a minute." He covers the phone again.

"You have any paperwork that shows you're the executor?"

"Yeah, right here." I open the file, thumb through it and find the papers I want.

Douglas rubs his chin, and studies everything. "Yeah, well, this all looks in order I guess." He pauses again. "What did you say your name is?"

"Evan Horne."

"Marge. While you're at it, pull up Calvin Hughes and print it out and send it upstairs, okay? Thanks." He hangs up the phone. "This won't take long."

He gets up and goes to one of the file cabinets and takes out a form and lays it on the desk in front of me. "You need to have the beneficiary fill that out and enclose it with the death certificate for payment. We'll run an item for the federation newspaper. You can write something if you want."

"Yeah, thanks. I'd like to do that."

Douglas sits back down and studies me, his hands folded across his stomach. "Evan Horne. I got it. You're the guy who broke that serial killer case with the FBI. I knew the name was familiar."

I nod. "Well, there wasn't that much to it as far as I was concerned."

"You're too modest," Douglas says. "Man the *Times* was full of that story." He hands me a slip of paper. "That's Jackson's last known phone number and address. His membership is lapsed."

We're interrupted then by a young black girl in jeans and a sweater top. She smiles at me and hands Douglas some printouts. He takes them and his chair creaks as he leans forward on his desk, studying them.

He tears off the top sheet and pushes in across to me. "There's your beneficiary. See, right there." He points to a space on the form.

Jean Lane.

I sit for, I don't know how long, staring at the name, then look up at Douglas.

"You okay?" he asks.

"Yeah, fine. I just don't recognize the name."

He leans back. "The sooner you find her, the sooner the benefits can be paid. She will have to file that form."

"Yeah I know." I gather up the papers and put everything back in the file folder. "Thanks for your help. I'll get something together for the union paper."

I walk in kind of a daze back to my car and I sit there for several minutes. I light a cigarette and roll down the window, and look at the insurance form again.

Jean Lane. Who the hell is Jean Lane? The name rings no bells whatsoever. I go back over the many conversations I had with

Cal but there's nothing I can recall about any woman named Jean Lane. Any woman at all for that matter. I always assumed Cal had never been married, never had any kids. I can't think of how to start looking for Jean Lane. There's nothing to go on but a forty-year-old photo.

Then I remember the two phone messages Dana told me about. Musicians, she thought they were. They must have known Cal, worked with him. Maybe they would know something. Maybe one of them was Barney Jackson from the photo, the third guy with Cal and Miles Davis.

I let all that swirl around in my mind for a few minutes. It's like looking through fog, catching a glimpse of something now and then. I shake it off.

First, there's something very unpleasant I have to deal with. I look through the file again for the number of the Cremation Society, take out my cell and dial the number.

I explain who I am for a pleasant sounding woman who assures me that Cal's remains, his ashes, will be held for sixty days for the next of kin or "so designated person," as she calls it. Designated is obviously the key word, and given Cal's morbid humor, I almost expect some bizarre name, like Jelly Roll Morton or Fats Waller. After sixty days, if they are not claimed, the ashes are disposed of at sea along with other unclaimed remains.

"A mass burial at sea? Is that what you mean?"

"Well, yes actually. However, you may choose to accompany a group for such disposal although there is an additional fee."

I think about that for a moment. I've been to a few funeral services, some memorials, but overall, this is a subject I'm not at all comfortable talking about. Now it's one I'm going to have to deal with directly.

"Mr. Horne?"

"Yes, sorry, I was just thinking."

"I understand. When you decide, please let us know."

"Thanks, I will." I make a tentative appointment with one of their counselors.

When I ask if Cal has designated a next of kin, there is another surprise.

"Checking now," she says. She's one of those people who, on the phone tell you everything she's doing. "Checking, checking, where did that sheet go?"

I hear a rustle of paper and then, "Yes, next of kin is listed as..." She pauses. "That's strange."

"What?"

"Evan Horne. That's you, right?"

Chapter Four

After leaving the union, I drive down Sunset till I find a coffee place with outside tables. I pull in, park, and go inside. Joining a fairly large line, I order a large coffee to go and take it outside to one of the tables where I call the number Harvey Douglas gave me for Barney Jackson on my cell.

"Hello," a young woman's high pitched voice says.

"Hello. My name is Evan Horne. I'm trying to reach Barney Jackson, the bass player—"

"Oh, you mean my father?" She pauses for a moment. "He passed away over a year ago."

I sigh, not quite sure what to say. "I'm sorry. Actually, I'm calling about an old photo he's in and I was hoping somebody could help me identify the other people. Maybe you—"

"Identify?" Her voice takes on a hesitant tone now.

"Well, recognize. I'm a musician too," I say quickly. "It's a photo of your father and Miles Davis, you know the trumpet player. And another man," I say quickly.

She laughs. "I know who Miles Davis is. I've seen him in some other pictures with my father."

"Look, you don't know me, but it's pretty important. Do you think we could get together. I'd like to see those other pictures, and have you take a look at this one."

"Sure, I guess so but you should really talk to my mother. She knows more than I do."

"That would be great. Is she home?"

"She will be in about an hour if you want to come by."

"Great." She gives me an address in Vanuys. "Thank you very much."

I light a cigarette and drink off half the coffee, feeling a little better about things. At least I have some place to start. I take the coffee with me and start for the Valley, hoping to beat the traffic going over the hill on the 405, but L.A. freeways are always busy and it takes me almost an hour to get there. The Jackson home is not far off the Ventura Freeway and easy enough to find. It's a small frame house with a large front yard. I park in front. A small slender woman in jeans and a t-shirt is dragging a sprinkler hose to another section of the lawn. She looks up as I get out of the car.

"Are you the man that called earlier and talked to my daughter?"

"Yes, thanks for seeing me."

She nods and looks at the grass. "Can't keep anything green out here." She walks over to me. "I'm Wanda Jackson. Did you know Barney?"

"Hi, Evan Horne. No, but I think a friend of mine who just passed away did."

"Oh, I'm sorry about your friend. I guess Beth told you we lost Barney over a year ago." She shakes her head. "Seems longer somehow."

I nod. She has a tired look about her, as if life has played a trick on her and she doesn't know how or why it happened.

"Well, come on in."

"Thanks, I won't take too much of your time." I follow her inside and we sit down in the small living room. It's dominated by a large screen television on one wall. She notices me looking.

"That was for Barney. He loved his sports." She blinks for a moment. "Can I get you something to drink?"

"No thanks, I'm fine." I notice a couple of photo albums on the coffee table in front of us. I open the file I've brought in with me and show her the photo of Cal, Miles Davis, and her husband. A small smile comes over her as she takes the photo in her hands.

"Oh my, this was taken a long time ago."

"Yes. Look, let me explain. The other man is, was, a friend of mine. He just died last week. I'm the executor of his estate. In going through his things I found this photo. Anyway, he had a life insurance policy with the musician's union."

She nods and frowns. "Yes, not even enough for a decent burial."

"I know, but I don't know who the beneficiary is, so this is all I have to go on. Do you recognize the other man in the photo. His name was Calvin Hughes."

She continues to look at the photo and shakes her head. "No, I'm sorry I don't. I think this was taken way before Barney and I were married." She puts the photo aside and opens up one of the albums. There are several of Barney Jackson with various bands, none of which I recognize, and none with Miles Davis.

"What was his connection with Miles? Do you know?"

She leans back and thinks. "Barney lived in New York before he came out here. I can't remember for sure, but I think he played in some big band with Miles, a rehearsal band. He wasn't the main guy I don't think, but he subbed with the band. You know how that goes."

"Yes, I've been there myself."

"Wait, I remember now. He was always telling this story about how he should have been on that record with Miles, *Birth of the Cool*, but he was out of town when it was recorded."

I feel the hair on the back of my neck rise as I think about the music sheets I'd found in Cal's house. I knew Miles had played on the west coast at the Lighthouse.

"Do you know if your husband ever worked with Miles out here?"

She shakes her head. "No, he took me to see Miles once, at Shelly's Manne Hole. He spoke to him briefly but he came back kind of annoyed. Miles hardly remembered him, he said. By then Barney was starting to do studio work, lot of television. He'd given up jazz or rather jazz had given up on him." She listed off several shows he'd played on and flipped through the photo album showing me various photos of Barney with studio and television bands. One has Carol Burnett standing, laughing with the piano player. Another was with him and Johnny Carson and Doc Severinson.

She sighs. "But it all ended eventually, and he wound up doing weddings, parties, that kind of thing, got his real estate license." She shrugs. "If you're a musician, you know how it goes."

"Yes." I lean back, thinking, disappointed that there's no more here. "Well, I won't take up anymore of your time." I write down my cell phone number. "If you think of anything, would you please give me a call?"

She shrugs. "Sure." She gets up and walks me to the door. "I hope you find who you're looking for."

Back in the car, I head for the Ventura Freeway, but of course, it's like a parking lot. I call Dana to tell her I'm going to be hung up in traffic for awhile.

"That's okay," she says. "I just got back myself. What are you doing in the Valley at rush hour?"

"I'm asking myself the same thing. It was a dead end. I'll tell you about it when I get there." Inching along I decide to use the time to make a couple of other calls.

"I left those numbers of the musicians you said called on the table by Cal's chair. Can you give them to me." In the glove box, I find a pen with the rental car company logo.

"Sure, hang on."

By the time she comes back on the line I've gone all of a hundred yards.

"Ready? First one is Al Beckwood. The other is Mal Leonard." I write the names and numbers on the front of the file folder beside me on the seat.

"Okay, thanks, Dana. I'll be there as soon as I can."

I try Beckwood first but there's no answer, not even a machine. I'm not sure but I think it's a New York exchange. For Mal Leonard, there is only partial success.

"Musicians' home."

"Hello. I'm trying to reach a Mal Leonard. What is this place?"

"Musicians' Retirement Home," a woman's voice says. "Mr. Leonard won't be back until sometime tomorrow."

"Does he work there?"

"No, he's a resident. He's with his daughter on an overnight visit."

"I see. I'm returning his call. He left a message a few days ago. Can I get him tomorrow then?"

"Yes, he'll be available then."

"Okay, thanks." I close the phone and drop it on the seat beside me. A musicians' retirement home. I didn't know there was such a place.

◇◇◇

Back at the house, I find a parking space fairly close and jog up the steps. Dana is in the kitchen, stirring a pot of sauce and I can smell shrimp sautéing in garlic and olive oil.

"Hey," she says. "Won't be long now. Why don't you open the wine." She nods to a bottle on the table. A corkscrew is lying beside it.

"Looks like you've done this before," I say as I open the wine.

"Oh I love to cook. Just haven't had the time or opportunity for awhile."

I pour us both a glass. "Merlot." I look at the bottle. "How did you know?"

She smiles. "Just a guess. It's about the only red wine I like." She gives the sauce a final stir and turns off the fire under the shrimp. She's in a t-shirt and jeans and sandals, her hair loose about her face. "So how did it go?"

I catch her up on things as she drains the pasta, mixes in the sauce and adds the shrimp in a large bowl. She doesn't ask any questions, just listens until we sit down at the table.

"Well, here's to it." She holds up her glass and I tap mine against hers.

"This is really nice," I say. "How about some music?"

I go in the living room and dig through Cal's records and put on *Birth of the Cool*. I listen for a minute. It's such an old copy there's a lot of noise and static.

"Cal used to play that a lot," Dana says as I return to the table.

"This is delicious," I say as the band moves through the tricky little line called "Boplicity." I tell her about the music sheets I'd found.

She looks puzzled. "Does that mean anything?"

"Well, they're very old but it could mean two things. Cal was either just writing out the line for himself, or, he possibly had a hand in the composing."

"But wouldn't his name be on the record?"

"Normally, yes, but there are a lot instances where the wrong people got credit, or the rights were sold. Sometimes it gets complicated."

There had been a persistent controversy over "Blue in Green" between Miles Davis and Bill Evans on the record *Kind of Blue*. Both had claimed to have written it. And there were others. "The Chase," by Wardell Gray and Dexter Gordon, who sold the rights for a hundred dollars. A similar story floated around about Oliver Nelson's "Stolen Moments," which had been recorded many times since the 1960s when it first saw light.

"A lot of groups recorded those tunes in the past forty years. That means maybe thousands in lost royalties for the person who didn't get credit."

Dana listens, takes a last bite, and pushes her plate aside. "So Cal might have written some of these tunes and never got credit?"

"Who knows. It was a long time ago." I listen for a couple of minutes, recalling the tunes then think of something else. "Is there a big record store anywhere near here?"

"Yeah, Tower down on Sunset and a couple of others in Hollywood. Why?"

"There's a newer version of this, a two CD set with a little booklet. I'd like to see it, see who the musicians are." I was mainly curious to see if Barney Jackson was listed.

I pour us both some more wine and light a cigarette. "There's something else I want to talk to you about, Dana."

Dana nods but looks a little wary. "You've changed your mind? You're going to sell the house?"

I laugh. "No, nothing like that. It's about Cal." I tell her about calling the Cremation Society, the scattering of ashes at sea. "It's something I want to get over with and I'd like you to go with me, since you were the last person to see Cal."

I study her for a moment. She holds her glass in both hands and looks down.

"I don't know," she says. "Isn't it really a more private thing for you? I mean I got to know Cal but—"

"No, I understand if you don't want to. Hell, I don't want to but I just don't like the idea of going by myself."

"It's not that, I just don't want to, you know, intrude."

"You won't be and I'd really appreciate it."

She smiles. "When is it?"

"I'll have to call them tomorrow to make arrangements." I feel an inner sigh of relief that I'll have some company.

"Look, let's leave the kitchen and run down to Tower and then I'll buy you a cappuccino or something. How about it?"

"Sounds like a plan."

◇◇◇

Sunset is crawling with cars full of cruising teens as we wind down toward Tower Records, past the clubs and restaurants. I manage to find a parking place in the crowded lot and we go inside. I almost wince as I hear the heavy, blaring band with a screaming vocal they're playing over the store sound system.

Dana sees my frown and laughs. "Not your thing, huh? Aerosmith." She takes off. "I'll meet you in the jazz section," she says.

Jazz is in the back, a couple of aisles worth with quite a selection. There's plenty of Miles Davis in the racks and several copies of *Birth of The Cool*. It's a two CD set and even includes a few of the tracks recorded live at the Royal Roost. I grab one and wander around looking randomly at all the new releases. Half the names I don't recognize. So much music, so little time. I'd about seen enough when Dana comes by.

"Find anything?"

She frowns. "Nothing I don't already have and nothing new I want."

I watch her browse through the jazz, her fingers dragging over several rows of CDs, then she lets out a little squeal. "Oh, look," she says. "You're here too."

I walk over and see she's pointing at one of the tabs separating each musician. Right between Red Holloway and Bobby Hutcherson is one with my name on it and a single copy of *Haiku*, the recording I'd done before I took off for Europe. Cal had been in the studio that day. I didn't even know Tower was carrying it.

Dana picks it up and looks at the front with my photo. I guess I'd been trying to look pensive at the time, but seeing it now, I think I look more puzzled than anything. Dana looks from the cover to me and back several times. "Not bad," she says, "but you look better in person. They'll order more if I take this one, right?"

"You don't have to do that. I can get you one of the promotional copies."

She shakes her head. "No, I want this one. I've never been in a record store and bought one with the guy who made it with me."

We both pause for a moment and then laugh at what she said. She even blushes a little. "Well, you know what I mean."

I start to take it from her. "At least let me buy it for you."

"No, this one I pay for myself. You can autograph it for me later."

We stand in line a few minutes and then a bored cashier in spiked purple and green hair rings up Dana. As the clerk starts to put it in one of the yellow plastic Tower bags, Dana points to me and says, "This is the guy who recorded it."

The clerk glances at me quickly, obviously unimpressed and says, "Awesome."

Dana waits by the door as I pay for mine. "Thanks," I say to the clerk, but she's already focused on the next customer.

"She's obviously not a jazz fan," Dana says, nodding toward the cashier.

"Yeah, there aren't many of us."

I drive back up Sunset. It's still warm as I pull into a spot in front of an old style ice cream parlor coffee house. Marble tables, wire chairs, and a white tile floor. It's been such a long time, I decide to indulge in my all time favorite—a hot fudge sundae. Dana opts for a frozen yogurt. I get two coffees to go with the ice cream and we find a place at one of the outside tables.

The sundae is delicious and I haven't felt this relaxed in a long time. Dana watches me eat and smiles. "Hmm. Doesn't like peas, loves hot fudge sundaes. I'm getting to know you, Evan Horne."

"You think?" I finish off the sundae and chase it with some coffee and light a cigarette.

For a few minutes we both just kind of space out, watching the people walk by, the traffic, and occasionally exchange glances over one wild hairdo or outfit. Finally, Dana says, "So tell me about your girlfriend."

"Andie? Well, she's an FBI agent. She was a profiler but now she's on bank robbery detail whatever that is."

"Cal told me a little about her. I don't think he liked her. He said you met when that serial killer thing happened. I remember seeing some of it on the news."

"Yeah, we did. She had to run a background check on Cal during that investigation. Just brought up some old wounds and bad memories I guess."

Dana continues to study me. "So, is this pretty serious?" She leans forward and touches my arm. "I'm sorry, I'm just curious. It is kind of a strange combination. A jazz musician and an FBI agent."

"Yeah I guess it is. I don't know how serious it is really." I suddenly realize I don't. "We each have our own place but we've spent a lot of time together since I came back from Europe. I guess neither of us is sure where it's going. We're just kind of playing it by ear."

Dana nods and looks away.

"How about you? No boyfriends on the horizon."

She shrugs. "There was a guy for awhile but it didn't work out, and I'm so busy with grad school I don't have time for a relationship. Casual dating is kind of boring and the only guys I meet now are as tied up with studying as I am."

"That's too bad," I say. "You have a lot to offer someone."

She smiles. "Why thank you. That's very nice of you to say."

My cell phone rings then. I dig it out of my pocket and see it's Andie.

"Hey."

"Hey, yourself," Andie says. "How's it going?"

"Well, I just had a hot fudge sundae. Trying to relax a little."

Dana gets up and points inside and mimes ladies room.

"Sounds decadent," Andie says.

"I found out Cal had a life insurance policy with the musicians union, but I have no idea who the beneficiary is or how to find her."

"It's a woman?"

"Yes. Someone named Jean Lane. Any chance you could do some digging for me?"

"Evan, I told you I'm swamped but when you get back and I can see that photo and all, I'll see what I can do."

"That would be good."

"When are you coming back?"

"Hopefully by the weekend. I'm going to go along on a boat to scatter Cal's ashes. Have to call them tomorrow to set it up."

"I'm sorry, Evan, about all of it. That's going to be hard. I wish I could be there with you."

"Dana is going to go. I figured since she was the last one to see Cal and all," then regret it immediately.

"Of course," Andie says, a decided chill in her voice. Dana comes back and sits down and stares at the traffic.

"Come on, Andie, lighten up."

"I'm sorry. I'm just frustrated at not being there and I've been so tied up here."

"I know." There's a long pause where neither of us say anything. "Well, I'll let you go."

"Yeah, I've got an early briefing. Call me tomorrow."

"I will."

"Night."

"Night."

I punch off the phone, and light another cigarette. Dana looks at me. "Everything okay?"

I shrug. "Andie has a little jealous streak about her."

Dana nods. "I understand that. It's good. It means she cares."

Wednesday morning I call the cremation society around nine and talk to the same woman. There's a boat on Friday morning if I'd like to make a reservation, she tells me.

"There will be two, another friend of Mr. Hughes."

"Fine, I think you'll be glad you decided on this, Mr. Horne."

"I'm not so sure I am," I say.

"Trust me," Mrs. Johnson says. "Friday morning at ten. The lower deck of Santa Monica Pier. One of our representatives will be there."

I hang up the phone and wander around the house for a bit. Dana is already gone and has left a note for me that she has classes but will be back later this afternoon if I need her for anything. She's even drawn a little happy face on the bottom of the page.

I have to admit her presence has made things much easier and she's a bright attractive girl and...

I don't finish the thought when my cell rings.

"So, am I picking you up sometime today?" Andie asks.

I tell her again about the excursion to scatter Cal's ashes. "It's Friday. I just have to have some kind of closure on this, Andie, and this seems the only way."

I'd sat up late thinking about all this. Although it was a done deal and what Cal wanted, there would be no grave to visit in the coming years, no visible signs at all. But maybe it was best to remember Cal as I'd last seen him.

Andie sounds disappointed. "You're right."

"I have a couple of other things to run down while I'm here but I'll try to make it back Friday night or Saturday, okay?"

"Well I can't promise I'll be around. This case I'm on may get heavy by the weekend."

We're both silent for a long moment. "Let's just play it by ear then."

"Not much choice," she says. "Let me know what you decide."

"Andie."

"Yes."

"I'm going to pursue this thing with Cal and try to find the woman, the child in the photo, with or without your help."

"I know."

She's quiet again then, "Evan, you may not like what you find."

I know what she means. I've heard it before.

I call the Musicians' Retirement Home again and try to catch Mal Leonard. I get the same woman who tells me he's expected back around noon.

"Are there any restrictions on visitors?"

She laughs. "No, nothing like that. I'm sure he'll be glad to swap stories with you."

"Good, just tell him I'm the friend of Calvin Hughes."

"Will do," she says and hangs up.

With time to kill I sit down at Cal's piano and go through some exercises and start thinking about tunes for the Roy Haynes date.

That still hasn't quite registered yet. A recording date with Roy Haynes. Big label, promotion, and very likely I'll be in some very fast company with top flight bass players as well as Roy Haynes.

I love playing ballads so it's not hard to come up with several possibilities I can suggest to Haynes. For something more uptempo, I decide on "Solar," the Miles tune, and a blues line I dredge up from memory called "Shifting Down," by trumpeter Kenny Dorham that has a kind of quirky, rhythmic line I know Haynes would love to play on.

It feels good under my hands and before I know it, a couple of hours have passed. I also get out the lead sheets I'd found that Cal had left and play them again. I'd have to check them with the recordings, but the chord changes all fit and sound like the original to me. What Cal was doing with them is something I still haven't figured out, but as I leave I slip them into the file folder with the rest of the papers and photos.

On the drive down to the musicians' home, I stop at a Kinko's and make several copies of both lead sheets.

The young clerk picks them up. "Man, these are really old and in pencil. Can't promise the quality is going to be very good."

"That's okay. Do what you can."

He's back in a few minutes with fairly clear copies. "I punched up the contrast," he says. "Not bad really."

"Thanks." I pay for the copies and drive down to the address of the home off Melrose.

I'm not sure what I expected. A rest home? A convalescent hospital? But it's neither. A couple of low stucco buildings with a courtyard and some grounds that look pleasant enough. There's a large porch-veranda kind of affair in front and several men are playing cards at small tables. A few others are relaxing in chairs, some look to be dozing.

Inside at a small reception area, the voice on the phone has a face, a woman in her fifties named Connie. She has glasses on a chain around her neck and is dressed in a long shirt kind of dress with music notes all over it.

"Hi, I'm Evan Horne. I called earlier about seeing Mal Leonard."

"Right, right," she says. "He just got back a while ago. He's having lunch. Down that hallway, then to your left."

I start to ask her how I'll know him but she anticipates my question. "Mal is black and the biggest guy in the room."

"Thanks." I walk down the hall and find the small dining room. There are only a few men sitting around in little clusters seated at the picnic table style seating. Mal Leonard is by himself near the window with a cup of coffee in front of him.

"Mr. Leonard? I'm Evan Horne. You left a message for Cal Hughes last week."

He turns to me and smiles broadly and stands up to shake hands. "I sure was sorry to hear about Cal. Sit down, man. I'll get you some coffee."

For such a big man, he moves gracefully. He gets up and goes over to a small table with a coffee urn, mugs and brings me back one. Cream and sugar are on the table already. His hair is salt and pepper and tightly curled and he could be anywhere from fifty to seventy. He sits down again and looks at me.

"So you were a friend of Cal's, huh?"

"I didn't see him as much as I should have and now of course—"

"I know what you mean," he says. "Damn if I had known he was around here I would have got up there somehow. You a piano player too?"

"Yes."

He nods. "Figures. Well you must be good. Cal didn't mess with people that couldn't play. So what can I do for you?" He smiles again. "I got my bass back in my room if you feel like playin'?"

"Well, I—"

He grins. "I'm just teasing." He flexes his hands. "This arthritis got me. I don't know why I even keep my bass. I tell you, getting old sucks."

He takes a sip of his coffee. "How can I help?"

I open the file folder and show him the photo with Cal and Miles and Barney Jackson first. He adjusts his glasses and studies the photo. "Uh huh," he says. "Well course we know that's Miles and Cal. Other guy is Barney Jackson, but I bet you already know that."

"Yes, I was at the Musicians' Union. One of the business reps recognized him, and I talked to his wife. He died over a year ago."

Mal blinks a couple of times. "You don't say. I don't know how I missed that. I knew Barney pretty well at one time. We used to trade gigs sometimes."

I take out the other photo. "This is the one I can't figure," I say as I show it to him.

He leans over close to peer at the photo and studies it for a couple of minutes then pushes it aside. "You know Cal talked about a woman in Kansas City but, well, I s'poze this could be her, but I didn't know nothing about no baby."

"You think this could be Cal's baby?"

"Could be, man. Could be. We spent a lot of time in Kansas City in those days. There was women everywhere." He turns and looks out the window, smiling, digging through memories. "Women, lot of bands, lot of music. There was a lot of scuffling, but we always had gigs in those days." He looks at me again. "What did you say your name was?"

"Evan Horne."

"And do you know Cal?"

The questions confuse me for a moment but then I realize Mal's short term memory is much less accurate than his early life.

"I'm sorry, man. I can remember gigs, conversations, even hotels I stayed at but sometimes I can't remember what I did yesterday." He shakes his head. "Just drives me crazy."

"Do you think this photo might have been taken in Kansas City?"

He looks at it again. "Oh yeah, no doubt about that."

I sit up straighter. "Really? Why are you so sure?"

He points to the OTEL sign in the photo with a thick finger. "That's the Carlisle Hotel. The H was shot out by this crazy trumpet player and they never fixed it." He laughs so hard then his whole body shakes. "Mmm, mmm. Billy Webb. That boy thought his girlfriend was up in one of the rooms. He was trying to hit the window and missed." He looks at me steadily, then points to the photo. "Right there to the left is 18th and Vine. Yep. Carlisle Hotel, Kansas City, MO. Charlie Parker, Lester Young. Why I remember one night—"

Then he's off for ten minutes recounting a jam session he was involved in before he realizes how long he's been talking. Or that I'm even there. I was just the trigger. He stops suddenly and then looks at me.

"Sorry, I get carried away sometimes. Are you Evan Horne?" He leans in closer. "Any chance you got an extra cigarette?" He notices the pack in my pocket. "We can't smoke in here and I'm not supposed to at all but hey, one won't hurt. Let's go outside."

In the back there's a garden area and a few wicker chairs scattered around. "Connie won't see us out here," he says, taking a cigarette and a light from me. He leans back in the chair and drags deeply on the cigarette. and looks at it. "Menthol. Lucky Strike was my brand."

"Do you remember a woman named Jean Lane? Somebody Cal knew maybe."

Mal leans forward. "Cal had a lot of women, they just gravitated to him like bees to a flower, but names? Man, I wish I could help you."

"Well you did. At least I know where the photo was taken. Jean Lane is listed on Cal's life insurance policy from the union."

"Oh I dig," Mal says, "and you trying to find her."

"Exactly."

He crushes out the cigarette under his heel and pockets the butt. "Can't leave no evidence for Connie," he says.

"Well if I was you, I'd put on some Count Basie and think about heading for Kansas City." He laughs and starts humming the tune.

"Thanks again, Mal."

He smiles and nods but doesn't get out of the chair.

On the way out, Connie catches up with me. "Did he talk you out of a smoke?"

"Ah, well, yes he did."

"That old rascal." She smiles and shakes her head. "He pulls that on anybody who comes here that smokes."

"Sorry, I—"

She waves her hand. "Don't worry, he doesn't get enough smoking visitors to matter much. What else has he got? Come back if you can, even if you don't find what you're looking for."

"I will."

I try Al Beckwood again but still no answer and I wonder if he might be out of town. He's certainly one of those rare ones who has no answering machine. I turn back toward Hollywood, unsure what to do next.

I've identified the people in the photo and thanks to Mal Leonard, it's reasonably certain the baby carriage photo was taken in Kansas City. But I'm no closer to knowing who or where I can find Jean Lane, if she's still around. Or for that matter, the baby in the carriage.

I think about what Andie said when I told her I was going to pursue this. You might not like what you find. Was it what I'd find, or was it that she knows more than she's letting on. She's obviously not eager to help in the search and surely, since the FBI had checked Cal out before, she could look at that file again. It was something we were going to have to talk about, I realize finally. That's maybe a conversation neither of us wants to have.

At a stop light on Hollywood Boulevard, a tiny piece clicks into place. The dresser drawer full of receipts and papers.

Suddenly I can't drive fast enough to get back to the house.

Chapter Five

A junk drawer. Usually it's that odd, extra drawer somewhere in the kitchen for those things we don't throw away but don't quite know what to do with yet. Old receipts, warranty cards that are never mailed, phone numbers on scraps of paper without names, special offers that have expired long ago. A key or two that we don't recognize or know what they open, old pencils, pens, a battery or two we never got around to using, a small screwdriver, pizza coupons, Chinese take-out menus. The list is endless. Everybody has one, and this is Cal's.

I'd taken everything from the drawer and put it in a shoe box earlier. Now I bring the box over to the bed, dump it all out, and start going through it piece by piece, first separating papers—receipts, menus, coupons, scraps—from solid objects. There are the usual pencil stubs, pens that don't work, two small screwdrivers, a Phillips head and one with a tiny blade for glasses, and the pocket watch I'd looked at earlier. I turn that over in my hand. It's gold with a white face and large black Roman numerals. No inscription, no marks, just a watch with a cover that clicks into place over the face of the watch.

There's also a silver cigarette lighter, the kind you don't see much anymore. Small, slim, compact, maybe a woman's, the body of the lighter done in black, alligator-like leather. On the bottom, Ronson Princess is stamped on it, and on a small silver plate, engraved in all caps is the name JEAN.

I weigh it in my hand and press down on the lever. Not even a spark. I lay it and the pocket watch aside and start with the paper items.

Most of them are cash register receipts of one kind or other. The printing has faded on most but they seem to be from L.A. businesses, or have no identifying marks at all. The larger pieces are bills, a couple of warranty cards for a coffee maker and a toaster, and several hotel bills. I sort through these and find three for the Hotel Carlisle, Kansas City, Missouri. The dates are 1959-1961. There are also passenger copies of two round trip train tickets from Kansas City to New York.

I stop for a minute and light a cigarette. Cal could and probably did live in both places at one time. Both cities figured prominently in the jazz scene, and many musicians gravitated to New York from Kansas City, Detroit, Chicago. Count Basie, Lester Young, Charlie Parker all had roots in Kansas City. Cal would have been in the thick of things in those days. On a whim, I dial the number on the Hotel Carlisle bill, but of course I get nothing but one of those weird tones and a voice saying, "Your call cannot be completed as dialed. Please try again."

I set the lighter, the pocket watch, and the hotel bills aside and dump everything else in the trash under the kitchen sink. The pocket watch I stuff in my bag, and for some reason, the lighter in my pocket, wondering if it can be fixed. The hotel bills I slip into the file folder I've been carrying around with the intention of making copies of them sometime.

I hear footsteps then and Dana comes in. "Hi. What's up?" she says.

"Just going through things from that drawer." I show her the lighter and bring her up to date on my visit to the union and the musicians' home and my visit with Mal Leonard.

"You've been busy," she says, dropping into Cal's chair.

"Yeah, but not accomplishing much."

Dana smiles. "Well, you know more than you did a couple of days ago."

"I guess. It's just, it seems like it's going to be a long haul. Too much time has passed."

She picks up the hotel bills and looks at them. "God, is this the one in the photo?"

"So Mal Leonard says. He even told me a story about how the H in the sign was shot out by a jealous boyfriend."

She nods and lays the bill down again. "Do you think Cal was staying there?"

I shrug. "Probably. It's certainly possible. I still haven't connected with Al Beckwood. I'll keep trying with that and, well, after that, I don't know."

She nods again and smiles. "It'll come. You just have to let it happen."

"Let's hope so. You have any plans tonight?"

"Well I should do some work on my thesis, but I can easily be talked out of that. What do you have in mind?"

I look away for a moment. What do I have in mind? The more I'm around Dana, the more I like her. "I'm sorry, with all this happening, I've never even asked what your thesis is about."

"Oh that," she says, laughing. "A close textual analysis of F. Scott Fitzgerald's *The Great Gatsby.* Colon—there always has to be a colon in academic titles. 'Daisy: Victim or Instrument of Gatsby's Death.'"

"Wow."

She laughs again. "Well I always loved the book, but finding something nobody has written about already is hard, so it's a stretch."

"It'll come. You just have to let it happen."

"Okay, you got me. Now what are you going to tempt me with?"

I think for a moment. "Want to hear some jazz? There's a place in the valley with pretty good food and usually a pretty good trio."

"Yes!" she says. She stands up. "Do I need to change?" She stands up and holds out her arms. She's wearing very form fitting jeans, a light sweater, and sandals.

"Not a thing."

◇◇◇

Conte's is on Ventura Boulevard in Encino. Nothing upscale but good food, at least the last time I was there, and they've maintained a jazz policy, despite the closing of many other clubs. They do it by using studio players who aren't concerned so much with money as they are with having a place to play, or new guys, just looking to make some gigs, stretch out, get away from the rigors and constrictions of recording or casual money gigs.

The first set is underway when we arrive. We get a booth fairly close to the band. I don't know the piano player or the drummer but I'm pleasantly surprised to see the bassist is Buster Browne. I catch his eye and wave as Dana and I sit down. He smiles broadly and nods then hunches over his bass and pulls off a couple of choruses on "Invitation."

"You know him?" Dana says.

"Yeah we go way back." We order two glasses of wine, salad, and the special of the day, a seafood pasta in cream sauce. We're just finishing our salads when the set ends and Buster comes over. I introduce him to Dana and he slides in next to her in the booth.

"So, Buster, how you doing?"

"Oh you know, gig here, gig there. Same old thing. I had a good run with Bonnie Rait for awhile. I heard you were in Europe."

"Yeah, I worked Ronnie Scott's in London for a week, then hooked up with a tenor player named Fletcher Paige. We landed a gig in Amsterdam that lasted three months. I'm living in the Bay Area now. Just down here for some business."

Buster frowns. "Fletcher Paige. Tenor player, right? Wow, I thought he was dead, man. He must have been over there a long time." Buster smiles at me. "You get into any trouble over there, any detective work?" He turns to Dana. "This cat can be scary."

I let it go, not wanting to get into the long story about tracking down Chet Baker and my friend Ace Buffington. I glance quickly at Dana. "No, everything was fine, Buster."

Buster looks at his watch. "We gotta go back. You feel like playing a couple? It's been awhile."

I glance at Dana. "Sure, if the piano player doesn't mind. Who is he?"

"Naw, he's cool. Joey Beal. He's been around awhile. You know this town and piano players. Never enough good ones, then too many." Buster gets up. "I'm going to get some air. Give me a nod when you want to come up, okay?"

"I'm excited," Dana says. "I get to hear you play." She's already downed her first glass of wine. "How long have you known Buster? Is that really his name? I won't ask about the shoes."

"Only one I know him by. We worked together a number of times. Last one was the concert in Las Vegas he mentioned."

"And you don't want to talk about that one." She holds up her glass and I pour her some more wine. "So how does this work, you playing with them. Are there some kind of rules?"

"Well, usually if one or other of the musicians knows you, and they like you, you'll be invited to play and it's fine. Buster will let the piano player know I'm here, and unless he's got some particular reason, he won't mind. It's just kind of an unwritten protocol. My part means I won't play more than two or three tunes."

"Camaraderie among musicians. You have your own little society don't you?"

"Yeah I guess we do."

We get through dinner and listen as the trio comes back. Joey Beal has a nice touch and I guess the three of them have been playing together for awhile. The trio has a kind of straight ahead feel as they play standards and blues. Nothing to really upset the dinner crowd but enough jazz to satisfy people who come for the music. When Buster looks over and raises his eyebrows, I nod and get up. "Back in awhile," I say to Dana.

Buster introduces me to Joey. "Hey, the detective piano player," he says but not in an unfriendly way. "The piano is pretty good. Enjoy, man."

I sit down at the piano and turn to Buster and the drummer, a young black man with a pencil thin mustache. "How about 'Sweet and Lovely'?"

Buster nods, the drummer nods, and we take it at a medium two tempo, Buster just floating behind me as the drummer stays with brushes for a couple of choruses. I lean in more as Buster starts walking in four and the drummer switches to sticks and we swing hard for two more choruses. Buster solos for two choruses and then we exchange fours with the drummer and take it out.

"Yeah," Busters says. "You're playing better than ever, man."

"Thanks." I flex my right hand. Not even a twinge of pain. "A ballad? Then I'll get out of here."

"Sure. What have you got," Buster says.

"'My Foolish Heart'?"

I play through one chorus out of tempo alone, then Buster and the drummer ease in as we take up the slow ballad tempo. Buster nods his head as I near the end of two choruses. He plays half then I come back in and we close it out.

"Thanks," I say. I stand up as Joey comes back to the piano.

"Very cool, man. Come by again if you stay in town. Good to see you," Buster smiles.

"You too, Buster." I shake hands with the drummer and Joey and return to the booth.

"That was amazing," Dana says. I see she's already ordered some coffee.

"Glad you liked it." We listen to a couple more tunes, then I get the check. I wave again to Buster as we leave.

In the car going back to the house, Dana is quiet. The radio is tuned to KLON and Bill Evans is gliding through the changes of "I Love You." I glance over from to time, see her just staring out the window. "Something on your mind?"

"What?" She turns toward me. "Oh, sorry, just zoned out for a minute."

"Thinking about your thesis?"

She laughs. "Hardly. That's about the last thing on my mind."

"What then?" We pass the 405 Interchange and head east toward Hollywood.

She sighs and leans back. "I was just thinking, these last couple of nights, seeing you play tonight. I'm going to miss you being around." She sits up straighter and turns up the volume on the radio. "Who is that? It sounds kind of like you."

"Thanks. That's Bill Evans." I stare straight ahead, light a cigarette and crack the window. "Are you going to be okay in the house?"

"You mean am I going to be spooked?"

"Well, yeah."

She smiles. "No, I'll be fine and I'll have Milton." She looks over at me till I feel her gaze. "Andie is a lucky woman."

Neither of us says anymore till we get to the house.

I wake up early in spite of sitting up for over an hour, just thinking, letting my mind run over things. Dana is gone when I get up. I make coffee and sit at the kitchen table with a pad and pen, trying to write Cal's obituary for the Musicians International. I look at what I've written so far.

> *Calvin Hughes—pianist, composer, teacher, died in his Hollywood home of natural causes. Born in Kansas City, MO, Hughes' career spanned six decades, as a pianist with a number of territory bands before moving to New York. In 1949, he became a member of a rehearsal band that eventually led to the recording of Miles Davis' Birth of the Cool.*
>
> *Hughes later moved to southern California where he was a staple at Los Angeles jazz clubs while teaching youth groups in Watts. In the early 80s, Hughes retired from active playing and lived quietly in Hollywood. Hughes is survived by*

I stop there. Who? Jean Lane? An unknown child? How to fill in those blanks? I stare at the pad for several minutes before I continue.

> *No funeral services were held. Messages, condolences can be sent care of Evan Horne.*

I add my address and phone in Monte Rio and as an afterthought, Cal's home address and phone. Not much but it's all I can think of.

I get a second cup of coffee and sit down to think about it some more when the doorbell rings. I go to the door and find a man in a three piece suit and tie. He's about thirty and carries an expensive looking tan briefcase. "Yes, can I help you?" I don't open the screen door.

He flashes me a big smile. "Evan Horne?"

"Yes."

"Hi, I'm Brent Sergent with Erwin, McCullough, and Bowers Developers. Do you have a few minutes?" He holds up a business card. I glance at it through the screen door and look back at him.

"What's this about?" I open the screen door and let him in.

"Thanks." He steps inside and gives the living room a quick once over. "Smaller than I imagined," he says. He looks back at me. "I understand you just inherited this place from a Mr. Calvin Hughes."

"Yeah, that's right. What about it?" I already don't like Sergent. He's just too slick, too presumptive. I know he's selling something. "How did you know?"

"Public record, Mr. Horne," he says almost too quickly. "My company is prepared to make you an offer, a very considerable offer I might add. I'm sure you are aware of property values in this area. Frankly, this place isn't worth the cost of razing it. But the land is extremely valuable."

"It's not for sale," I say.

He gazes at me. "Can we sit down for a minute?"

I shrug. "Sure, but you're wasting your time."

Sergent sits down on the small sofa and snaps open his briefcase. He takes out a document and hands it to me. "Just take a glance at this, Mr. Horne. Please."

I take it from him and look it over. It's an offer for sale and the amount is mid six figures. I look up at Sergent. "Are you serious?"

"Very," Sergent says. "Of course that offer is negotiable."

"Of course."

Sergent frowns. "Did you have a higher figure in mind?" he says cautiously.

"I had no figure in mind. Like I said, it's not for sale."

"But surely, Mr. Horne, you can't—"

"Yes I can. There's really nothing to talk abut. I've already rented the house and the new tenant has moved in."

"I see." Sergent gives me a disappointed sigh. "Well, will you just hang on to that, think it over maybe, and get back to me."

"I can do that, but I'm afraid my answer will be the same."

Sergent nods and closes his brief case. "Thanks for your time." He heads for the door, pauses as if he's going to say something more, then thinks better of it.

"Mr. Sergent."

"Yes? Brent, please."

"Okay, Brent. Call before you come next time."

"Certainly."

He goes out and I stand at the door for a minute watching him walk down the steep steps. He brushes past Dana, then turns, and gives her an appraising look.

"Who was that?" she says, nearing the door."

"Some builder's rep, wanting to buy the house." I hand her the offer.

She takes it from me and scans over it then her eyes go wide. "Oh my God. $650,000?"

"They want to tear it down and build condos probably."

"What did you tell him?"

"I said it's not for sale."

"I may be cutting my own throat, but Evan, are you crazy? That's a lot of money."

It was. More than I'd ever seen or probably ever would see, and I admit I felt more than a twinge of temptation, but it didn't feel right. Why hadn't Cal sold it? He must have had similar offers over the years and I bet from the same people.

"I know but, I hadn't even thought about it until he showed up. I'm just not comfortable with the idea, at least not now, so soon after Cal's death."

Dana nods but still looks skeptical, shaking her head. She sets the document down on the table.

"Where did you go anyway?"

"Oh just down to get some donuts." She hands me a bag.

I look inside. "Mmmm chocolate. How did you know?"

"I watched you wolf down that sundae the other night, remember?"

"You are very observant. Okay, well let's do these in. Coffee is already made. Then we have a boat to catch."

There's no easy way to get to Santa Monica from Hollywood. I could either go south to the Santa Monica Freeway, which meant a lot of traffic signals, or take Sunset to the San Diego Freeway. At this time of morning, I opt for Sunset.

We get lucky and make the drive to Santa Monica in record time. As I start down the steep incline of Santa Monica Pier fifteen minutes ahead of schedule, I begin to feel some misgivings about the whole thing. Maybe I should just skip this part entirely, make a U-turn and...

Dana touches my arm, sensing my thoughts. "It's going to be okay, Evan."

I nod and sigh and keep going. It's less crowded than I thought and I manage to find a parking space in a lot by the merry-go-round. How many times had I ridden that as a kid?

We get out and I lock the car and start walking toward the end. The pier has always had a special feeling for me. I'd spent a lot of time here as a kid. Riding the carousel, eating snow cones and hot dogs, even once jumping off on a dare. But not all the memories were good.

At the end of the pier, I catch sight of a man in a dark suit. There are several small boxes stacked near him. His tie flaps in the breeze and behind him, the water looks choppy. The sky is slate gray and getting darker. I catch his eye as we near. "Are you from the Society?"

He steps forward. "Yes," he says. "Arthur Cummings." He holds out his hand.

"Evan Horne," I say. "This is my friend Dana Trent."

He nods at Dana and checks off my name on a clip board he holds in one hand. "We're waiting for one more person," he says. He turns to the small boxes, picks one up and hands it to me. There's a typed label with Cal's name and the logo of the society. "If you'd like to join the others." He indicates several other people standing nearby. "We'll be underway soon."

"Thanks." We walk over and nod, exchange sympathetic looks with each other and wait. Nobody is talking much. I light a cigarette, glad I'd brought a jacket as the wind whips up. I can't wrap my mind around the fact that all that remains of Cal is in this small box.

The box is dark maroon plastic with a flip top lid sealed shut with a notice stating the state of California's regulations regarding disposal of remains. Inside, in a clear plastic bag, are the gray ashes of Calvin Hughes. There's a label on the top with the Society's address. I close the lid and look around for Dana. She's gone over to the railing, her hair blowing all over, staring out over Santa Monica Bay.

A few minutes later, a woman rushes up, slightly out of breath and checks in with Cummings. He comes over with her. "Now if you'll just all follow me," he says, "we'll be on our way."

We follow him down a flight of steps to a ramp below the pier at water level and step aboard a small motor launch with bench seating in the back and a small enclosed area in the cabin. The motor is already running and the captain, a craggy faced man in a baseball cap is manning the wheel.

We all get aboard and find seats. I count nine people in all. The captain guns the motor, gets a nod from Cummings, and we pull away from the pier heading for the break in the bay.

With the wind and chop, the ride is pretty bumpy and a couple of people already look queasy. I begin to have second thoughts about this again as we clear the bay and head for the open sea.

Cummings stands by the wheel house, talking with the captain, his white hair blowing in the wind, hanging on to the side of the door, periodically checking on all of us.

We go probably a mile or two then the boat makes a looping turn. The engine slows and finally we come to a stop and idle, the boat rocking up and down. No sound but the water lapping against the boat and the low rumble of the engine. Instinctively we all took toward Cummings, awaiting his cue. I feel Dana's hand on my arm.

Cummings bows his head for a moment, says something but his words are lost in the wind. He looks up then and smiles.

"Take your time ladies and gentlemen. We're in no hurry." One by one we stand up and get close to the side of the boat. I look down at the box. It weighs maybe five pounds. There's a sliding top. I pull it back a few inches and see the gray ash. A woman next to me suddenly starts crying as she opens her box and holds it up. The wind catches the ash and blows it quickly away in a small cloud. I follow suit, numb, not quite knowing what to think. "Good bye, Cal" is all I can manage in a soft whisper, as Dana grips my other arm to steady herself in the rocking boat.

Everyone except one man finishes in about ten minutes. He just sits, unable to move. Cummings watches and moves toward him, talking quietly. The man doesn't look at Cummings, but his head bobs up and down. He finally stands up and opens his box, Cummings' hand on his shoulder, and flings it up in the air. Ashes and box fly, both whipped by the wind. There's a small almost unseen splash as the box hits the water, then the man sits down again, his head in his hands.

Cummings gives the captain a nod and we start back. Nobody talks. Total silence except for the whine of the engine, the water crashing against the hull, a few squawking gulls until we get back to the pier. Cummings has a bag to dispose of the boxes and I wonder if they are used again. I start to put mine in the bag but at the last minute, I decide to keep it. A few other people cling to theirs. The final bit of ceremony is Cummings handing us a small card with the latitude and longitude of where the ashes were scattered.

Dana and I climb back up the stairs with the others. I walk over to the end of the pier and stare out toward the spot where we just were. Two men alongside me have fishing lines in the water and coolers filled with beer and bait. Finally, I turn back to where Dana is waiting and we walk to the car. We get in and I just sit for a moment, thinking, lighting a cigarette. The whole process has taken less than an hour.

"You okay?" Dana says.

"Yeah, I guess so." I sit up and start the car.

"I don't know about you, but I could use a drink."

We're both quiet during lunch at a Mexican restaurant in Santa Monica, sitting somberly, sipping margaritas, eating chips as we wait for our order.

After awhile, Dana reaches over and touches my arm. "Tell me to shut up if you want, Evan. But really, there's nothing more you could do. Cal was sick a long time and he knew what was coming."

I smile at her and nod. "I know. I guess my reaction is fairly normal, huh?"

"Of course it is. I only knew him a short time so I can imagine what it's like for you."

We order another margarita when our food comes and lapse into silence again as we eat. Finally, I push my plate aside. "I'm going back today, Dana. If I can't get a flight, I'm going to try standby."

Dana just nods, avoids my eyes. She leans back in the booth and sighs. "You want to get home, see Andie. I understand."

"Well, yes. I—"

Dana gets up quickly and heads for the ladies room. "I'll be right back," she mumbles.

I get the check, pay it, and stand outside smoking, waiting for her. When she comes out she's more together and smiling.

"Okay, I'm ready," she says.

We drive back to the house without talking, the radio play-ing, both of us lost in thought. Inside I call Southwest and get reasonable assurance I can get on standby to Oakland at four. I check my watch and start gathering up my things.

"Can I drop you off?" Dana is watching me throw things in my bag.

"Well, no. I have the rental car to return."

"Oh, right. Well, I guess we'll say goodbye here then." She looks away and shakes her hands. "I'm sorry. I'm being stupid."

"No you're not." I walk over and hug her. "Thanks for being here and thanks for taking care of Cal, and thanks for taking over the house."

She nods, then her arms go around my neck. She leans back, looks at me and kisses me lightly. "You take care of yourself."

"I will. And you call me if you need anything. Promise?"

She nods. "Now get out of here."

I grab my bag and turn and go out, jogging down the steps. I get in the car and look up the steep stairs. Dana is standing at the top, looking down, waving.

I wave back and pull away, wondering not if I'll see her again, but when.

At Burbank Airport, I return the rental car and check in with Southwest. Still looks good for standby the attendant at the gate tells me.

"Stay close," she says, as she types into the computer. "We've had a few cancellations so you're in luck."

"Thanks," I say and go looking for coffee.

Now that I'm here at the airport, I'm anxious to get back, see Andie and hope I can get her to dig a little for me on Cal's back-ground. If anybody can find Jean Lane, it should be the FBI.

I pace around the gate waiting for the plane to arrive, drinking coffee and wishing I could slip outside for a quick smoke. Finally the arrival announcement is made and I watch the passengers getting off in Burbank. A few minutes later, boarding begins.

Another ten minutes passes, then the gate attendant calls me and four other passengers on standby. Before boarding, I make a quick call to Andie and leave a message on her voice mail, hoping she'll get it before I arrive in Oakland. I turn off my cell and grab the first available seat. I doze off once we're up, miss the drink service. When I look out the window, we're already on final approach into Oakland.

Hurrying through the terminal, I finally make the baggage claim exit and scan the cars lining up for Andie. But getting out of a car and walking over is not Andie but a man in a dark suit, who I know immediately means trouble. Ted Rollins, another agent who worked with Andie on the Gillian Payne case in L.A—I'd clashed with him from the start. Rollins had disapproved of me being involved in the case and even more so, when Andie and I started to hit it off.

His face is grim as he comes up.

"What?" I say, setting my bag down and digging for a cigarette.

"I'm here to pick you up," Rollins says. "Car's over there."

"What happened?" Rollins is maddeningly laconic.

"It's Andie," Rollins says quietly. "She's okay but she was involved in a shooting this morning during a bank robbery. She's going through debriefing now."

"Dammit, Rollins, is she okay?"

Rollins smiles. "She's fine but the bad guy isn't."

Chapter Six

We get in Rollins' car. He swings into the traffic flow, ignoring the security guy's hand waving as a light drizzle starts to make the street wet and send people scurrying for cover, dragging bags, holding briefcases and purses over their heads. Before I can ask him anything, his cell phone chirps. He stabs at a button.

"Rollins. Yeah, he's right here." He listens for a moment. "About forty minutes depending on the traffic." He listens again, glances over at me then says, "Right, I'll tell him." He turns off the phone and slips it in his coat pocket, his eyes straight ahead, his hands gripping the wheel as we snake out of Oakland Airport and onto the access road for I-880.

"Well? Tell me what?"

"That was Andie's supervisor," Rollins says. "I'm taking you to the hospital."

"The hospital? You said Andie—"

"I said she was okay. I didn't say she wasn't injured. She's out of surgery and doing fine."

I shake my head and smile. "Nothing much has changed has it Rollins?" I dig for my cigarettes and light one.

Rollins looks sharply over at me. "This is an official FBI car," he says. "That means no smoking."

I roll down my window halfway. "I'm not in the FBI. Guess you'll have to charge me."

Rollins shakes his head. "Nothing has changed with you either. Still the smart ass jazz musician." He rolls his own window down and waves his hand at the nonexistent smoke.

I first met Ted Rollins when some looney tune started knocking off smooth jazz musicians and leaving jazz related clues at the crime scenes. When the killer had struck in Santa Monica, Danny Cooper's territory. I agreed to help, but only as an observer, and only because it was Coop asking to help the FBI. So I did.

My involvement had gotten deeper with subsequent murders and that's when I'd met Ted Rollins, as well as Wendell Cook and Andie Lawrence.

Rollins felt I was a waste of time. The FBI didn't need a musician in the mix, he'd argued, but he'd been overruled and then acted like it was my doing. I helped Andie work up a profile and we spent more time together. Then, when the killer actually contacted me, the FBI made me a conduit. It had been a terrifying experience and Rollins had made it worse with his constant harassing that increased when Andie and I hit it off so well. Rollins had a thing for her, I realized, and he saw me as both a threat and a nuisance.

It had turned out well, all things considered, but Rollins never got over it and I can see now, he's in the same mode, loving the control, making me ask for information, like he's in charge.

I think about all this and finish my cigarette, flipping it out the window on the I-880 freeway under Rollins' disapproving gaze. "Hey, I didn't want to get your FBI ashtray dirty," I say. Rolling up the window, I turn slightly facing him. "What did happen?"

Rollins is silent for a moment, gauging I suppose, how much to tell me but probably realizing Andie will tell me everything eventually. "You knew about her being on this bank detail, right?"

"Yes, but believe it or not, she doesn't talk much about her assignments."

Rollins nods. "Yeah, she's a good agent." He changes lanes, following the signs for San Francisco and heads for the Bay

Bridge maze. "I don't know the whole story, but the bureau has had these two guys under surveillance for some time. We knew they were getting ready to roll on one and this morning they did. We let them in the bank and started to move in when one panicked, spotted a car or something. I'm not sure."

"Andie was one of the first ones moving in as one of them came out of the bank with a shotgun. He opened fire immediately, hit Andie but, she caught him on the way down and the rest of us moved in."

"Jesus." I watched the traffic, trying to visualize the scene.

"She was lucky, far enough away so the blast only caught her in the leg. Lot of blood, looked worse than it was."

"They get both guys?"

"Yes, we got them. The other guy just threw himself down on his stomach and yelled at us not to shoot him. Nobody in the bank was hurt either so it was a good show."

I look at Rollins. "A good show?" He just nods, as we snake through the maze toward the toll booth and finally get through and onto The Bay Bridge. The traffic in the city is not quite so bad and we make it to the hospital in less than the forty minutes Rollins estimated.

At the admitting desk, Rollins flashes his badge and we're directed up to the third floor where a nurse tells us Andie is in recovery and wants to know who I am, if I'm a relative.

"We live together," I tell her, noticing Rollins almost flinch.

The nurse nods. "You can see her briefly in about an hour. I think the doctor is still around if you want to talk to him."

"Yes, I would. Thanks." She picks up the phone and dials. "I'll see if I can get him."

Rollins turns to me and hands me a ring of keys. "We brought her car here," he says. "I got things to do."

"Thanks for the ride." Rollins turns and heads back for the elevator. I turn to the nurse. "Where is the cafeteria?"

"Basement. Coffee is terrible but it's hot," she laughs. "Doctor Muckle is already there. Dark curly hair with a white patch. Can't miss him."

"Thanks."

I share the elevator with an orderly and patient on a gurney headed for surgery and find my way to the cafeteria. Grabbing a sandwich and large coffee, I scan the cafeteria and find Dr. Muckle at a corner table, eating soup and crackers.

"Excuse me, doctor. I'm Evan Horne. You just operated on the FBI agent with the gunshot wound."

He looks up. "Yes."

"We're not married but I guess I'm the closest thing to next of kin. We live together."

"Oh, I see. Well, sit down, please."

I sit down and unwrap my sandwich and add cream and sugar to my coffee as Dr. Muckle finishes his soup. "The wound was largely superficial," he says, pushing the bowl aside. "Some blood loss but she'll be fine with plenty of rest. She's a lucky young woman. The shot wasn't a direct hit." He shakes his head and frowns. "In broad daylight, right in San Francisco. I guess I shouldn't be surprised anymore."

I just nod, imagining the scene, Andie on the ground, bleeding, waiting for paramedics.

"I don't think there's anything else I can tell you," he says. "Couple of prescriptions to fill for pain and see she takes it easy."

"I will. Thank you, doctor." I get up and take my coffee, go up to the lobby, through the main entrance and outside. I find a space on a concrete wall in the circular driveway. There are several nurses and doctors in scrubs drinking coffee, talking and smoking. Somehow that doesn't make me feel so bad when I light up in front of a hospital.

I get about half the sandwich down when my cell phone rings.

"Evan? It's Dana."

"What's up," I say, more sharply than I intended.

"I just wanted to make sure you got back okay. Is something wrong? You sound funny."

"Sorry, little chaotic here. Andie was shot this morning during a bank robbery attempt she was working on."

"Oh my God, is she okay?"

A couple of the nurses turn and look at me. I walk a few feet away. "Yeah, I think so. I haven't seen her yet. She's in recovery now."

"Well that's good. The other reason I called is that developer guy that was here, Brent Sergent, called me, wanted to know about the house. I told him it was your business, I'm just a tenant and—"

"Are you serious? I told him I would call him. Look if he calls again or comes by just refer him to me. Don't let him in the house. I'll take care of it."

"Oh I will. Don't worry. He's kind of creepy. Asked me to lunch to talk about it."

"Don't go. How's Milton?"

"He's fine, but I think he misses you. He kind of wanders from room to room, looking. I'm sure he wonders where Cal is."

"He'll get over it. Listen, I have to go but I'll talk to you later, okay?"

"Sure. I hope Andie is okay."

"Thanks, Dana. Bye." I press the off button and pace around for a minute thinking about Brent Sergent. Then I dial Coop's work number and get transferred to his office.

"Coop, it's Evan."

"I was just going to call you," he says, "maybe have dinner, tonight?"

"Sorry, I forgot to tell you. I got a standby flight. I'm already back in San Francisco."

"Ah, quick getaway."

"Yeah, well I walked into it here." I tell him about Andie and the bank robbery.

"Hmm, sounds like she was lucky," he says with typical cop coolness.

"I haven't seen her but it sounds that way. But that's not why I called. Dana just called me. A developer came by yesterday, making an outrageous offer on Cal's house. I told him no and not to call or come by again, but he called Dana, hit on her about it."

"Uh huh. And?"

"He's from a company called, Erwin, McCullough, and Bowers. Know anything about them? Brent Sergent is this guy's name?"

"I've seen their billboards around town. They have offices in Santa Monica too." He pauses a moment. "There was something about them in the paper fairly recently, but I can't remember now what it was."

"Can you run it down for me? I'd like to put some heat on this guy."

"Well begging you to take money and calling Dana isn't exactly a crime."

"I know. I'd just like to know who I'm dealing with."

"Okay, I'll see what I can dig up. My best to Andie."

"Thanks, Coop."

Leaning over Andie's bed, I kiss her on the forehead. Her eyes flutter for a moment then she focuses on me. "Oh, I'm so glad you're here." She manages a weak smile. "I'm so sleepy."

"Got you drugged up huh?"

"Yeah but I'm not complaining." She smiles again. "Did somebody pick you up?"

"Yes, my old buddy Ted Rollins."

"Oh God, I bet you enjoyed that." She shifts in the bed and pulls the covers back. Her left thigh is swathed in bandages. "Nice huh?"

"Doc says you were lucky." Her eyes close briefly then open again.

"What? I'm sorry I can't stay awake."

"That's okay, you need the rest. Look I'm going to run down to Monte Rio, pick up some things and I'll be back this evening okay? You need anything? They say they're going to keep you for a couple of days."

"Yes, I—" Her eyes close again.

On the way out, I pass the nurse and tell her when Andie wakes to tell her I'll be back later this evening and write down my cell phone for her.

"She'll be out awhile," the nurse says. "You go do something."

I find Andie's car in the parking lot after a lengthy search, having forgotten to ask Rollins where it was parked. It's another tan Ford Taurus sedan. I gas it up and head for the Golden Gate Bridge and the long haul up 101 to River Road, thinking more about Andie, Brent Sergent, and everything I'd covered in L.A.

By the time I make the River Road turnoff for Guerneville, it's dark, but at least there's no traffic as I cruise through Guerneville and continue another four miles to Monte Rio. The post office is already closed so no chance to pick up any mail. I cross the little bridge to Bohemian Avenue and turn into my place.

Inside it's stuffy from being closed up for a week, so I go around opening windows and airing it out. I put on some music, Keith Jarrett's *Kolon Concert*, and rummage around in the fridge for something to eat, but decide in the end to get some Chinese takeout from a place a couple of blocks away.

I eat and watch the news, smiling as I pick the peas out of the fried rice. It makes me think of Dana and I decide to call her later.

I get up, stretch, and go out on the deck for some air before I call the hospital. The nurse on Andie's floor tells me she's been given more sedatives. "She said to tell you not to bother tonight," the nurse says. "She's had enough visitors today already."

"Oh, who was there?"

"Mr. big shot FBI man. Rollins, I think he said his name was. He's a bit annoying."

I laugh. "I know what you mean. Please tell her I called and I'll be back tomorrow."

"Will do."

I make some coffee and take the phone out on the deck to call Dana.

"Hey, it's Evan," I say when she answers.

"Hi. What a nice surprise. Everything okay?"

"Yeah, I saw Andie. She's knocked out with drugs now." I sketch in what Rollins told me about the shooting, the bank robbery attempt, and Andie's scheduled recuperation.

"Wow, your girlfriend leads a dangerous life."

"Yeah, I guess she does. So what are you up to?"

"Trying to make some headway on the thesis. I've been looking at this computer screen for twenty minutes and only typed two words. It's not going well."

"No, how come?"

"I don't know. I'm just…distracted I guess."

"How so?"

"Well this has been quite week for me. Getting my own place, getting a dog now, and," she pauses a moment, "meeting you."

"Dana—"

"No, don't say anything. Just let me, I don't know, absorb things, okay?"

I laugh. "Okay. I'll let you get back to your thesis."

"Evan, can we just talk awhile?"

"Sure." I hear some clicking sound.

"There," she says. "That's better. I just shut down my laptop."

We talk about everything. Music, grad school, her thesis, old boyfriends and girlfriends, and of course, Cal. But I realize she knows much more about me than I do about her. Forty minutes goes by before I hang up the phone.

I sit in the darkness a long time, smoking, thinking, drinking coffee, listening to the sounds of the night, wishing I could just stay here. I've gone from Venice Beach to Amsterdam and now to a redwood forest on the Russian River.

What's next?

When I check my box at the little post office just off the Northwood golf course, there's nothing much in the way of mail. I get back home, pack a bag for the stay at Andie's. I'm almost out the door when Coop calls.

"Hey, Sport, I got little info on your developer friends."

"Shoot."

"Erwin, McCullough, and Bowers are a big high pressure outfit. Shopping malls, condos, planned communities, that kind of thing. They're not exactly paragons of virtue though. There was an incident a few months back where some construction workers and a couple of unions picketed one of their job sites, claiming unfair practices, cutting corners on building materials, that kind of thing. They were even taken to court but nothing was ever proven."

"How about this guy Sergent? Anything on him."

"No, no record, seems to be clean but probably caught up in the business. You're best bet is to forget them," Coop says.

"I plan to, but I don't want him harassing Dana anymore."

"Let me know and then we can pay him a little visit. If it gets out of hand, she could file against him. Just curious, but how much did he offer?"

When I tell Coop, he just whistles. "They must want it bad. You know best. Well I gotta scoot. How's Andie?"

"She's doing okay. Bringing her home today. Thanks for the help, Coop."

I lock up and head for the car and throw my bag in the back seat. I have to push a box of files aside and wonder if they have to do with the bank case. I'm too curious not to look, but when I do, I see there's nothing about bank robbers.

The whole box is about what the FBI called the "Bird Lives!" killer.

One of the folders has my name on it.

I get to the hospital a little after noon. In Andie's room, I find her already dressed, sitting on the edge of the bed, impatient to leave.

"Thank God," she says. "I hate hospitals, especially when I'm the patient."

"All signed out?"

"Yes, just have to let them know I'm ready to leave." She reaches for the call button and the nurse arrives shortly. She fusses over Andie for a minute then turns to me.

"If you'd like to bring your car around, I'll arrange the wheel chair to bring her downstairs."

"Okay. See you in a minute," I say to Andie, and take off for the elevator. I pull the car around to the entrance and Andie is already there with an orderly, his hands on the chair handles. I have to lift her in the front seat. She settles in and I stow the crutch she's been given in the back.

She glances over her shoulder, sees the box of files. "I forgot I had those. I have to get them back to the office sometime." Her eyes meet mine for a moment then she looks away. "Maybe you better put them in the trunk."

I nod, take the box out and open the trunk, then I get in and start the car. "Well, don't worry about it now. Something you were working on? We can stop and I can drop them for you."

"No," she says quickly. "I'll figure something out."

"Secret stuff huh?" I pull out of the drive.

"No, but you can't just drop off FBI files at the bureau for me."

"Whatever you say."

Andie leans her head back on the seat and closes her eyes, doesn't say anything for several minutes as we slug through the traffic heading to 19th Avenue.

"Andie."

"Yes."

"I looked."

She doesn't open her eyes but says, "Is that why you were late?"

"Yes." I turn on to 19th Ave and seem to catch every red light till we get to I-280.

She sighs, opens her eyes and sits up. "I was going to tell you."

"When?"

Most of my file had to do with the background check the FBI did on me. There were two short reports on Natalie Beamer, Gene Sherman, and Jeff Powell, my drummer and bass player at the time of the case. There was nothing on Calvin Hughes.

"I thought you ran a check on Calvin too. I remember a couple of his friends calling, telling him they'd been questioned." Andie says nothing, just stares through the window.

"C'mon, Andie. What gives?"

"I don't know," she says. She turns her head and looks at me. "Really, I don't know, Evan. Ted Rollins did the follow up on Hughes."

"Shouldn't the file be in that box with everything else?"

"Yes it should," she says. "That's why I brought the box home. I was hoping to find out before you got back." She sighs and shifts in the seat. "I didn't plan on getting shot, you know."

We crawl past San Francisco State University, crossing the BART tracks, and finally break though to the 280 south toward San Jose.

"Did you ask Rollins last night? The nurse said he had been there again when I called."

"No, it was just more questions about the robbery attempt and the shooting."

I nod and move into the center lane, merging with the faster traffic. "If you don't ask Rollins, I will, Andie. I mean it."

She waves her hand in the air. "No, no, I'll do it but I told you there wasn't anything much anyway. At least not the kind of thing you're looking for."

I light a cigarette and roll down the window as we get to Andie's exit. Winding back under the freeway, I drive the few blocks to her street in silence, angry but trying to keep it together. I know she's been shot, drugged, had surgery, but the big question still looms heavily in my mind. We pull in the drive of her apartments and I park.

"Well, here we are." I get the crutch out of the back seat and open the door for Andie. She swings her legs out and stands leaning on me, then hobbles to the stairs.

"Shit," she says, looking up. "I don't know if I can make that."

"No problem. Put your arm around me." I pick her up and carry her up the short flight of stairs.

"Oh, Mr. Horne, this is so romantic," she says smiling at me.

"Don't make me laugh or we'll both go flying." I set her down, get the door open and she makes it inside and to the couch where she plops down and sighs.

"God, I'm going to hate this," she says. She puts her hand on her leg and rubs it. "Can you get my bag out of the car. I need some drugs. My leg is throbbing."

"Sure." I get the bag and set it on the coffee table. Andie rummages around inside and pulls out a small zippered plastic bag and finds the bottle of Percodan. I bring her a glass of water and she swallows a couple and takes a gulp of water.

"Do you want to get in bed?"

"No, I'll stay here for now." She stretches back and lets me take off her shoes. I get two pillows and a blanket from the bedroom. I put the pillows under her head and cover her with the blanket. Before I finish, she's almost asleep.

I make some coffee and wait a few minutes, then go back down to the car and get the file box and bring it upstairs. I sit at the kitchen table and go over everything again to see if I've missed anything, but an hour later I haven't found a single mention of Cal anywhere.

I go out on the balcony to smoke and think about it. Why? The whole case is in that box, everything but what was supposedly a routine background check on Cal. Why is that one thing missing? Do I believe Andie? I want to, but with Rollins involved it's difficult.

Before I can form another thought the phone rings. Ted Rollins.

"How's she doing," he asks without even a hello when I answer.

"Okay. She took some pills and she's sleeping now."

"I need to talk to her again. Okay if I come by? Couple of points we have to go over her statement."

"Do we have a choice?"

"Actually no." I can almost hear the smirk in his voice.

"You know where she lives I assume."

"Yeah. Let's say around five."

"See you then," I say, and hang up.

I let Andie sleep another hour or so then wake her up with some hot tea.

"Hey," she says blinking her eyes. "What time is it?"

"Going on five. Rollins called. He's coming over. Something about your statement."

She closes her eyes for a moment and then sits up and takes a sip of the tea. "God I hate this," she says, then smiles. "Nurse Horne. You're taking such good care of me."

"Can't you put him off?"

"No, report has to be filed, Bureau policy and all that jazz. Better to get it over with."

I nod. "You hungry?"

"No, maybe later, after Rollins leaves." She looks over at the kitchen table and sees the file box then looks at me. "You find anything."

"You know I didn't, but I had to see for myself. Are you going to ask Rollins about the missing info on Cal. Because if you don't I will. I—"

She puts her hand up to stop me. "Yes, I'll ask." She puts the tea down and starts to stand up. "I've got to pee and wash my face."

I help her up and she hobbles to the bathroom. I stuff the files back in the box and put it in the bedroom closet. A few minutes later she comes back looking slightly refreshed. "God, my mind is so fuzzy. All I want to do is sleep."

"How's the leg?"

"Not so bad." She stretches out and props her leg on the coffee table just as the doorbell rings. I go to the door and let Rollins in. The suit is gone and he's in khakis, tee shirt, and a windbreaker.

He walks in, nods to Andie and looks around. "Well this is cozy."

I watch him, pretty sure he's never been here before, then wonder why I thought he might have been.

"How you doin', babe?" he asks Andie.

"I've been better, *babe*," she says, bristling a little.

Rollins takes a pad and pen out of his jacket and looks at me. "Can you give us a little time? This is FBI business."

I look at Andie. She shrugs. "It's better, Evan really."

Rollins watches me, that smirk beginning again.

I grab my jacket and head for the door. "You got thirty minutes." Then I'm gone, jogging down the stairs to the parking lot, remembering then I don't have the car keys. I decide to walk off my anger at Rollins and at Andie for going along with it. At the bottom of the hill there's a small strip mall with a dry cleaners, a convenience store, and a small book shop. I go in and wander around, aimlessly looking at titles, warding off a bored clerk who is ready to close up.

I grab a Coke at the convenience store and stand outside, looking at the headlines in the newspaper racks, checking my watch every couple of minutes. I decide to persuade Andie to go with me to Monte Rio for her recuperation. I want to get to the piano, make calls, and I can't do either at her place. I check my watch again and start back up the hill.

At the apartments, Rollins' car is still in the guest parking, but as I reach the stairs, he's coming down and I hear Andie's door shut. We meet halfway.

"Get what you want?"

Rollins pauses a couple of steps above me and looks down. "Yeah, we got it pretty tied up now. Just the formal report to file."

"Good." I brush past him up the stairs.

"Horne?"

I stop and turn around.

"I'm just doing my job." He goes on down to his car and I watch him drive away.

Inside, Andie is on the couch, her head back, her eyes closed. "You okay?"

"Yeah," she says. "I'm just tired of talking about it."

"You hungry now?"

She opens her eyes. "Something light maybe. Eggs and toast?"

"Sure. Coming up." I go into the kitchen and get things started. Andie uses the crutch and makes her way to the table. "Scrambled?"

"Perfect," she says, watching me. "I missed you last week."

I look up at her and smile as I beat two eggs in a bowl. "Me too."

"I'm sorry I wasn't with you, Evan. I know that must have been rough."

"It was okay." I stand waiting for the toast to pop up, stirring the eggs. "How about some juice with this?"

"Sure, that would be nice."

I bring it all over to the table and sit down opposite her, watching her eat with some gusto. She finishes and pushes the plate aside. "Wow, that was good. Hospital food sucks."

I don't say anything for a moment, just letting her do it in her own time. She downs the last of the orange juice and looks at me.

"Okay. Ted says he doesn't know what happened to the file," she says finally.

Well, there it is. I could push it, but to what end? Either Ted Rollins or Andie or both don't want me to see whatever was in that file on Cal, and that's that. I try to give them the benefit of the doubt. Maybe it was just lost, except it's too much of a coincidence that it's Cal's file that's missing. I don't believe in coincidences like that, and the FBI doesn't just misplace files.

"Thanks for asking."

Andie looks at me to gauge whether I believe her or not. "Look, when I get back to the office I'll check around some more myself. I promise."

"Okay, no problem." It's hard to be mad at someone who has just been shot. "You need to get some more sleep, eh?"

Andie nods and pushes back from the table. "I want some more Percodan and my bed." She tries on a weak smile. "This is not how I planned on your homecoming."

"Don't worry about it."

I help her get undressed and into bed and bring a glass of water and her pills. "Night, babe," I say. I kiss her lightly on the lips.

She smiles. "I'll get better fast," she says. "I promise."

Chapter Seven

Persuading Andie Lawrence to do anything she doesn't want to do is not easy. She's tough and fiercely independent, but as an FBI agent, she has to be. It takes a lot of coaxing, logic, and reasoning to get her to agree that a few days at my place would be good for her recovery both physically and mentally. She'd be away from bureau business, Ted Rollins, and reminders of the shooting.

She hadn't talked about it much, but I know, tough or not, the shooting had shaken her. How could it not? I wanted to hear about it myself. But on the way to Monte Rio, despite my cheerful, tour guide efforts, she alternately dozes and complains about the drive.

"Are we there yet?" she says, in a whiney, little girl voice, stretching and sitting up in the seat. "God it's such a long trip."

We're on River Road now, heading toward Guerneville. "That's the idea," I say. "It'll do you good to see some beautiful scenery, breathe some fresh air. This is wine country, babe. People come from all over to vacation here. We're on the home stretch now."

"It feels like *we've* come from all over."

From just about anywhere in San Francisco, Monte Rio is about a two hour drive, depending on the traffic and time of day. A lot of people had vacation places there for long weekends or summer getaways, but over the years the area had changed a great deal according to my crusty landlord, morphing finally into a varied blend of artists, writers, musicians, old hippies trying to hang on to the days of Haight Ashbury, a significant gay population, a share of good ole boys with pickup trucks and dogs, and a small drug culture. It's a strange mix but so far, everyone seems to get along and mind their own business and accept one another for what and who they are.

Between Guerneville and Monte Rio, about a mile from my place, is the Northwood Golf course. Lush, green, dotted with towering redwood trees the nine-hole course is surrounded with an eclectic variety of expensive homes. My plan is to show Andie as much as I can while we're here. Until now, she's only been down a couple of times and both were at night.

As we pass the Korbel Winery, I glance over and see her use two hands to move her leg around in a more comfortable position. "How is it?"

"I'll be ready for a pill when we get there," she says, "if we ever get there." She leans back and stares out the window as I hit the play button for a CD. The first sound is a clean, crisp, crackle of sticks on a snare drum, playing an intricate little pattern then the intro to "If I Should Lose You" by bass and piano. I turn up the volume as the trio goes into the first chorus, the cymbal beat clear and sharp nudging behind the piano and bass.

Andie turns her head. "Let me guess. That's Roy Haynes, right?"

Nodding, I smile. "Very good. How did you know?"

"Because he's the guy you're recording with and that's about the tenth time I've heard it."

"Sorry, thought you were asleep."

"It's okay. It's growing on me. I kinda like it," Andie says. She leans back against the seat and closes her eyes again.

I've been thinking about and listening a lot to Roy Haynes, the upcoming recording session, so I'm trying to familiarize myself with his playing. The time is always there, but it's often just implied, broken up, floating behind the soloists. Haynes is a master at it. After the bass solo, Haynes rips off two deceptively simple choruses, then brings the piano and bass back in for the fade out as we slow and glide through Guerneville.

Andie sits up again and looks around. "Ah, civilization. Look, a Safeway, a pizza parlor, a pharmacy." She sees me frown and laughs. "Relax, I'm just pushing your buttons."

We leave Guerneville and continue on the curving two lane road toward Monte Rio with the Russian River on our left. Even Andie is impressed with the greenery and the way in some places the big redwood trees on either side of the road lean toward each other, almost forming a tunnel.

We pass the golf course and finally round a bend into Monte Rio. Andie takes in the convenience store, Chinese restaurant, the two cabin like motels, and a hardware store. At the stop sign, the road splits. On my left is a large Quonset hut with a mural painted on the side.

"What's that?" Andie asks.

"Movie theater. First run movies too."

"You're kidding."

"If we were to continue down 116 about ten miles or so, we'd be at the ocean."

Andie swivels around and looks back. "That's it? That's Monte Rio?"

I laugh and drive on under the large sign that says Monte Rio Vacation Wonderland, then turn left over the bridge spanning the Russian River. "Oh no there's more." On the other side of the bridge I turn right and show her the Pink Elephant Bar and the small grocery store and make a U-turn. "Now you've seen it all."

"This is like the Twilight Zone," Andie moans.

I turn back onto the bridge road, left again on Bohemian Avenue and pull into the drive. "Now we're here." I get out of the car and stretch and walk around to Andie's door. "C'mon, I'll help you up the stairs."

"No," she says. "You go ahead. I have to get used to doing this myself."

I shrug. No point in arguing with a determined FBI agent. I get the bags out of the back and drag everything upstairs and open the doors to the deck. The sun has broken through and it's warm enough to sit outside. I pull one of the big chairs I'd rescued from a thrift shop in Guerneville outside, facing the sun and finally, Andie's head appears at the top of the stairs.

"That's a lot of stairs," she says, hobbling over to me. She sits down in the chair and props her leg up on the ottoman and sighs. "Okay, this is where I'm staying for awhile."

I get a blanket, some water, and her Percodan from her purse. She gulps down a couple and leans back. "You're right, this is nice."

"You need anything else?"

"No, I'm fine. You go ahead and do whatever you have to do. I'm going to get a nap."

"Okay. Just holler." I get the file folder with all the papers and the lead sheets I'd found at Cal's and go up to the loft room and sit down at the piano. I'd given up on the idea of getting a real piano up here and had settled on an electronic keyboard. They're greatly improved from the days of the old Fender Rhodes. This model has a surprisingly good piano sound and the keyboard action is very close to a real piano feel. With headphones, I can play day or night and not bother anybody.

I keep the volume low as I run through some exercises before I try out a couple of tunes, wondering how much say Roy Haynes will have in the final selection. I want to do one ballad and finally settle on "My Foolish Heart," "If you Could See Me Now," and "Goodbye Porkpie Hat." All three feel good under my fingers.

I get the lead sheets I'd found at Cal's then and play through them again, confirming my original reaction that they are from *Birth of the Cool* and *Kind of Blue*. They're on onion skin paper that's almost transparent, the kind you hardly see anymore, but they've held up considering they're over forty years old. I'd have to check with the records, but I'm sure the chord changes are exactly right.

I stop then, lean back and stare out the window at the towering redwoods, trying to come up with a valid explanation for these tattered lead sheets, done in pencil from recordings that were made over forty years earlier.

Had Cal simply written out the melody and the chord changes for his own reasons, taking them from the records, or was it just the opposite? The recording was made from these sheets that were actually used at the session. Another possibility was these were rehearsal sheets Cal had just kept as souvenirs of dates he hadn't made. Did Miles Davis, Gil Evans, Gerry Mulligan, John Lewis, or anybody else on the sessions write these tunes? The best bet was if I could try to find some of the musicians who had done the dates, if that was possible, and ask. The thought that Cal might have written one or more of these tunes and not been credited haunts me, makes me want to pursue it until I find out for sure. I put the sheets away and turn off the piano, and go downstairs to check on Andie.

She's asleep, her head turned to the side, but it's a little cooler now, so I cover her up with the blanket and make a pot of coffee. I drag a chair out for myself. When the coffee is ready I take a mug outside, put my feet up on the railing, light a cigarette, and think about the other problem—finding Jean Lane.

I hear Andie stir on the chair and turn and look at her. "Hey, sleepy."

She sits up and stretches. "Mmmmm, that was delicious," she says, eyeing my coffee. "Got some for me?"

"Sure." I bring her back a mug and turn my chair facing her.

She takes a sip and looks out at the trees. "Okay," she says, "maybe this was a good idea."

I smile. "I won't even say I told you so."

"Good. Don't. You know what else? I want a cigarette."

"What? You never told me you smoked."

"There's a lot I haven't told you."

I give her one from my pack and light it for her. She takes a deep drag, coughs a little, but doesn't give up.

"Been a long time." She takes another drag, and makes a face. "I don't like menthol."

"You're not thinking of starting up again are you?"

"No, just wanted to see if it's as good as I remember." She takes another couple of drags and stubs it out in the ash tray.

She takes another drink of coffee, her expression a faraway look. "Half a cigarette is nothing to compare with a shotgun. Instead of relaxing here I could be…" Her voice trails off.

"Want to talk about it?"

"No. Well yes, I mean, I don't know. Yeah maybe I do."

I nod. "Tell me about it."

She rubs the bandage on her leg. "I was so lucky. A lot of it's hazy, which is probably a good thing, but when he pointed that thing at me, I remember thinking, you're cool, you have the vest on, but looking down those double barrels, they looked like big wide pipes." She shakes her head. "I was stupid, moved in too fast. The guy panicked when he saw me." She looks away for a moment. "That's how you get killed."

"I heard Rollins or one of the guys, yell 'Gun!' and then I heard the blast and fired. It was like somebody kicked me in the leg, knocked it out from under me." She closes her eyes, remembering. "Ted says I hit him in the stomach with my shot. Then I was looking up at a paramedic in the ambulance." Her eyes meet mine. "I was scared, Evan. I really was."

I don't say anything for a long moment. "Was that the first time? Have you been shot at before?"

"Never. Never even fired my gun before this except on the range and I hope it's the last." She manages a smile. "Anyway, how was your day?"

"Fine. Did a little practicing, thinking, you know."

"About?"

"Cal, finding this woman Jean Lane, the recording session."

"It's important to you isn't it? The recording session. I'm not going to pretend to know how significant the recording session or Roy Haynes is."

"Well imagine I'm a rock keyboard player and I got invited to record with Eric Clapton or—what's that noisy band you like—U2?"

"Okay okay, I get it."

I laugh. "It is important, but so is Cal and so is finding Jean Lane." I look at her. "Want to have a conversation about that?"

Andie sighs. "I guess we need to."

"Yes, we do."

"Okay, let me go to the bathroom first."

I start to help her but she waves me off. "I can make it."

She comes back in a few minutes and sits down again. I refill her coffee and lean against the railing facing her. "Okay, where do we start?" she says.

"I have to know about that file, Andie."

"Evan, honest to God, I have no idea what happened to it, and I did ask Ted. He has no explanation but I've been thinking about it. There wasn't much in it. It was just routine, a background check, wants, warrants, little history, but nothing that would help you find this Jean Lane woman or how she was connected to Cal."

"You don't think it's too much of a coincidence that it's that particular file that's missing? I mean this is the FBI. They're not sloppy filers. Isn't everything logged in or something."

"I don't know what to tell you otherwise."

"What about Rollins? He doesn't like me and the feeling is mutual."

She waves her hand in the air. "I pulled that box before he even knew about it."

I sigh, knowing I'm not going to get anymore. "Okay, but can you help me out on this or not?"

"I can try."

"Fair enough." I run upstairs and bring back a manila envelope and drop it on her lap. "The photo I told you about, the note Cal left, it's all in there. Take a look and think about it. Maybe you can come up with something."

Andie nods. "Okay."

"I'm going to take a shower then we'll get some dinner. How about Mexican? There's a pretty good place in Guerneville."

Andie licks her lips. "Oh, tacos, enchiladas, you read my mind."

I head for the shower wishing I could.

◇◇◇

"So what do you think?" Andie is wolfing down her second enchilada and spooning beans and rice on a tortilla.

She nods and swallows. "I like Guerneville already. This is so good." She leans back and takes a long pull on a Corona.

It's good to see her eat. Probably her first real meal since the shooting. "Better watch it mixing beer with those pills."

We're at a family owned restaurant I'd heard about and the food is good. It's the kind you line up and order, then they bring it to your table. "Now that I've plied you with food and drink, what about my questions?"

Andie leans back and looks out the window, then back at me. "Look, I know this is important to you, I understand that, but I just don't know how much help I can be. I looked at the photo again and I agree with Coop. It's most likely Cal's baby in the carriage, and given the note he left, I'd say he was feeling considerable remorse and regret. He knew his time was up and wanted somehow to make amends, or at least try in his own way. He made you the instrument, but something was left out, something he couldn't bring himself to tell even you, either in person or in the note."

I take out the lighter I'd found among Cal's things. "I found this too," I say, handing it to Andie.

She turns it over in her hands and looks at the inscription. "Kind of makes it all real doesn't it?" She hands it back to me.

I nod. "Can you remember anything from that missing file at all?"

Andie shakes her head. "What I do remember is there was nothing in there that pertained to this Jean Lane woman. Like I said, it was a routine background check. We didn't go very deep." She looks away again then back at me. "We just wanted to know who you were hanging out with. 'Known associates' is the Bureau term." She sees me frown. "Come on, Evan, that's the way the Bureau works. We were bringing you in to help with profiling on a case no civilian had any business being involved with."

I sigh and know she's right but it still bothers me. "So what about searching those data bases? Maybe you'll get a hit."

"I can try to swing it, but these records are scrutinized carefully. There are a lot of restrictions now. I can't just log on and go searching without some justification, some connection to a case. Every time an agent logs in, it's there for the record and I'd have some explaining to do."

"So that's a dead end too?"

She shakes her head again. "Look, I'll do what I can, maybe see if I can clear it with Wendell Cook. He liked you. But even if I can get authorization, there are no guarantees. There is so little to go on and Jean Lane could be anywhere, remarried, dead, who knows."

She reaches across the table and squeezes my hand. "I'm sorry, baby, that's the best I can do."

"I know, I just wish I had that file on Cal. Maybe something in there would trigger a thought, an idea." I put my hands up. "Okay, I'll stop for now. You want to go?"

Andie smiles. "Yes, I want to go home and lounge on that comfortable couch with you and fall asleep watching a movie. How does that sound?"

"Like a plan."

Back at the house, Andie struggles up the stairs, leaning on me heavily. While she changes into a thick robe, I find there are two messages on my machine. One from Dana, the other from Roy Haynes' agent Larry Klein, to call as soon as I can. It's already after midnight in New York, so that one will have to wait till morning, and I'm not about to call Dana with Andie hovering around.

We settle on the couch and find an old movie on Turner Classics. Ten minutes and Andie is already yawning, her head against my chest, my arm around her. "You want to go to bed?"

"No, I just want to stay right here for now."

A half hour later, she's sound asleep. As carefully as I can, I slip my arm out from under her and get up. She stirs briefly but stretches out and I cover her with a blanket. Taking the phone with me I go out on the deck and light a cigarette and call Dana.

"Hi, Dana. Hope I'm not calling too late."

"No, not at all. How is Andie doing?"

"Fine. She's conked out already. Mexican food, beer, and a couple more Percodan."

"Lethal combination. The reason I called is that guy Al Beckwood called. It's a good thing you had your calls referred to the new number."

"What did he say?"

"Not much, just that he wanted to know who I was and send his condolences about Cal."

"Did he leave a number?"

"Yes. It's a different one than before. Got a pen?"

"Hold on a sec."

I go in the house, glance at Andie, and grab a pen and pad of paper.

"Okay, go." I copy down the number but don't recognize the area code. "Any other calls?"

"Yes, some agent for Roy Haynes. He wants you to call as soon as possible."

"Yeah, he called here but we were out." I hope Haynes hasn't changed his mind or something. "And nothing more from Brent Sergent."

"Nope."

"Good. Let me know right away if he contacts you again."

"I will, don't worry."

"Thanks, Dana."

"Do you have to go?"

"Yeah, I really should. Got to check on Andie."

"Well good night then."

I catch the note of wistfulness in her voice. "We'll talk again soon. Night."

◇◇◇

Andie is still asleep when I get up at seven. I make some coffee, take the phone out on the deck, and call Larry Klein. I get his secretary but she puts me right through.

"Evan, Larry. Thanks for getting back to me so soon. We need a favor."

By we, I assume he means Roy Haynes and himself. I try to form a mental picture of Klein, legs up on his desk, phone head set, stack of messages to get through. "Well, if I can, sure."

"Outstanding. We've got a conflict on dates. As I'm sure you can imagine, this is a nightmare, scheduling a half dozen busy piano players. Anyway Herbie Hancock has had to cancel the date we booked him for, last minute thing he can't get out of, and Roy has a conflict with the alternative date Herbie suggested, and we have studio time booked while Roy is in New York, so—"

"You want me to drop out."

"Drop out? Oh no way, man. The gig is solid, a commitment. We want you to take Herbie's date. We were originally going to schedule you for later. Just want to move it up. Any way you can swing that?"

I look back into the house and see Andie limping toward me, a cup of coffee in her hand "Sure, I guess so. When's the date?"

I hear some movement, as if he's swung his feet back down to the floor. "This is the killer. It's next week. I know it's a drag to hit you with this so last minute, but, hey, you know, shit happens. Can you help us out?"

What choice do I have? If I say no I could get cut out later with somebody else's cancellation and I do want this gig. When, if ever, will I have a chance to record with Roy Haynes? I glance at Andie. She is leaning on the railing of the deck but I know she's listening. "Okay, next week is fine."

"Outstanding. That's just great. Roy will be very pleased, and I am forever in your debt. I'll send you the tickets and book a room. You and a guest for the weekend. My treat. It's next Friday, two o'clock at Avatar Studios." He double checks my address.

"By the way, who's the bass player?"

"Hang on, let me check." I hear him shuffling through some papers. "Eddie Gomez or Ron Carter. Not sure yet. Gotta scoot. Call me if you need anything, and thanks so much. You're a prince."

He hangs up before I can say goodbye.

Andie watches me sipping coffee. "Next week is fine for what?"

"The Roy Haynes recording session. The date has been moved up. I have to go to New York." I watch Andie's face for some reaction but there's none. "Look, I can call him back and—"

"No, no," Andie says. "I'll be fine. I can get around and by next week I'll be much more mobile. I know this is important."

"Want to go with me? They're booking a room for the weekend and it's on them."

Andie sips her coffee, looks away for a moment. "No, I don't think so. You'll be busy and I won't be much good hobbling around New York City, getting in and out of cabs."

"You're sure?"

"Yes." She smiles. "I'll be fine. Really, Evan, it's okay."

I still feel a little guilty, but I take Andie at her word. "Okay." I look around. "You hungry? I'm going to walk over to that little market and get a few things, maybe take a walk, stretch a bit."

"Sure," Andie says. "I feel almost ready to join you." She runs a hand over her leg. "I would like to get this bandage changed though. How far would we have to go to find a hospital?"

"Guerneville. There's a clinic there. I'm sure they could do it. I can call."

"I'll do it. I can give them my insurance number. Do you have any cellophane wrap or plastic bags?"

I shrug. "Plastic bags for sure. What for?"

"I'm going to wrap something around my leg and take a shower."

Under the sink, I find several plastic grocery store bags and hold up a couple. "These do?"

"Perfect. Go to the store and take a walk. I'm going to try and get my old self back."

"Okay, see you later." I grab my cell phone and trot down the stairs and out to the street. At the bridge, I start to turn toward the store, but then decide to walk across the bridge and check out the movie theater. I'd never been there but it might be a good diversion. Maybe I can talk Andie into a movie.

I stop in the middle of the bridge and lean over the concrete railing, looking at the Russian River flowing below. It seems higher than usual and I'd been told about flooding but it's still way under the bridge. With the redwoods and hills as a backdrop, the scene is like a postcard. Farther up the river I can see houses lining the shores and wonder what they do in high flood water.

Continuing across the bridge, I check out the movie marquee. There's a fairly recent thriller playing with a starting time of seven. I stand for a minute, debating on whether to walk the mile or so to the post office but decide against it, and retrace my steps back across the bridge and turn right to the small family run grocery store.

I get a bagful of things—bacon, eggs, milk, some lunch meat and cheese, and a few bottles of beer. I start back to the house when my cell phone rings. Setting the bag down in front of the Elephant Bar, I open it.

"Evan, it's Roy Haynes."

"Oh hey, how are you?"

"Much better. I checked in with Larry and just wanted to thank you for helping us out on Herbie's cancellation."

"No problem."

"Well it would have been, so I appreciate it. Got some tunes down?"

I tell him my three ballad choices.

He pauses a moment. "Let's go with 'Porkpie Hat.' It's not recorded enough."

"Cool. How about Invitation for the up tune?"

Haynes laughs. "That would work fine. We're all set then. I'm looking forward to this. See you Friday, and thanks again."

"My pleasure. Bye, Roy."

The bag feels lighter in my hand as I walk back to the house. I feel the surge of excitement flow through me and it increases as I see Andie. Her hair is still damp and she's wrapped in my big terry cloth robe. She comes over and reaches up on her toes to kiss me.

"God I never thought a shower and washing my hair could feel so good," she says. She eyes the grocery bag. "Goodies?"

"Bacon, eggs, toast sound okay?"

"Mmmmmm, yes, I'm starving."

"Coming up," I head for the kitchen.

"I called the clinic. I can get in at one o'clock."

After breakfast, Andie finds something to read while I run through "Invitation," trying out some variations on the changes, then call her upstairs. "What do you think of this?"

I play through "Goodbye Porkpie Hat," as Andie listens. Even on the electric keyboard it sounds good to me.

"Beautiful," she says. "Just gorgeous. I've never heard that before have I?"

"Not unless you know Charlie Mingus." I tell her about the tune, how it was written for Prez.

She nods. "Makes you think about Cal, doesn't it?"

"Yeah, it does." I turn off the piano. "Let's get you to the doc."

The clinic is right off Main Street in Guerneville. We get out of the car and Andie eyes the steep stairs. "Not very good planning," she says, but I point to the ramp entrance so it's not nearly as bad.

Inside, the nurse-receptionist has Andie fill in a form and checks her insurance card. The nurse's eyebrows go up a bit when she sees the attached FBI identification. "The doctor will be with you shortly."

There's only one other person there, a young woman who looks over six months pregnant. She and Andie exchange smiles as we sit down to wait. When Andie is called in, I flip through some very out of date magazines, then finally go outside and have a cigarette. As I start back in Andie comes through the door.

"I'm all set," she says. "The doctor told me the wound is healing just fine and I should do a little walking so it doesn't stiffen up." She links her arm in mine as we start down the ramp. "He also told me as long as you don't lean on me too hard, we can do it tonight."

I look at her. "You asked him that?"

◇◇◇

Despite her brightened spirits, and mine, Andie takes another long nap while I do some more practicing on "Invitation," and "Porkpie" feeling as good as I have in a long time. When I finish, I pick up the rubber ball I used for so long when I was rehabbing my hand and wondering if I'd ever play again. I squeeze it hard and smile.

When Andie wakes up, we have a sandwich and she seems well rested and eager to try the movie theater. "Good test for my leg," she says. "I can make it across the bridge."

She only has to stop once as we walk over and find a large crowd in the lobby waiting to go inside. Everybody seems to know everybody. Andie takes it all in. "Nothing like a small town is there."

She eyes the snack bar and catches sight of a handwritten sign about homemade sausages. "Goodies," she says. "I want one of those, some popcorn, and a coke."

"My we are feeling better, aren't we."

"You better believe it, Buster, and I hope you are later."

We get our food and drinks and go inside where animated conversations are going on all over the theater. Andie glances at her watch. "Isn't it supposed to start at seven?"

A woman next to her overhears. "Yes, hon, but the owners know everybody is always a little late, so they hold things up till everyone gets here."

"Of course," Andie says and glances at me. "Isn't it cute. Just like Mayberry."

The lights finally go down and we get ten minutes of coming attractions before the feature. Andie hooks her arm in mine and leans on my shoulder. "Wow, this is just like a date isn't it?"

Twenty minutes later she's asleep. When the lights come up, she glances up at me sleepily. "Was it good?"

"Come on, you, let's go home."

Crossing the bridge, we stop and look at the lights, hear the low sound of the river flowing under us as a few cars pass by.

Andie turns and kisses me. "Thank you for bringing me down here," she says.

"My pleasure."

"It will be as soon as we get home."

Chapter Eight

By Tuesday, tired of bucolic life in Monte Rio, Andie is anxious to get back to the city and her own place. We'd spent the weekend lounging around—Andie napping, me practicing—eating out, exploring the shops in Guerneville, but I could see she was antsy. For her, it was like being on a cruise ship. She liked the ship well enough, but was anxious for the next port and home. We went for longer and longer walks along the river. She pushed herself, sometimes I thought too hard, like an injured athlete desperate to get back in the lineup, but it was good to see her recovering so quickly.

My ticket and hotel reservation for New York had arrived by express mail from Larry Klein. I'd been booked on a red eye flight Wednesday night, so I'd have all day Thursday in New York, so said the note Klein had enclosed with the ticket. He'd signed it with a large flourished scroll. That made it all the more real. I am going to New York to record with Roy Haynes. The adrenaline rush makes me feel like I've won the lottery.

As for Andie and I, we'd come to a sort of truce on the search for Jean Lane. She promised to do what she can when she returns to work, already moaning about being on a thirty day desk duty assignment the bureau mandates after an agent involved shooting.

"I'll have plenty of time," she said, "and yes I'll try to track down Cal's file." That was still the sticking point for me, that nagging feeling that something wasn't right. Something was missing, even though she's assured me there was nothing relevant or anything that could help with tracking down Jean Lane in the file. I haven't mentioned it again.

Since I'm going to be in New York, I decide to check in with my folks, maybe take a run up there while I'm in the area. While Andie wanders around the bookstore next to Guerneville's answer to Starbucks—a wooden table and chairs place run by guys in tee shirts and pony tails—I call late Tuesday afternoon, hoping to catch them after dinner time. It's my dad who answers.

"Hi, Dad, it's Evan."

"Evan, how are you? We got your postcards from Amsterdam. Sounds like you had a good time."

"Yeah, it was a good trip."

"Good, good. Well let me get your mother."

Still a man of few words, little interest, even less time I think to myself, although we never had much to say to each other since I was a teenager. He had no affinity for music, knew nothing much about what I did, and didn't care to know more. I'd resigned myself to that long ago. My mother had once been a decent pianist, and I think once longed for a career in music, but life caught up with her and she transferred her enthusiasm to me, usually over protests from my dad.

One afternoon when I was about twelve, I came home from school and found her at the piano, playing some classical piece, sheet music and books spread everywhere on the floor and tears streaming down her face. I watched her for several minutes. Then, I guess feeling my presence, she stopped suddenly and turned, looked at me, then just sat there till I left the room. I never knew why, but after that, she hardly played again.

"Evan?" Her voice draws me back to the countless arguments between her and my dad, the peacekeeping attempts, the apologizing for my father.

"Hi, Mom. How are you doing?"

"Oh just fine. Where are you?"

"Right where I live now. That's one of the reasons I called, to give you the new address and phone."

"Great. I've got a pen and paper right here."

After she copies them down, she asks, "So how are you? Everything going okay with your music? How do you like living in San Francisco?"

"I love it. Nice change from Venice. Just been going through a few things lately though."

"Oh?"

"Yeah that old friend of mine, Calvin Hughes, died and made me his executor, so a lot of legal paperwork." She doesn't say anything for a long moment. "Mom?"

"What? Oh, sorry. Yes, the piano player from Kansas City."

"Yeah. He left me his house in Hollywood and some money. I found out there was a life insurance policy through the musicians union, and I've been trying to find the beneficiary. It's all kind of a mystery." I leave out the way Cal left the note and don't even mention the photo.

"Still playing detective are you. That always gets you in trouble."

"Well not this time, it's just that there are no leads on the woman he named in the policy so I'm trying to track her down. Andie is helping me."

There's another pause. "Well the FBI should be able to do that I would think."

"I'm going to give it a try. I owe that much to Cal. The other reason I'm calling is I'm going to be in New York next week for a recording session. I thought I might run up and see you guys if it's convenient."

"Next week?" She pauses again, sounding unsure.

"If it's not, or you're not going to be around, that's okay. I just thought—"

"No, no we'll be here. That would be nice, Evan. You can tell us all about Europe. You're dad may be away on business but I'll be here. We haven't had a good talk in a long time."

"No, we haven't."

"Is Andie coming with you? I'd like to meet her."

"No. Ah, she was, ah, shot, during an attempted bank robbery."

"My God! Shot? Is she all right?"

"Yes, she's fine but she's recovering well and going through rehab now."

My mother laughs. "Your life is like those television shows your dad likes."

"Who got shot?" I hear my dad say in the background.

"Evan's girlfriend," my mother says, "but she's okay.

"Yeah I guess it is sometimes. Anyway, I'll call you when I get to New York and see where things are." There's another long pause. "Everything okay, Mom?"

"What? Oh yes, everything is fine. I look forward to seeing you, son."

"Me too. Bye, Mom."

"Bye. I love you, Evan."

Son? I can't remember the last time she called me son. I press the off button and sit for a minute thinking about the call, like I'd missed something, something my mother had said, or hadn't said, but I can't put my finger on it. The pauses, the kind of unsureness in her voice, but maybe it was just the aging process. My mother is generally very sharp, but she'd sounded distracted, not quite with it.

"Hey, earth to Evan." Andie stands over me, passing her hand in front of my eyes. "You look like you were zoned out there." She sits down next to me with a coffee and a paper bag from the bookstore. "I bought you a present."

She hands me the bag. Inside is a book called *Kind of Blue*.

"Isn't that the music Cal left that you've been talking about?"

"Yes." I flip through the book and quickly read the jacket flap that claims to tell the behind the scenes story of the recording session. On a whim, I quickly scan the index for Hughes, Calvin, but no. It isn't going to be that easy. "This is fantastic. Thanks. I didn't know about this."

She leans over and kisses me. "No problem. So what had you in a trance?"

"Oh, nothing really. I just talked to my mother, told her I might visit her while I'm back East. She just sounded, I don't know, funny."

"How so?"

"I don't know really. I told her about Cal dying, the insurance policy. There was something she said that was off, but now I can't remember what it was that made me think that."

"Let it go. It'll come to you when you least expect it."

"Yeah, maybe it will."

"C'mon, we got packing to do."

We have an early dinner, watch a movie, then Andie goes to bed around ten. I sit up late, listening to all the records I have of Roy Haynes playing, and finally fall into bed after midnight.

We get the car packed up, stop for breakfast in Guerneville and two hours later, we're on the road and just barely beat the rush hour along 19th Avenue through San Francisco. I'd packed clothes, the file folder of legal papers on Cal, and the copies of the music sheets I'd found in the piano bench at his house. I plan to read *Kind of Blue* on the plane, maybe do a little digging around while I'm in New York.

We pull into Andie's place in late afternoon. Her mail box is stuffed with several days of bills, junk mail, and a couple of things from the bureau which she goes through quickly. I watch her unfold one letter and read intently. Then she sighs and lays it aside.

"I'm scheduled for a review board on the shooting Friday. Just as well we came back when we did."

"Is that a problem?"

"No, just more bureau crap. I'll wear a short skirt so they can see my bandage," she says laughing.

"Did the guy you shot, did he…"

She shakes her head. "I don't know. I'll have to call Rollins and find out."

I frown at her. "Give him my regards."

I shower and change, have a sandwich with Andie, and get ready to leave for the airport.

"You want me to drive you?" she asks.

"No, I'll just leave my car in long term parking. You just take it easy."

She stands up and gives me a mock salute. "Yes, sir." Then she folds into my arms and mumbles against my chest. "I'm going to miss you."

At San Francisco International, it's relatively quiet, so even the security check doesn't take as long as usual, although I do have to take my shoes off again. I make the long trek down to the gate and check in at the desk for my boarding pass with forty-five minutes wait till boarding. I grab a cup of coffee from a small snack bar and settle down with the book Andie bought me.

As I sit down, I glance over at a man working on a laptop computer. He looks up and our eyes meet for a moment in one of those don't-I know-you looks, then he's back to his computer screen, and I start flipping through my book, trying to think where I might have seen him before. I scan the preface, but my mind isn't on it. I glance at my watch, then grab my stuff and wander over to a corner and call Dana.

"Dana, it's Evan."

"Oh, hi," she says.

"Just thought I'd check in with you. I'm at the airport, getting ready to fly to New York. I'm doing a recording session there."

"I'm impressed," she says. "Is Andie going with you?"

"No, she's still recovering but doing fine."

"Well, that's good. How long are you going to be gone?"

"Just a few days. If you need to get me, you can call on the cell or leave a message. Everything going okay? How's Milton?"

"Fine and Milton has settled in pretty well. He's used to me now but I'm sure he'd like a visit with you."

"Well, who knows. Maybe I'll get down there soon."

"I hope so," she says. "Have a good trip, Evan."

"Thanks. Bye."

When I come back to the gate, the guy I thought I knew is waiting, looking at me.

"Evan Horne, right?" He's standing in front of me, the laptop in a case slung over his shoulder, a small carry on bag in his hand. He's in jeans, a light sweater, and some expensive looking loafers.

"Yeah, I was just trying to remember where—"

"That party on top of the mountain." He sets his computer case on the floor and sits down next to me. "Cameron Brody." He holds out his hand.

"Oh yeah, you were with that girl in the…dress."

He grins. "You remember her better than me, huh? Haven't seen her since the party. So what are you doing in New York?"

"Recording session with Roy Haynes."

"Whoa. That should be cool." I explain the project and mention some of the other players. "Nice, very nice."

"How about you?" I remember his business card now, that he works in some kind of capacity for ASCAP.

"Checking on some royalties, trying to track down a blues singer who has some coming and maybe doesn't know it."

People are starting to gather up their things as the attendant at the desk makes the preboarding announcement.

"Where are you sitting?"

We compare boarding passes and discover we're seated only a couples of rows apart. "Hey if you want to talk I'll see if I can trade seats with somebody," Brody says.

"Sure, but I have to get some sleep too."

He notices my copy of *Kind of Blue* then. "Interesting story. Jimmy Cobb, the drummer is the only one left from that band."

Brody was right. Miles, Coltrane, Cannonball Adderley, Bill Evans, Wynton Kelly, and Paul Chambers were all dead. "Well, I have a kind of personal interest in this." But before I can explain, we're called for boarding. "I'll tell you about it after we get on. Maybe you can even help me."

"Cool, I like mysteries."

We file on board and I find my seat about halfway down, by the window. I stow my bag in the overhead rack and settle in just as Brody comes up. So far, the middle seat is empty. A guy in a rumpled suit drops into the aisle seat and glances over, looking like he's ready to sleep the whole way.

"Excuse me, sir," Brody says. "I didn't know my friend was on this flight and we'd like to sit together and catch up. I have a window seat just a couple of rows up where you won't be bothered."

"Hey, sure," the mans says. "Lead me to it."

He gathers up his things and follows Brody, who is back before I can glance at the airline magazine. "Okay, we're set," he says, throwing his small bag in the rack and keeping his laptop to push under the seat in front of him.

We buckle up, listen to the safety lecture, and settle back to wait our turn on the runway. "So," Brody says, "How can I be of service."

Cameron Brody brims with confidence and congeniality. He has a quick disarming smile and the good looks to be very successful with women, I imagine, if that girl at the party was any example.

In the twenty minutes or so we wait to take off, I briefly run down Cal's legacy. The note, the photo, and the music sheets.

"Have you got them with you?" Brody asks.

I have everything in an accordion style plastic filer. He rubs his fingers over the thin, almost transparent paper, squints at the notes and chords and begins to hum. I watch him nod his head. "You a musician too?"

He shrugs. "Not really. I thought I was going to be. Played a little in college, but…" His voice trails off, then he hands me back the sheets. "So you found these at your friend's house?"

"Yes, along with some other music from *Birth of the Cool.* You familiar with that?"

"Sure. And you think he might have written these?"

"It's possible." I explain the other possibilities, I'd already gone over in my own mind. "Like I say, he could have just copied them off the records, but I found out he was in the *Birth of the Cool* Band, at least as a sub during rehearsals, and I have a photo of him with Miles."

He nods and grips the arms of the seat tighter as the engines rev and we start down the runway. Then we're climbing out of San Francisco into the night sky. The plane banks slightly as we continue to climb and Brody starts to relax. "I hate takeoffs."

"I can tell."

We level off and over drinks and a light meal, we continue talking. He's a good listener and obviously intrigued and fascinated by the whole idea. "Have you checked the copyright on these tunes?"

"No. Not sure how to do that."

"There I can help you. I have access to several data bases— ASCAP, BMI, some independents, but I'm guessing these are mostly on BMI. They always did more jazz than ASCAP." He looks thoughtful for a moment. "You know there is some precedent for this. You'd be amazed at what I've found digging through recording dates, personnel. Record companies didn't keep very good records in those days. A lot of people didn't get what they were due. It adds up."

"Well, it's not the money I'm concerned about. Cal is dead, just last week, but it would be nice to know if he was the composer of one of these tunes."

"I'm sorry," Brody says.

The attendants collect our trays and the cabin lights are dimmed. "Movie time," Brody says.

"I'm going to pass. I need some sleep." Brody nods and adjusts the head phones and leans back. I cram the pillow between my seat and the window and try to get comfortable. I close my eyes, and try not to think of anything. I can usually sleep pretty well on planes. The darkness, the low whine of the engines kind of lull me, but tonight, there's too much on my mind and it seems like a long time before I drift off.

Voices, people moving about, and a sliver of sunlight in my eyes wakes me up. The sliver turns into a wide swath as the sliding port goes up and I hear Brody's voice. "Hey, breakfast is on the way."

I blink and sit up, stiff and sore, the side of my face cold from the glass. The flight attendant's pushing a cart down the aisle toward us is only a few rows away. I glance at my watch and see we're only an hour or so from New York.

"Let me out for a minute. Grab me a tray if I don't get back in time," I say, crawling over Brody and head for the toilets. There's a line in both aisles but it moves pretty fast. I stretch, do a couple of knee bends and by the time I'm back at my seat, I'm feeling more with it.

Brody has already wolfed down the breakfast and is eyeing mine as I gratefully sip hot coffee and cold orange juice. I pick at the plastic dish of fruit but pass on the barely thawed roll and rock hard butter. "Help yourself," I say, pushing the tray his way. Everybody is awake now, readjusting their clothes, slipping into shoes, gathering up their belongings as we get the first announcement that we're on approach to Kennedy.

"So where are you staying?" Brody asks.

"Ramada Inn, midtown, for two nights anyway. If I want to stay longer, I can probably swing it. How about you?"

"Friend of mine has a pad in the Village. He's out of town so I have it long as I want. You can always crash there with me if you want."

I nod, not sure how long I'll be in New York. "I may run up to Boston for a couple of days and see my folks too."

"When is the session?"

"Tomorrow afternoon at two."

"Nervous?" Brody grins.

"Should I be? It's only Roy Haynes and Ron Carter." Now, as New York looms below, I feel that adrenaline rush again and yes, the butterflies too. "If I can't sound good with those two, I might as well give it up."

Brody shakes his head and smiles. "Wow, Roy Haynes. That's who I wanted to be."

"You play drums?"

Brody shrugs. "Well, I thought I did. I took private lessons from a guy in San Francisco, played in my high school stage band, and when I went to Berkeley, I kept at it. Formed a group." He pauses for a moment, looking sheepish. "We called it The Jazz Bears."

"Catchy."

"Well the Jazz Messengers was already taken." Brody looks away for a moment. "We played some frat parties, got in a couple of local clubs but…" His voice trails off.

"What?"

"You ever see the movie *Amadeus* about Mozart?"

"Sure, several times."

"Well, I'm Salieri. Lot of desire, some training, but the talent just isn't there. Took me awhile to realize that, but it finally sank in. So, I was prelaw at Berkeley, started reading up about copyright, that kind of thing and decided the way to stay involved with music for me was this gig I have at ASCAP. Most of it's bullshit work, but occasionally I get to track down some talented musician who got screwed out of royalties and show up on his doorstep with a check." His eyes meet mine. "I would love to investigate this music you've got, see if your friend did write some of it. Wouldn't that be a kick if he did?"

The fasten seat belt announcement comes on then as we feel the plane bank. I hold the arms of the seat with both hands, and look at Brody watching me. "It's landings for me."

We share a cab into Manhattan, feeling the hum of the city already as we cross over the Triborough Bridge. Midtown is chaos as usual. I get out at the Ramada, leaving the cab to Brody. He hands me a card with a phone number. "Let's get together for dinner later, huh? I know some good places in the Village, maybe catch some music."

"Sounds good. I'll call you." I start away then turn back. "Look, I'll make a call, see if you can come with me to the session if you like."

"Way cool, man. Way cool," Brody says as the cab pulls away.

All goes smoothly at check in and there's a message to call Larry Klein, which I do first thing.

"Evan, you made it. Everything okay with the room and all?"

"Fine, Larry. Just a little tired and jet lagged."

"Well just take it easy today. There's a rehearsal studio on 56th, not far from the hotel. Nice piano there if you want to run through anything. Just tell the guy I sent you over. I called them already just in case."

"Great, I'd like that. By the way, I ran into a friend on the flight. Okay if he comes to the session? He's a big fan of Roy's."

"Sure, I don't see why not. There'll be some other people there anyway."

"Thanks, Larry."

"See you tomorrow afternoon."

I hang up the phone and sit on the bed for a minute looking out the window at mid town Manhattan. On the road again. Calls made, nobody to see, nowhere to go, just time to kill. I put my clothes away, grab the file of papers, the book I never opened on the plane, and head out for a late breakfast.

I walk over to 9th Avenue and find a diner and a booth by the window. A heavy set guy in a white apron comes over and swipes at the table with a damp rag. "Okay, my friend. You going to order or what?"

Ah, New York. I order bacon, eggs, toast, and coffee, lingering for over an hour, reading, eating, smoking through two cups of strong coffee. I love walking in New York and with a vague, general destination I start downtown, following what I've read in the book. I turn east on 30th Street and find 207. It's a large condominium complex now. I stand across the street and try to conjure up in my mind how it looked then, an abandoned Orthodox Greek Church that became the Columbia recording studio where Miles and his band gathered one August afternoon to record five of the most important pieces of music in modern jazz history.

I imagined Jimmy Cobb, lugging his drums inside, setting up, waiting for Miles and Cannonball and Coltrane. Paul Chambers, unzipping his bass cover, leaning over, running through the famous line to the opening of "So What." Bill Evans, arriving later, sitting down at the piano, going through Miles' sketchy outlines for the music that would make up *Kind of Blue,* wondering if he'd been aware that Wynton Kelly, who had taken a taxi all the way from Brooklyn, had already come and gone so "Freddie Freeloader," could be recorded first.

I get into things like this, fascinated by historical events, tuning in, listening for echoes of the past, wishing I'd been there, been a part of it. I'd always wanted to visit the site of Custer's last stand, the piece of ground in Montana. What would I hear there? The voices of dying soldiers, shouting Indians as they closed in on Custer and his men?

Here on 30th Street I hear in my mind the voice of producer Irving Townsend. "The machine's on…here we go: no title, Take 1…" and the magic began, a magic that has not lost its luster in over forty years, and never fails to resonate for me in a way no other record ever has.

I must stand there for fifteen or twenty minutes, visualizing that session until I've had my fill and move on, walking back up town to the 56th rehearsal studio.

I give my name to the guy at a small desk and he hands me a key, a newspaper in front of him that he never looks up from. "Upstairs. Number 4," he says.

It's strictly no frills, just a small room, wood floors, an open window, a tin ashtray on the decent upright piano. I sit down, light a cigarette and go over "Goodbye Porkpie Hat," making some notes on chord changes as I go. It feels good but I don't want to overdo it. I want it to be fresh for tomorrow. I try "If You Could See Me Now," and end up trying a few other up tunes, spending an hour or so just playing. It all feels good. I'm ready.

I meet Cameron Brody in the Village at a small Italian bistro with checkered tablecloths, a candle on every table and grumpy waiters in black vests. He's already got a carafe of red wine and is dipping chunks of bread into a dish of olive oil as I sit down.

"Hey," he says. "Get over the lag yet?"

"Pretty much. Got a short nap in later this afternoon." After the session in the rehearsal studio, I'd wandered around some more and finally drifted back to the hotel and dozed off watching an old *Rockford Files*. By the time I'd gotten awake, it was time to shower and change and head for the Village.

"So what's good?"

"Everything," Brody says. "It changes every day." He points to a small blackboard with the names of dishes scrawled in a shaky hand. "I don't think anybody in the kitchen speaks English. This is the real deal."

We settle on soup and something that seems like seafood gumbo over the best pasta I've ever tasted. The place gradually fills up as we get through our dinner, the carafe of wine. Over coffee, I tell Brody he can come to the recording session.

"Awesome," he says, smiling. "Let me buy dinner then."

"No, you got the cab. This is on me."

He shrugs. "Whatever. But thanks, man. I appreciate it."

I sip the strong coffee and light a cigarette. Brody wrinkles his nose but the waiter brings an ashtray. He's chosen apparently, one of the remaining places smoking is allowed.

"I did a little digging this afternoon. I don't think your friend wrote any of the tunes on *Kind of Blue*," he says. "'So What,' 'All Blues,' and 'Freddie' are all solid Miles. You're right. There was controversy on 'Blue in Green' with him and Bill Evans, and Evans has been on record that 'Flamenco Sketches' came from something he'd done earlier, but Miles got credit."

"Yes, I've been reading about it. Evans seems pretty adamant. I've been thinking. Cal may have done the same thing many musicians did. Write out the tune trying to figure out what they were doing and how they did it."

"Exactly my thought," Brody says.

"Flamenco Sketches" was a very unusual structure. With *Kind of Blue*, Miles had wanted to get away from the typical

American song book of standard tunes. "Flamenco" was based on a series of five modal scales, each played as long as the soloist wanted until the cycle had been completed. Much different from playing say a Cole Porter song and taking two, three, or four choruses. This was different altogether.

"Plus," Brody went on, "there were only six people in the band and this was really a Miles-Evans collaboration. Cannonball and Coltrane were still getting into it, but Miles and Evans were the architects. *Birth of the Cool*, however is a different story, at least from what I've found."

"How do you mean?"

"Bigger band and they rehearsed for weeks. A lot of musicians contributed tunes even though the brain trust was Miles, Gil Evans, Gerry Mulligan, John Lewis, John Carisi, maybe even some others. The personnel changed all the time, depending on who could make the rehearsals, who had a gig and who didn't. It was also ten years earlier."

I knew a lot of what Brody said was true. Rehearsal bands are notorious for many of the band pulling out something they'd written or sketched out. Sometimes they got played, sometimes they didn't. Some stuck, some didn't. It was like a workshop according to the liner notes of the recording.

"Then there's the odd tune, like 'Boplicity,'" Brody says. "Cleo Henry. What happened to him. Writes one tune and it gets recorded, becomes kind of a signature thing for the album. Lot of room for shared composing credit on the others." Brody looks at me. "If you could confirm that your friend made some of those rehearsals, well…" He lets that hang in the air. "Boplicity, duplicity, complicity, multiplicity." He shakes his head. "Can't think of anymore, but that was a different era. Records weren't kept well, credit got sold, switched around, who knows what really happened and when and by whom."

I take a drag on my cigarette and finish my coffee. "So you're saying what."

"I'm saying officially, ASCAP, BMI records show the copyright registered for all the tunes on the recording are valid. The individual composer would file for each but since Miles ran things, well, people forget."

The idea I'd been floating around in the my mind, now had greater importance. "What if I could find somebody who made some of those rehearsals, who knew Cal?"

"That," Brody says, "would be a good start." He smiles.

"What?"

Brody grins. "Nothing. I guess the guy who sorted out a missing tape of Clifford Brown could do that."

Chapter Nine

I get a taxi to Avatar Studios in midtown, and arrive early. Cameron Brody is already there, pacing in front of the building, drinking coffee from a paper cup. "You sure this is okay?" he asks, as I come up. "I mean I don't want to get in the way or anything."

I smile and pat him on the shoulder. "If it wasn't, they would have told me. Come on."

We go inside and check in with a security guard, who consults a clipboard. "Evan Horne and guest?"

"Yes."

He has Brody sign in and sends us upstairs to Studio B. Inside, it's all wood paneling, wood floors, and two isolation booths with sliding glass doors. In the center of the room a drum set is centered on a red rectangular carpet, the cymbals gleaming in the overhead light. Cameron Brody stops and walks all around the drum set like a little kid. "Far out," he says. "This is so fucking cool."

I glance up at the glassed in control booth that overlooks the studio. A young guy in a dark sweatshirt and longish hair is seated at the board, scanning dials, while another older man in a suit is talking, gesturing, pacing. Has to be Larry Klein.

One of the booths is dark but I can see the grand piano inside. A handwritten note is taped to the glass that says: Do Not Touch. In the other booth, I see who's going to play bass.

Tall, slim, studious looking in a tweed coat, pale blue shirt and yellow floral bow tie, just as I've seen him dressed in many photos, Ron Carter sits on a high stool. The bass is cradled against him as he gazes at some music on a stand in front of him. How many times have I heard him with Miles, that great quintet of the sixties, and now, here he is, waiting for me.

I walk in the booth. "Ron? Evan Horne."

"Hey," he says with a friendly smile. He stands up and holds out his hand. "Just looking over your tunes," he says. "I'm doing a television show later," as if to explain his coat and tie. He points to the music. "Anything I should know about this?"

"No, I use the original changes on 'Porkpie' and 'Foolish Heart.' We've all played that. I'll just play maybe four bars in front before the melody."

He looks up. "Yeah. Roy gave me a cassette of yours. Some very nice playing."

Before I can say anything, the man in the suit comes in. "Evan, Larry Klein." He's all smiles and enthusiasm and frenetic energy. He nods to Ron Carter, who just glances up from the music and begins working on his bass lines. "Come on, let's check out the piano," Klein says.

I follow him over to the other booth. He flips on the lights and I sit down at the grand piano. And it is grand. The sound is gorgeous and the action feels very comfortable under my fingers as I run through some chords.

Klein beams, listens for a moment, then turns as we both see Roy Haynes come in with a woman and another man. Haynes waves and comes over. Always known for his dapper attire, he's dressed casually but expensively in a sweater and slacks and soft looking tan loafers.

"Hey," he says, smiling at me. "You ready to make some music?" We shake hands. "I'm sure glad you could make this."

"I'm looking forward to it."

And I am. A kind of calm had descended on me the minute I walked in the studio. I felt relaxed, confident, and I know even then it's going to go well.

"Okay, let me see if they set my drums right." He walks out of the booth, over to his drums, and unzips a small black bag that holds sticks and brushes and mallets and sits down at the set. He taps on the snare drum, moving the stick around the edge, listens and makes some adjustments with a drum key, then turns and waves to the control booth.

The engineer's voice comes over the playback speakers. "Okay, guys, put on the phones, let me get some levels. You first, Evan."

I nod and put on the headphones and begin to play the opening to "Goodbye Porkpie Hat," looking toward the booth. The woman that came in with Haynes is talking to him now. She has a notebook in her hand. I see her glance over at me and write, but I see Haynes look up and smile as I start to play.

"Okay, that's fine." The engineer's voice comes through the headphones. "Ron, you next."

I listen as Carter plays some deep long tones, then walks for a few moments. "You going to bow any?" the engineers asks.

Carter looks over at me and I shrug. "Maybe on the ending?" Carter nods and tries the bow. "Got it," the engineer says. "Roy?"

Haynes nods to the woman as she walks away and sits down near the wall with Brody and the other man. Haynes taps on all the drums, plays a little time on the cymbals and hits the bass drum a few times. "Thanks," the engineer says.

The first time I recorded like this it was weird, hearing everybody only through headphones, but I got used to it. We can all see each other through the glass and the isolation booths make doing the final mix more precise. I'd read once that Benny Goodman's band had been recorded with one microphone and a reel to reel tape recorder at Carnegie Hall. Things have changed.

The engineer comes on again. "Okay, let's do something together so I can get a mix."

"How about a blues," Haynes says. I can see his lips move and hear his voice in my ear. "Go ahead, Evan, pick something, you start. But remember not too fast. I'm old." He laughs.

I nod and play four bars in a medium tempo and go into "Israel," a Bill Evans tune. Carter is in on the fifth bar as Haynes plays some little crackle thing on the snare, his right hand is on the ride cymbal. I'd already seen it was one he favored. A flat one, with no bell, the definition so precise you could hear every tick of the wooden tip stick distinctly.

We play a couple of choruses and the rush is so strong I want to keep playing, but Haynes stops. "Whoa, listen to this cat," he says. "Let's save some of that. You got enough, Buzz?" he says to the engineer.

There's a pause then, "Yeah, we're fine."

Haynes nods. "Let's do 'Porkpie' first, okay?" And to me, "Right on it?"

I nod in agreement and wait for the cue from the engineer.

"Okay, we're rolling. Roy Haynes, take 1, 'Goodbye Porkpie Hat.'"

I count…1..2..slow ballad tempo and play the first chord of the melody. Carter's bass pulses in my ear and Haynes, brushes in hand, swirls in circles on the snare, implying the tempo. It feels so relaxed it's like playing at home, or that day I was at Cal's house, only now I have one of the best drummers and bass players in jazz. I play two choruses, glance up at both of them to signal I'm going out and we end with Haynes rolling with mallets on the cymbal and Carter drawing out a long bowed line on the last note.

We all freeze for a few seconds, allowing time, then hear a click and the engineer's voice. "Fuck, we gotta keep that one," Buzz says.

Haynes says, "Definitely. You okay with that one, Evan."

"Yeah, unless Ron wants to solo one."

Carter shakes his head. "No, thanks."

Haynes says, "Let's hear it back, Buzz."

I get up and walk out to the drums to listen with Haynes, knowing I'll never play it any better. As the playback fills the room, Haynes nods, smiling, shaking his head. "Beautiful, man. Just beautiful."

When the playback finishes, Buzz, the engineer, comes in the studio and moves one of the microphones on Haynes' drums slightly. "The up tune now, right?"

"Yeah," Haynes says. Ron Carter joins us and we talk over tunes and how we'll do it, but Haynes has another idea. "You know 'I Hear a Rhapsody,' right?"

"Yes, play it a lot."

"And 'All Blues'?" He looks at Carter. "I know I don't have to ask you," he says. Some six years with Miles, Ron Carter must have played it hundreds of times, and of course I know it too. "Cool, I got an idea. You'll see what I mean. Come on." We go back into the booth with the piano. Haynes explains, snaps his fingers for the tempo he wants, and has me play the "All Blues" intro which is a repeated vamp in 6/8. "There," he says. "That last note of the 'All Blues' vamp is the first note of 'Rhapsody.' See what I mean? Then after each section, we go back to that as a kind of interlude."

I play it down a few times and marvel at how easy it fits. "You see?" Haynes says. "It sounds like we're going to play 'All Blues' then we go right into 'Rhapsody.' It can mess with cats trying to sit in." He laughs heartily.

"Mr. Haynes, you are so clever," Carter says, with a grin.

"Why thank you, Mr. Carter." Haynes bows slightly

Not at all what I'd planned to play, but sometimes, even in recording, it happens this way. The leader will pull a new tune out of the hat to raise the level of spontaneity, create something we didn't know we would do.

Haynes and Carter go back to their places and we run through it together with no problem, then decide on a format for solos. "Evan, you do a couple or three choruses, Ron, you take a couple, then we'll do some eights and take it out, ending with the 'All Blues' interlude, okay? And at the beginning, we'll just vamp on that interlude till you're ready, Evan."

He turns and looks up toward the booth. "Okay, Buzz, let's get one."

There's silence for a few moments, then Buzz: "We're rolling. Roy Haynes, 'I Hear a Rhapsody,' take 1."

Carter and Haynes poise for my cue and I begin the vamp. For a moment, I'm lost in the dream that Bill Evans played these exact same chords on *Kind of Blue* in 1959. I nod, feeling Haynes and Carter watching, and we go right into "Rhapsody." I do three choruses, glance at Carter, who takes two, his beautiful tone singing through the headphones, then two choruses of eight bar exchanges with Haynes. He's all over the drums but in such a melodic way, it's always clear where he is in the tune, and more than demonstrating his nickname "snap crackle." We take it home and play the "All Blues" interlude, vamping again until Buzz's voice comes over. "I'll just fade on the interlude, okay Roy?"

We all stop then. "Perfect," Haynes says, "but let's do one more since we got time. How about the thing we did for the level check, Evan. 'Israel.'"

"Sure."

We take it fairly up, like Bill Evans did with his later trios. Haynes pushing and prodding like we're walking along a path in the woods with his hand on my back, guiding the direction, and Carter's deep low tones anchoring everything. In a little over an hour, we're done and everybody is happy with the playbacks.

"Damn," Haynes says. "It's going to be hard to choose between those two." He hugs me and beams. "That ballad was beautiful, man." He looks at me quizzically. "You got somebody important you just lost?"

"Yeah, I do," I say, surprised at his insight.

"Uh huh. I can always tell. You know Mingus was thinking about Lester Young when he wrote it."

Carter already has his bass packed up and he's heading out. He stops and shakes hands. "I enjoyed it much," he says. "Later, Roy."

Cameron Brody comes over then, standing back expectantly, waiting for an introduction. "Roy, like you to meet a friend of mine. He's a drummer too. Cameron Brody."

Haynes turns and smiles and shakes hands with Brody. "Well, all right then," he says. "Want to check out my drums?" He winks at me, and Brody looks like he's going to faint.

"Thanks again, man," Haynes says to me. "I'll let you know how the mix comes out." He points to the woman he'd been talking to earlier. "She's from *Downbeat*, going to give us a little nudge on this project."

"My pleasure." I watch Brody circle the drums and tentatively sit down.

"Go on," Haynes says. "Let's see what you got."

I signal Brody I'll wait downstairs. Outside on the street, I light a cigarette and lean against the building, letting the euphoria wash over me, savoring one of those rare moments when I've done just what I wanted. I watch the traffic rush by, but my mind is still on the session, the sound of Ron Carter's bass buzzing in my ear, and Haynes' crackling snare and precise cymbal play. It takes me awhile, but by the time Brody joins me I feel like my feet are on the ground again.

"That was fucking awesome," Brody says. "Man, can he play or what!"

I smile and start walking, letting Brody have his moment. He stops then, touches my arm. "That ballad was fantastic, Evan. You were really on."

"Thanks." I nod and keep walking toward midtown.

"We gotta celebrate, and I'm buying. Let's get a real expensive dinner tonight." He checks his watch. "I got a few things to do so let's meet later. I know a place or you can choose."

"Just tell me where," I say. "I'm going back to the hotel and make a couple of calls."

"Okay. Why don't you come to my place and we'll go from there." He writes down his address on a card and hands it to me. "See ya." He makes me laugh as he suddenly whirls around and points, then goes on down the street.

I stroll slowly back toward the hotel. I pass a coffee place near Times Square, and bring a tall one to an outside table. I take out my phone and call Andie.

"Hi," she says. "How did it go?"

"Couldn't have been better. It's easy to play with great musicians and I just recorded with two of the best."

"Oh, I'm so happy for you. Congratulations, babe. Wish I could have been there."

"So how are you doing?"

"Pretty good. I took another walk today. My leg feels fine and I'm having a check on Monday. What are you doing now?"

"I'm going up to Boston to see my folks for a couple of days. Probably come back Monday or Tuesday."

"Did you figure out what was bothering you about your mother?"

"Not yet. Maybe when I see her."

"It's been awhile. Evan?"

"What?"

"Nothing. Just let me know how it goes, okay."

"I will. You take care."

"You too. I love you."

"I love you too."

I hang up and once again feel something is off. First my mother, now Andie. Maybe I'm imagining things, but both nag at me and I can't put my finger on either. I finish my coffee and make one more call.

"Dana? It's Evan."

"I was just thinking about you," she says. "Did you do the recording already?"

"Yeah, just finished awhile ago. Everything went fine. Anything new with you."

She sighs. "No, just trying to get this thesis done and I'm bored. Are you going to be coming through L.A. on the way back?"

"I hadn't planned on it, why?"

"Oh I just thought it would be nice and Milton misses you."

"Well give him a pat for me. I'm going up to see my mother for a couple of days. I'll see how things go. You haven't had any more calls or visits from Brent Sergent have you?"

"No, not a word."

"Okay, well get back to work."

"Yeah, I will. Bye, Evan."

Back at the hotel, I call around the airlines and manage to get a round trip to Boston on a shuttle without too much trouble, going up Saturday morning and coming back late Sunday evening. I call my mother to let her know.

"That's fine," she says when I give her the flight information. "Your dad will pick you up."

"That's not necessary, mom. I can get a cab."

"No, he wants to."

"Well, okay then. See you tomorrow."

The apartment Cameron Brody is staying in is in the West Village. He buzzes me in and I walk up to the second floor. The door is open and Brody is sitting on the couch, leaning over his laptop computer.

"Be right with you," he says. "Just doing a little research."

I sit down next to him and watch his fingers fly over the keys, the screens changing like a slide projector. He finally ends on a screen with a lot of figures and dates, mumbles something, then shuts down and closes the lid.

"Okay."

"What was all that?"

"The reason I'm in New York. I've been tracking this blues singer. He doesn't know it but he's got a valid claim for some royalties on something he wrote years ago. With all this nostalgia thing happening, some newer group recorded one of his songs and it took off. So I got a check for him but he moved and didn't leave any forwarding address."

"And you can do all that on the computer."

Brody smiles. "It's amazing man, just amazing what you can do with one of these puppies if you know where and how to look."

"Ever do any family history searches, genealogy, that kind of thing?"

He shakes his head. "No, but I can. Got somebody you want to look up?"

"Maybe later. Let's get some dinner."

Brody leads me to a steak house near the Village Vanguard. It's down a few stairs below street level and about half full as we're early. We get the whole scene—Caesar salad, baked potato, and a juicy New York cut of course, grilled to perfection. We share a carafe of burgundy and finally lean back sated and satisfied.

"So what are you plans now?" Brody stirs as coffee arrives.

"I'm going up to Boston to see my folks for a couple of days, then I guess back to San Francisco. What about you?"

"I have to take care of this royalty thing. I have an open ticket so I can go anytime. You coming back to New York or going straight from Boston?"

"I'll come back here, I guess." I realized how pumped I still was from the recording session, the energy of New York, and although I was anxious to get back to Andie, at the same time I was reluctant to leave the city.

Brody studies me a moment. "How serious are you about tracking down the *Birth of the Cool* recordings, seeing if your friend was responsible for some of the tunes?"

"Very. Why?"

"While you're in Boston, let me do some searching. Hell, they were done right here. Why not check it out? The family search you have in mind, the woman you mentioned. What was her name? Lane?"

"Yeah, Jean Lane. Well, I don't want to put you to any trouble. You have your own work."

"Are you kidding? I love a good mystery too, and I owe you for Roy Haynes. You know what that would mean if we could find out your friend wrote any of those tunes?" He was grinning now, excited at the idea of the hunt. He takes out a small notebook and pen from his pocket. "Give me as much as you got."

I give him Cal, Jean Lane, Kansas City, any other things and then I remember another name. Al Beckwood.

Brody looks up. "Who's he?"

"I'm not sure, but he called a couple of times after Cal died. He left a number but I've never been able to get him." I dig the number out of my wallet and he adds it to his list. He looks at the number for moment. "Something familiar about this name." He shuts the notebook and puts it away. "It'll come to me. Doesn't sound too hard, man," he says. "It's not easy to disappear these days. People leave paper trails wherever they go."

"Thanks. I appreciate this," I say.

"Don't mention it. I met Roy Haynes, played on his drums thanks to you. That's worth a lot. Oh, give me your cell phone number too, in case I need to check with you."

We walk outside and amble back toward Brody's borrowed apartment.

"Want to catch some music? There's the Vanguard, the Blue Note. Not sure who's there."

I catch myself yawning. "No, I think I'll pass, just get some sleep. I've got an early flight in the morning and I'm still on west coast time."

At his street, we shake hands and I wave down a cab. "Thanks again for dinner."

"No problem. When you come back, you can crash with me. The couch is pretty comfortable."

No calls or messages back at the hotel. I watch a little television but nod off a couple of times and finally turn it off. After that, I don't remember a thing.

Chapter Ten

At Logan Airport in Boston, I catch sight of my dad's dark blue van, emblazoned with *Horne Printing & Copy Centers* as soon as I come out of baggage claim. He pulls over and opens the door for me and claps me on the shoulder as I climb in. "Hey, Evan, good to see you."

"You too, dad." I throw my bag in the back and we're off. Neither of us has much to say, the old awkwardness still there, as he maneuvers through the airport traffic, out into the city's maze of one-way streets, working his way north, toward I-90. It's only a few minutes till we're on I-60, merging with the Saturday morning traffic headed for Medford.

"How's mom?" I ask, reaching for my cigarettes. I still have that nagging feeling that something is wrong.

"Oh she's fine, looking forward to seeing you. I have to run down to the Cape so you'll have some time together. I won't be back till late tonight."

"Oh?"

He doesn't respond, just keeps his hands on the wheel, and pulls the Red Sox baseball cap down more over his eyes.

"You mind if I smoke?"

"No, just crack the window if you will."

Rolling down the window, I light up, holding the cigarette outside for the most part, watching the half familiar scenery fly by, feeling the chilly fall air rushing in despite the bright sun. The leaves are starting to turn bright orange and red.

I hadn't spent much time here. My folks had moved from Santa Monica long after I left home, so I'd never actually lived here. There were some weekends when I was studying at the Berklee school in Boston, but never any long visits. It was a different life, a different world from the beach in Santa Monica, the small house just above Wilshire, where Danny Cooper and I had spent countless hours playing pool in the garage and shooting baskets in the driveway.

It takes less than a half hour from Logan until we pull up in the driveway of the Horne house. Like the others on the street, it's white clapboard, shutters, and a large front porch. The house looks freshly painted and the shutters are a dark green now. I see my mother sitting on the front porch, a cup of coffee in hand. She stands up and waves as I get out of the van. I turn to my Dad and reach behind the seat for my bag, but he's still got the engine running, waiting for me to get out.

"Aren't you coming in?"

"No, I have to get going." He's looking straight ahead. "You need to spend some time with your mother for this."

I get out and look at him, before I close the door. "For what?"

But he's already backing out of the driveway and pulling away. I look up at my mother. She's standing now and briefly waves at the departing van, then turns to me. "Hi, son. Come on in."

She has on a denim smock kind of dress with oversized pockets over a red turtle neck sweater. I walk up the few steps to the porch and hug her, then step back, my hands still on her shoulders. "What's going on, Mom? Are you sick or something?" I search her face, flashing on everything possible—heart, cancer, stroke, some kind of surgery.

But she manages a smile and shakes her head. "No, honey, I'm fine. We just need to talk." She motions to the two chairs. "Let's sit out here and we can both smoke."

I see an ashtray, a package of cigarettes and matches on the small table between two chairs. "When did you start smoking again?"

My mother had smoked much of her adult life, at least as far back as I can remember. I used to sneak cigarettes out of her packs of unfiltered Pall Malls, but she'd quit some years ago.

She sighs and looks at me. "I guess the day you called to tell me you were coming. Can I get you some coffee? I just made a fresh pot."

"Sure." She takes her cup and goes inside. I sit down, more puzzled than ever. Since the day I called? I was still trying to remember the uneasiness I'd felt after that call, about something she'd said, but I still haven't figured out what it is.

She comes back out carrying a small tray with two mugs of coffee, two spoons, a half pint carton of half and half, and a small bowl of sugar. She sets everything on the table and leans the tray against her chair. "So how did the recording go?"

"Fine. Look, Mom what's going on?"

She sits down. I see weariness on her face now, although she still looks good. Her hair is grayer and the glasses, attached to a chain around her neck seem thicker, but otherwise she looks healthy.

"Evan," she begins tentatively, "I don't hardly know how to tell you this." She takes a cigarette out of her pack and nervously strikes three matches before she can get it lit. Taking a deep drag, she blows the smoke out. She looks at the cigarette and smiles. "It's so easy to start again, isn't it?"

I wait, watching her, trying to read her expression. "Are you and dad splitting up? Is that what this is about?"

She laughs and shakes her head. "No, this isn't about your dad and me. This is about you." She takes a folded piece of paper out of one of the large pockets in her dress and hands it to me. "I've been carrying this around with me since you called, wondering how I was going to do this." She gets up and walks to the other end of the porch.

I open it and look at it, suddenly feeling like I did when I found Cal's note. Scanning over it quickly at first, then focusing more closely. Thicker than regular paper with some official looking seals and signatures, it's creased from many folding.

A birth certificate. In the middle of the page is my name, only it's not my name.

Evan Douglas Hughes Date of Birth: 9-27-58
Father: Calvin William Hughes. Mother: Susan Jean Lane.

I don't know how long I stare trying to make sense of it. I look away then back several times. My mother is staring straight ahead, the cigarette in her hand. Then suddenly, it hits me, what I was trying to remember when I'd called her from Guerneville, when I'd told her about Cal's death. *Oh yes, your friend from Kansas City,* she'd said. And that's what had been wrong. I'd never mentioned where Cal was from, then or ever.

I stand up and pace around the porch, the paper in my hand, looking at it again and again but still unable to digest what it means. "I don't understand, Mom. What is this?"

She comes back, sits down and stubs out her cigarette and sighs deeply. She won't look at me. "We, I, should have told you a long time ago, I know that, but we put it off, hid it, I don't know. The longer we waited, the harder it was to do. Then you were gone and..." Her voice trails off and she shrugs.

I lean back against the porch railing and close my eyes, my stomach churning.

When I was about thirteen or fourteen and learning to body surf, I took a wave one hot afternoon that was way too big. Two of my buddies shouted—Danny Cooper was one I think—"No, not this one," but it was too late. I was already shooting down the face of the wave, my arms at my sides, feeling its force and power take me. I don't know how long the slide was, but for a second, as the wave began its curl, I was in the air for a few seconds, suspended, between the crest of the wave and the flat dark surface of the water that seemed so far below. Then, I hit the water flat, felt tons more fall and crush me, throwing me around like a toy. Under water, the whirling and churning continued, the salt water stinging my eyes. My lungs ached for air. I fought in a panic, but I was so disoriented I didn't know where the surface was. Whirling and twisting and being thrown about, till I saw a faint light and dug for the surface. I broke through, gasping for breath, trying to keep my head above water, but I was thrown around by two more waves till I finally washed up on the beach and crawled up to the dry sand. I lay there, gasping, spitting up water, trying to get my breath back. That's how it feels now as I look at the birth certificate again, my birth certificate.

My mother's eyes finally meet mine. "I'm sorry, Evan, I'm so sorry."

"But how? Who else knew?"

"Most of the family, some close friends. We had two anniversary dates to account for you. The real one when your father," she pauses and corrects herself, "your stepfather and I got married, and another one to take in your birth. You were two when Richard and I got married."

Richard. Dad. Yes, suddenly the man I believed to be my father is now somebody else. Somebody called Richard Horne.

"Whenever you needed your birth certificate for school or something, we always took care of it. We had adoption papers, and since I was your birth mother, well, it wasn't that difficult and you were too young to worry about it."

I sit down again and feel the questions swirling around in my mind. Such an elaborate scheme to cover things up, keep the truth from me. The truth that Calvin Hughes, whose ashes I had scattered in Santa Monica Bay was my father.

"But why, Mom?" I look again at the certificate. "And Lane isn't your maiden name, or is it?"

She sighs again. "No." Her eyes well up then. She takes a swallow of coffee and lights another cigarette. "I was married again briefly, just a few months, between…between Calvin and Richard." She glances at me briefly then looks away. "I didn't want you to know about that. I made such a terrible mistake, I know that. Richard wanted me to tell you so many times, but I just couldn't bring myself to do it."

I stare dumbly at her. "So all these years you let me think I was somebody else, that somebody else was my father. Didn't you think I had a right to know?" I feel the anger rising up in me now as the truth starts to seep in my mind. "Jesus Christ, Mom, I had a right to know. You should have told me."

"Oh I know. Don't you think I know that? Don't you think I spent so much time trying to think how I'd tell you. I...I was trying to protect you, but I see that was wrong."

"Protect me? From what?"

She sighs again, her voice is quieter. "Calvin, your father, wasn't always a nice man. There were other women and I didn't want..." She doesn't finish for a moment. "When you first told me you'd met him, were studying with him, I knew then this day would come. He never said anything, hinted at it?"

I think back, trying to remember, but no, there was never anything. Just my surprise that Calvin agreed to take me on as a student, and later, a friend and mentor.

"No, there was nothing." I reach for my bag, unzip it and pull out the file folder with Cal's papers, the music sheets and the photo. I hand the photo to her and point. "That's me isn't it, in the carriage," I say, hearing my voice tremble.

She takes the photo and looks at it, puts her hand to her mouth as tears slide down her face. "Yes." Her voice is almost a whisper. "Where did you get this?" She wipes away the tears and looks at me.

"I found it with Cal's things." I tell her about the note and the photo, how Cal had left it.

She nods, studying the photo. "And he kept it all these years." She shakes her head again and looks up at me. "You're right, Evan, you did have a right to know and for that I'm so sorry. I just...I just hope you can find some way to forgive me."

I can see her steeling herself as she lights another cigarette. I hope I can too. I fish the lighter out of my pocket. I'd been carrying it around. "This is yours too."

She curls her fingers around it, her head bows slightly. "What do you want to know?"

"Everything."

"I was working in Kansas City," she begins, "my first time away from home, going a little wild I guess if you can imagine that. I shared an apartment with two other girls. There were parties, going out to clubs and dances, everything I'd never been able to do. One night we went to hear this band. Calvin, your father, was the piano player. I don't know why I was so drawn to him. I just stood in front of the band listening to the music, watching him play.

"He caught me looking at him a couple of times, smiled at me. We talked during the intermissions and later, we went out for something to eat. He was so ambitious, so dedicated to music, I was just...mesmerized. I'd never known anybody so passionate about something. Music, playing the piano was important to me, but nothing like that, and I never had any idea of a career in music."

I sit very still just listening to her, hearing for the first time about another life altogether.

"I met him again the next night and nearly every night for the two weeks they played. Then, well, things happened. I fell in love but the band was going on the road. They'd be gone for a month he said, but they were coming back to Kansas City. It was one of those territory bands. They traveled on a bus. It was a hard life but Calvin loved it. He called a lot, wrote me notes, cards, and I could hardly wait till he got back.

"The band he was with got another long term job in Kansas City, but he wanted to leave the band, go to New York. He said he'd missed his chance once and it wasn't going to happen again. I never knew what he was talking about and he never explained what he meant."

"We spent nearly two months together and finally, on his day off, we got married. Just the two of us and a couple of friends from the band as witnesses. Then he was gone again, another road trip, leaving me alone in a small studio apartment we'd found."

I glance over at her then, watch her sigh deeply.

"When he came back again, I was pregnant with you. He wanted to go to New York. That's all he talked about and he wanted me to go with him, but I was scared. I didn't want to be stuck in New York while he traveled, not knowing anybody, so I stayed in Kansas City. At least I had a few friends there. Then he called, said he had a chance to go to Europe on a tour and couldn't turn it down."

She stops then, sighs and lights another cigarette, takes a drink of coffee. "I knew it was a big chance for him, he was so determined to make good, but it was months before he came back. I waited, working as long as I could, until just before you were born. He didn't even call me at first, but I found out where he was playing, where he was staying." She points to the photo. "That's when that photo was taken, right outside his hotel. I don't know what happened while he was in Europe, maybe another woman, but he was different somehow. I realized then how foolish I'd been, but it wasn't just me now. I had a child."

"We spent a week talking about things, what we were going to do and finally I made him choose. You and me. His baby, or the road. It wasn't going to be any life I wanted. He'd be gone all the time and it was too lonely for me. Well, you can imagine what his choice was. He went back out on the road again and that was the last time I saw Calvin Hughes. He wrote occasionally, sent me money but I never responded. I was working, trying to raise you, trying to forget how silly I'd been. It was just too much. I couldn't cope with it all."

My mother slumps back in her chair and rubs her eyes. "Then, this man in the office I was working in, Jim Lane was his name, started asking me out. By then I'd filed for divorce and of course Calvin never appeared when I went to court. I was lonely, feeling abandoned so it was easy to fall into things with Jim, but it was a mistake from the start even though we got married."

"It lasted about six months and one day I simply took you on a Greyhound bus and went to California. One of the girls I'd roomed with was out there and she got me a job where she worked. I wrote Jim that it was over, saying I would agree to a divorce, that he could file anything he wanted. He tried to talk me out of it but finally gave up."

She pauses again, such a faraway look in her eyes then turns to look at me. "So there I was, strictly raised small town girl, married and divorced twice with a baby. Who would have thought. Sometimes I can't believe it myself."

She seems calmer now, having finally unburdened herself as she continues. "Then your dad, Richard, came along." She stands up then, leans against the porch railing, her hands in her pockets, staring out over the tree lined street.

"Richard was everything I thought I wanted at the time. Solid, hard working, and he accepted you like you were his own child. My life before with Calvin and Jim Lane seemed like a bad dream, and now I was waking up. We got married, moved into that house in Santa Monica and his business flourished. He was ambitious in his own way, but well, you know he had no affinity for music, that kind of life, although he never pressed me about Calvin. He thought I should tell you early on that he was not your real father, but like I said, I kept putting it off."

She sighs and turns back toward me. "Evan, I knew this day would come sometime, but can you understand I thought I was doing the right thing at the time. Please don't think badly of me for not telling you. I'm not making excuses but it's just something I can't undo now."

I don't trust myself to speak for awhile. My mind is churning, questions rising to the surface, so many I can't sort them out. Finally, I get up and put my hands on the railing and lean on it. "No, I don't think badly of you mom. I wasn't there, but to learn now that Calvin was my father, that Richard…. Do you have any idea what this feels like? I just wish you'd told me sooner."

I look into my mother's eyes and see the pain, the regret. "I just have to get used to the idea, Mom. It's not easy." I hug her to me for a moment. "Do you have any other photos of him, anything?"

"Yes, I've been looking for them since you called."

"I want to see them, Mom, anything you have."

She nods. "I think I know where they are."

"I need to get away for awhile, okay? I think I'm going to take a walk, kind of digest all this."

"Sure, honey. You go ahead. I'll fix us some lunch when you come back." She hugs me close and is still watching when I look back as I start down the street.

It's not every day you find out you're not who you think you are, the people you thought you knew are not who you thought they were. It's all different now and nothing can be changed. Nothing, I realize suddenly, will be the same again. I feel cheated, betrayed, lied to, and the feeling won't go away.

I walk for almost an hour, through the streets of Medford, trying to process everything, sort out my feelings. Memories flood my mind; little incidents come into focus, snatches of conversations that puzzled me at the time but now suddenly make sense, understanding now why I'd never connected with my dad, why he'd never understood my obsession with music. How could he? He was a businessman who owned a chain of photo copy instant printing stores. His life was the bottom line, facts and figures, hiring, firing, employee benefits. Mine was music, the piano.

As I walk, not really aware of direction, things come back to me in a rush. The many arguments, the threats, my mother trying to keep the peace with Richard while encouraging me to practice. It was all from her. The envy I'd felt with friends whose fathers seemed to have such good relationships with them, not knowing that at that very moment, my real father, Calvin Hughes was doing exactly what I wanted to be doing.

I look around, getting my bearings when it starts to rain suddenly and hard. I turn toward the house and when I get back, I'm drenched. I find my mother seated at the dining room table, looking through a shoe box of photos and a scrap book. She looks up at me. "Oh, you're soaked," she says, getting up. "Get out of those clothes. I put your bag in the back room."

I dry off, and change and come back and sit down with her, seeing photos of Cal, newspaper clippings she'd saved spread over the table.

"I want you to have these, Evan. You should have had them long ago."

I nod and smile at her. "Well, I've at least found Jean Lane."

"You've found more than that."

While my mother makes sandwiches, I look through the photos, seeing Cal, my mother as a young woman, and Cal gradually changing and aging, knowing I'll always wonder how I would view these if they'd told me earlier. How would my mother have explained things then?

I also have to accept that he never tried to see me or contact me. It wasn't until I began taking lessons with him that we began to form a bond. Why didn't *he* tell me then? I drifted in and out of his life for a few brief years, a student, friend, and never knew, never once guessed he was my father.

"Here we are," my mother says. She sets down plates with sandwiches and potato salad. "You must be hungry."

I take a bite of the sandwich but it's tasteless. "Did he know you moved to California?"

She shrugs. "I'm not sure, probably." She looks at me again. "But no, he never contacted me, never asked to see you. The only person I ever heard from was his friend." She looks up. "I'm sorry, Evan, but that's the truth. I think it would have been too hard for him by then, and he probably worried about what it would do to you, and I like to think, me. He wouldn't have known if I'd told you or not, but I suspect he knew where we were. He must have followed your playing career."

"What friend?"

My mother frowns. "Oh what was his name. He was a bass player, in the band with Cal when I first met him. Al...Beck, Becker, Beckwood. Al Beckwood."

I stop and look up at her. "Are you sure?"

"Yes. Every once in awhile he'd call or send me a card. I think Cal put him up to it."

"Do you know where he is, how I could contact him?"

She shakes her head. "No, it's been years now. I have no idea."

We finish lunch as I continue to look through things, but my mind is on Al Beckwood. Maybe he'd have some answers. Finally, my mother gets up and clears the table. "I've made some fresh coffee and there's beer in the fridge," she says. "I'm going to lie down for awhile."

"Sure, Mom, go ahead."

She leans over and kisses me on the forehead and squeezes my shoulder. "Take whatever you want, Evan. They're yours now."

I'm still sitting on the porch when my dad's, Richard's, van pulls into the driveway. He gets out, joins me on the porch and drops into a chair. "So. Now you know, huh?"

"Yeah, now I know." Even in the shadows, I see the weariness in his face. "You want a beer?"

"That sounds good."

I'd spent the afternoon and evening looking at photos, reading clips on Calvin my mother had somehow come across. I'd tried to call Andie twice but only got her voice mail and what I wanted to talk about couldn't be left on a machine. So much was still missing. What did Cal mean when he told my mother he'd missed his chance once in New York? I needed someone to fill in the blanks.

I go inside and get two beers and bring them back and hand Richard one. "Mom says you wanted to tell me before. Is that true?"

He nods and shrugs. "I went back and forth on it, but the bottom line is we should have told you as soon as you were old enough to understand." He takes a long pull from the beer. "It's worse now isn't it?"

I light a cigarette and take a drink from the bottle. "You can't possibly know what this feels like."

"No, I guess I can't," he says. "But look, it doesn't change who you are, you have to know that. It's just a name, Evan."

I turn and look at him, seeing my dad's face in shadows. "Just a name? Yes, just a name, but not my name. You and mom lied to me everyday you didn't tell me. You orchestrated a conspiracy with your friends and relatives to keep the truth from me for all these years."

He doesn't look at me but just nods. "Yes, you're right. We thought we were doing the right thing, protecting you, but obviously, we were wrong." He looks at me then. "Listen to me, Evan. You're still the same person, but I'd understand if you chose to be Evan Hughes. It's your decision."

"Yes it is." I want to be angry at somebody, but who? My mother, who simply did what she had to do when Cal abandoned her—and me. Or did he? Couldn't my mother have followed him to New York, or was she just too scared? Richard, who despite our often stormy relationship, raised me like I was his own? "I don't know what I'm going to do yet. It's too soon. I have to get used to the idea first."

"Yes, I suppose you do." He takes another drink. "Think what you want of me, Evan, but don't be too hard on your mother. She agonized over this many times. It was a past she'd buried, wanted to forget. She's always said the only good thing to come out of her time with Calvin Hughes was you."

He gets up and stands for a moment. "What time is your flight tomorrow?"

"Late afternoon."

"Okay. I'll drop you at the airport."

"Thanks."

He starts in the house then stops, puts a hand on my shoulder. "For what it's worth, I'm sorry about Calvin," he says. "I'm sorry about a lot of things. Maybe someday we can talk about it."

I nod, not trusting myself to speak, waiting for the click of the screen door. I'm sorry too for not being able to acknowledge Cal, good, bad, or indifferent, as my father, but it's too late for that now.

I think of spreading his ashes over the water in Santa Monica Bay, remembering the gritty feel in my hands, and my eyes film over as I stare into the darkness.

Chapter Eleven

At Logan Airport, I pace around waiting for the flight, trying Andie again on my cell, but with no luck. Danny Cooper is out of the office. I start to leave a message but don't. Even Dana is out. On the short flight back to New York, I just stare out the window, hardly aware of anyone around me, more anxious than ever now to see Cameron Brody, let Brody do his computer magic, and help me find Al Beckwood. When we touch down at La Guardia, I already have my hand on my bag.

I get a taxi and ignore the driver's effort at conversation. He gives up eventually, a loud talk radio show blaring from his radio for the rest of the trip into Manhattan. I tune it out and go over what my mother told me about Cal, Al Beckwood. He could be the key to finding out a lot of things that were on my mind. Maybe he could fill in some of the gaps, which seem even bigger now. Maybe know something about the *Birth of the Cool* sessions and rehearsals.

But when we pull up in front of Cameron's building my mind shifts. There's the flashing lights of a paramedic truck and a blue and white police car.

"Trouble everyday in this city," the driver says as I get out and pay the fare.

Cameron is sitting on the front steps, a white bandage around his head, a paramedic examining him. Two uniformed cops stand on the sidewalk, talking, laughing as I come up.

"What happened?"

"Whoa, pal," one of the cops says, putting up his hand.

"He's my friend," I say, looking over the cop's shoulder.

"All right," the cop says, glancing at Brody and stepping aside.

"What happened?" There's still some blood on his face. The paramedic, a husky woman with short brown hair snaps off her latex gloves and glances at me.

"He won't go to the hospital," she says. "I've done all I can do here." She shrugs. "No concussion but, maybe you can talk him into something." She closes her bag and heads for the truck, nodding to the two cops.

They come over and one takes out a pad and pen.

"Hey, Evan." Cameron smiles, one hand on his head. "Guess I look pretty goofy, huh?"

"Are you sure you're okay?"

"Yeah, I'm fine." He glances up at the cop, who has one foot on an upper step, his pen poised over the pad. He looks bored by the whole thing and his partner wanders away, checking out the passersby and the traffic. They were probably on the way to dinner when the call came through.

"Okay, Mr. Cameron Brody, want to tell us what happened?" His eyes quickly take me in with a dismissive look.

I light a cigarette and sit down on the step beside Cameron and listen.

"I don't know really," Brody says.

"You don't know?"

"Well, I had just unlocked the door and was going in when he hit me on the head from behind."

"He? You saw him?"

"Well, no, but it must have been a man because—"

The cop cuts him off. "We'll leave it at that for now. What happened then?"

"I fell down, but I don't think I was out. I remember him—okay, or her—climbing over me and then again on the way out."

"So a few seconds? A minute? Help me out here." The cop looks up from his pad.

Brody nods. "Less than a minute."

The cop nods, and continues writing. "So he went in, then right back out?"

"Yes, it was all very quick."

"Anything missing from your person?"

Brody smiles. "From my person? No."

"Have you checked the apartment? Anything from there?"

Brody sighs. "Yeah, my laptop computer."

The cop looks up, glances at me, then his partner, who's been listening. He walks over closer now. "Sir, would you mind showing me what's in your pockets, please?"

"My pockets?"

"Yes. If you would."

Brody stands up, puts his arm on my shoulder to steady himself. The second cop starts to reach out but Brody puts up his hand. "It's okay, I'm all right."

He takes out his cell phone from his jacket pocket, keys, change, a wallet thick with credit cards, and some folded bills.

"How much money?" the cop asks.

"I don't know," Brody says. He unfolds the bills, counts them. "Seventy two dollars."

The cop nods, exchanges glances with is partner again. "You didn't know this guy or recognize him?"

"No," Brody answers, looking puzzled now.

I look at Brody, then the cops, knowing where this is going. "He knew you."

"What?"

"You have seventy two dollars in cash, a wallet full of credit cards, an expensive cell phone, but he didn't touch them."

"He was in a hurry," Brody says, confused now.

"Exactly my point," the cop says. "He knew exactly what he was going for. All he wanted was your computer. You see what I'm saying?"

Brody nods, awareness spreading over his face now.

There are a few more questions, some doubling back over the ones already asked, and Brody is told to stay alert and that he probably won't see the computer again.

"I'd be very careful if I were you," the cop says.

"Why, he got what he wanted—the computer. They're stolen all the time."

"Yes they are, but he didn't just want your computer. He wanted what was on it."

Brody and I stare at the cop.

"If what he wanted isn't there, he'll be back," the cop says.

I help Brody inside and settle him on the couch. Looking at the head wound. It's swelling and raw around the bandage. "You sure you don't want to have that looked at more closely."

"I'll be fine." He leans back against the couch. "Can you get me some water?"

"Sure." I go in the tiny kitchenette, find a glass and run some water in the sink, then fill the glass and take it back.

"Thanks," Brody says, taking the glass. "In my bag, in the bathroom, there's a prescription bottle."

I get that, glancing at the label on the way back. Percocet, but an old prescription. Brody pops two in his mouth and leans back again, a slight smile on his lips now.

"Never know when you need Percocet," he says. "I'm going to crash for a couple of hours. Make yourself at home. How was the trip? Your mom okay?"

"Yeah, she's fine. Lots to tell you but we'll do it later."

"Oh yeah," Brody says. "Much later. I feel a little woozy."

While Brody lets the pain killer take over, I wander around the tiny apartment. There are books and typed manuscripts everywhere, on nearly every surface. One wall is all shelves and some books are stacked on the floor. The tiny bedroom is the same, on both sides of the bed. Nothing else there but a small dresser and a night table, also stacked with manuscripts. Once in the bathroom, it's hard to even turn around. I wonder how much a place like this goes for.

I check on Brody. He's stretched out now and totally out. I go outside and sit on the stoop to have a cigarette, wondering what this was all about, but knowing the cop was right about the computer. I had hoped Brody would have something that would help track down Al Beckwood, but that's gone now.

I think about calling Andie but I'm not sure what I'm going to say yet. I still haven't digested everything my mother told me and I want my mind clear when I confront Andie. I know now, that's what it's going to be. A confrontation. Some or all of what my mother told me had to be in Cal's FBI file, and if it was, then Andie had to know.

I smoke a couple more cigarettes, get some coffee from a deli across the street and go back in the apartment. There's a small TV. I turn it on low and find the news, catching up on the day's events, but my mind is really not on it.

Brody stirs, sits up and looks at me. "What time is it?"

I look at my watch. "Little after four. How you feeling?"

Brody smiles. "Like I've got cable going on in my head." He touches his head and winces. "Fuck, I wonder what he hit me with."

"You have a lot of important stuff on the computer?"

Brody says, "Yes, but it's cool."

"How so?"

"I back up everything, including my system software. The disks are in my suitcase."

"So you're really just out a computer then."

"Yeah, and this bump."

"You think the cop was right, about whoever did this knew what he was looking for?"

Brody thinks a moment. "Yeah, it doesn't make any sense otherwise, but I'm surprised he didn't just wait till I was gone, break in, and take it without the confrontation."

"That's weird too." I think for moment. Maybe it was some kind of warning, but for what? I don't mention it to Brody. "What was on the computer?"

Brody shrugs. "Lot of ASCAP files, projects I was working on, and the last disk I saved had a lot on you. Those names you gave me, the *Kind of Blue* and *Birth of the Cool* sessions. That got me intrigued."

"Al Beckwood? Was he one of the names?"

"He was. But how would anybody know that?" Brody leans forward and puts his head in his hands. "I don't know. You have more experience in this than I do."

"Tell me how ASCAP works."

"Okay, but first tell me about your trip." He leans back, his head against the couch and closes his eyes.

I lay out the whole thing. My mother's confession about Cal being my father, her second marriage, the photos, clippings, her stories about life with Cal in Kansas City, the talk with my dad, Richard, all of it. Somehow it feels like a story I'm telling about someone else. When I look over at Brody, he's sitting up again, his hands folded on his knees.

"Whoa, that's incredible. And you had no idea, never suspected anything?"

I shake my head. "Never had any reason to."

Brody nods. "You haven't told me everything."

I look up. "What?"

"How you feel about it."

I sigh. "I don't know. I haven't really digested everything yet. It's just hard to wrap my mind around all of it. I keep remembering things that happened, little fragments of memory that now make it so obvious, but they were good about keeping it from me."

Brody looks away. "Wow, finding out you're not who you're think you are at this late date. Has to be mind blowing."

"Oh it's more than that."

Brody nods and gets up. "Want to get something to eat?"

"Sure. We can talk about this some more."

We go to a diner around the corner, the kind only to be found in New York, and we wolf down burgers and fries, push the plates away and order some coffee.

"So tell me how ASCAP works exactly."

"Well you've written a few tunes, right? You file with ASCAP—or BMI—confirming authorship, get it copyrighted, then anytime anybody records your tune, they have to pay."

I nod "I know that much, and it covers movies, television?"

"Right. Anybody uses your song for anything, they have to get permission and pay for the privilege. You hold publishing and composer rights."

I was trying to remember a story I'd heard somewhere about a pop star who had recorded a jazz musician's song. Made him rich overnight. "Man, I didn't know there was that much money in music," so the quote went.

"And if somebody wants to use even part of your tune on a beer commercial or something, well, dude, you're set."

"What about live performances?"

"Theoretically, yes."

"So you mean every barroom pianist who plays 'Stardust' or 'Melancholy Baby' has to pay?"

"Well, as I say, theoretically, yes, but, you can't police every neighborhood bar and lounge. It's just not possible. ASCAP would need an army for that and it wouldn't amount to much. It's mainly sound recording, radio airplay we go after. Sometimes though, the composer loses touch, isn't even aware his or her song has been recorded, so we try to track them down so they get their money."

I lean back and light a cigarette. "You said you were working on some projects. Was it something like that?"

"There was some question about composer, false filing. In other words, somebody wasn't getting their bread."

I look at him for a moment till he makes the connection.

"You think that's what the mugging was about?"

"Possible isn't it. Why else would someone randomly clip you and take only your computer?"

"Somebody who didn't know you can save files. I guess it could be about that."

The waiter comes over then, a short stocky guy in a long white apron. "So, you boys going to take up space all day or you want something else?" He looks from me to Brody.

"Got any pie?" Brody asks

The waiter smirks. "Got any pie? Yeah we got pie. What's your pleasure?"

"Apple?" Brody looks at me and raises his eyebrows.

"No thanks, I'll pass."

The waiter gathers up our plates and swipes a damp cloth over the table. "One apple pie coming up."

"Sure different from California, isn't it?" Brody smiles.

I smile. "Yeah, I can't imagine him saying, 'Hi, I'm Al, your server today,' and that whole, 'our specials today are' speech."

The waiter comes back quickly and drops Brody's pie on the table without missing a step as he passes our table. "There you go, pal," he says.

I sip my coffee and watch Brody wolf down the apple pie. Finally, he sighs and leans back. "Mmmm, nothing like it."

I laugh. "Want a glass of milk too?"

"I'm tempted. But to tell you the truth, I'm fading fast. Want to get out of here?"

"Sure." I catch Al's eye and mime writing for the check. Brody and I get up and meet him at the register. I glance at it, and leave him a twenty.

He grins, rings it up and pockets the change when I hold up my hands. "Always a pleasure, gentlemen."

We walk back to Brody's place, both of us scanning the street but there's no one but the evening crowd strolling through the Village streets, and nobody lurking outside or in the building.

Brody unlocks the door and we go in. He grabs the bottle of Percocet, pops two more and turns to me.

"Sorry to be a drag, but I'm going to crash. My head is throbbing now."

"No problem."

"Just make yourself at home and you can take the couch if you want." He points to the TV and the CD player. "Help yourself."

"Thanks, I appreciate it. Get some rest."

He goes in the bedroom and that's the last I see of him.

I check out the CD collection. It's an eclectic mix of pop, Reggae, vocals, and a few jazz things, including several by Miles Davis. *Kind of Blue* is one of them. Who doesn't have a copy? It's like finding an old friend. I plug in the headphones even though I doubt Brody would hear anything, and settle down in a chair and close my eyes, letting the music wash over me.

By the time "Freddie Freeloader" comes on my mind is totally focused, as Miles, Coltrane, and Cannonball state the theme. Two note phrases, the rhythm section like a rolling sidewalk under them. Three guys walking down the street, totally in sync, then they meet Wynton Kelly, and his solo is kind of an agenda for the conversation they're about to have. Here's what we're going to talk about fellas, that crazy bartender Freddie, for whom the song was written.

Miles goes first, slow, lots of space, measuring his words, but gives the others plenty to think about. Cannonball is next, like he's saying, well that's interesting but have you considered this? His alto so clean and bluesy, while Coltrane bides his time, impatient, finally jumping in like he's arguing the point in complex lines. I picture them all joining in then, restating the simple theme and then walking away, disappearing around the corner.

The solos never fail to knock me out. During the few moments of silence before the next track, I hear the faint sound of my cell phone ring. I pull off the head phones and flip open the phone, look at the window. Andie.

"Well, finally," I say. I reach up and stop the disk, a little relieved, a little annoyed to finally hear Andie's voice.

"I know. I got your messages, I just got hung up doing things and wanted to wait till I got home."

"How are you feeling?"

"Pretty good. Doing some rehab, walking a little, just short trips down the hill and back. The doctor says I'm doing fine."

"Well that's good. Don't overdo it though."

"I won't." She sighs. "I'm sick to death going over the shooting again and again. God, the bureau is so anal about this stuff even though Rollins was right there and saw the whole thing. His statement corroborates mine so it's going to be okay."

"Speaking of Rollins." I try not to let my voice bristle. "Has—"

"No," Andie says, "nothing on the file and that's getting to be a sticking point. So far nobody knows about it but me and Rollins, but tell me about your trip. Is your mom okay?"

"Yeah she's fine."

"And?"

"I hardly know where to start, Andie."

"Why? What happened?"

I take a deep breath and reach for a cigarette, get it going. "I know just about everything now. Calvin Hughes was my father." I say it slowly, still not used to the idea of the words.

"Oh, Jesus, Evan."

I catch myself listening for genuine surprise in her voice and it's there. "She showed me the birth certificate, told me the whole story. I also found out she'd been married briefly, a few months, before, before my Dad. Before Richard Horne."

"Baby, you caught it all. Are you okay?"

"Yeah I guess. Just haven't really got my mind around it yet."

"That file doesn't matter now does it?" she says quickly.

"Well, no I guess not, but—"

"Believe me, Evan, all we were doing was running a check on—excuse the term—your known associates. Calvin Hughes was one, as was Natalie Beamer, but being a cop she was easy. We ran Hughes' name, talked to a few people, looked for red flag items. Remember, we were bringing you in on a big case. It's just standard procedure. Nobody would have cared who he was married to or paid much attention." She stops for a moment, maybe realizing how fast she was talking, that turns into a long pause.

"What?"

"It's been so long, hard to remember, but it would have shown he was married and…what's your mother's maiden name?"

"Shaw."

"See I didn't know that. I hardly knew you then. There would have been no reason for you to tell me your mother's maiden name at that stage. I wouldn't have connected it with you. See what I mean?"

I feel a wave of relief sweep over me. Andie was right. All this suspicion, this nagging feeling that Andie was holding something back, I've been carrying around is groundless.

"You said your mother married again. What was his name?"

"Lane. James Lane."

"Doesn't ring a bell at all."

"No reason it should. I didn't know about it till yesterday. I'm sorry Andie. The whole thing has just made me crazy trying to figure out everything."

"I'm sure. You've been hit big time. I don't know how I'd handle something like that."

"You still have to account for the file don't you?"

She sounds more casual now, almost relieved. "Yeah, but truthfully, I was worried about it more for you than the bureau. Hey, files go missing for a lot of reasons." She pauses again. "I wanted you to know that I wasn't holding out on you. I wouldn't do that."

"I know." I put out my cigarette, feeling like some small crisis has been resolved.

"God," she says. "I forgot. How did the recording with Roy what's his name go?"

I laugh. "Haynes, and it went very well, even better than I expected."

"I was sure of that," she says smugly. "So what are you going to do now?"

Good question. Despite what my mother told me, there was still a lot missing, unexplained, and I want to pursue the music angle, determine once and for all if Cal had anything to do with either the *Birth of the Cool* or *Kind of Blue* recordings. Now, I realize I want it even more.

What if I could show that Calvin Hughes, my father, was the uncredited composer of even one of those songs? It was something I could do for him. I also want to know as much as I can about Cal's life and Al Beckwood is the only lead on that. I explain that much to Andie.

"I can understand that. You might find some things about him you won't like though. You know that don't you?"

"I already have."

"Anything I can do to help that would get you home sooner?"

"Only if you could look up Al Beckwood without getting in trouble."

"Hang on. There are probably plenty of Al Beckwoods."

I wait, listening to her put down the phone and then come back on.

"Okay. Let's narrow it down. He's a musician I take it."

"Yes, or at least was."

"A ballpark age?"

"Like Cal. Late sixties, early seventies."

"If he's alive."

"If he's alive."

"You know I might run into a dead end," Andie says. "You may never find out what you want to know."

"I know, but it's important to me to try."

"I just don't want you to get your hopes up, but I'll see what I can do."

"Thanks, Andie."

"Evan?"

"Yes?"

"I love you. Don't ever forget that, no matter what you find out."

"I won't. I love you too."

I wake up to Cameron Brody's voice on the phone.

"I know, I know," he says. "Hey I didn't plan it." He glances over at me curled up on the couch, notices I'm awake and holds up one finger, nods. "Cool. I want to pick it up by noon, so make the call. Yes, I reported it to the police." He listens then says, "Thanks." He hangs up the phone and turns to me.

"I got ASCAP to spring for a new laptop. They're sending authorization to a computer store here, so we're in business." He gives me a look when I don't move or react. "Well come on, man, get up. We're going to track down Al Beckwood."

I sit up and run my hand through my hair, check my watch. "What time?"

"They said by noon so we got time to get some breakfast," Brody says. He's up, pacing around the small living room in boxers and a t-shirt.

"I'm going to get a shower first." On the way to the bath-room, I get my cell phone and charger and plug it into an outlet. Standing under the shower wakes me up and I feel refreshed, having had the best sleep in days. I change into some clean clothes—jeans, denim shirt, and light sweater, ready for whatever the day brings. Brody is dressed and ready when I come out, a small vinyl case crammed with computer disks.

We go back to the diner where we'd had dinner and tear into a couple of omelets, with toast and several mugs of coffee on the side. I watch Brody. He seems none the worse for wear. "How's the head?"

"Better." He touches the bandage. "Still got a headache but I'm cool."

"I was thinking, maybe we should get out of that apartment." "Why?"

"Well whoever stole your computer might be back."

Brody shakes his head. "I don't think so. He got what he wanted and no way he could know I had everything backed up."

I nod and light a cigarette. "Maybe. Any idea who it could have been or why?"

"I'm not sure. Main thing of interest is some royalty records, accounts owed, that kind of thing. I had a whole data base on there." He pauses. "Course I did have some stuff on you too, but I think it's ASCAP stuff he was after. I want to do a search on your dad too."

He looks at me. "You getting used to that idea now, that Cal Hughes was your dad?"

"No, not yet." And it was true. I'd have occasional flashes that it was all a mistake, but then I'd remember that birth certificate and it would all come flooding back.

Brody nods. "It's heavy, heavy stuff."

"Look, Cameron, I appreciate the help but this is not really your thing. I know you probably have plenty of other things to do and—"

He leans forward. "Are you kidding. I'm so into this. If we can show that your dad wrote even one of those songs from *Kind of Blue* or *Birth of the Cool*, well, I want to be there."

We pay the check and head back to the apartment, so I can get my phone. I unplug it and I barely get it turned on when it rings. It's Andie.

"Hi, baby," she says. "Got some news for you. Grab a pencil."

I motion to Brody for paper and pen and he shuffles through the desk for both.

"Go," I tell Andie.

"Okay. This has to be your Al Beckwood. Played trombone and bass, about the same age as Calvin Hughes, lived in New York and Los Angeles at various times. All this came up because he has a record. He did some hard time for possession with intent to sell."

I listen and write fast as Andie spits out the information. "Where?"

"Jean, Nevada. Medium Security facility near Las Vegas. In the seventies. Nothing much after that."

"Any last address? Is there any mention of—"

But she cuts me off. "Shit. Gotta go." She hangs up.

I look at the phone for a moment. Maybe she was at her desk and someone came by she didn't want to hear or see the printout if there was one.

I tell Brody Andie's news. "Good start," he says. "We can check with the musicians union here. Maybe they have something."

My mind whirling now, excited at the prospect. If I can talk with Beckwood, someone who actually knew Cal. Maybe he was in the Cool band too.

"Let's go," Brody says, already starting for the door. He locks up and we check the street before we step outside but it looks all clear. "Okay, let's split up. You go to the union, I'll pick up the computer and meet you there. We'll get a taxi and I'll drop you."

We step out in the street and flag down a cab without much trouble. "Musicians Union 802," I tell the driver as we get in. "It's by Roseland Ballroom on West 48th Street."

The driver nods and roars away, cutting off two cars in the process, and heads uptown through the heavy traffic. Brody and I sit back, each lost in our own thoughts. I try to keep from thinking that it could all be a wild goose chase but I have to do this, run down every lead, find Al Beckwood, and all I can about Cal. For once, I think, this is not a favor to someone else. This is only for me.

At 32nd Street, we're mired in a gridlock of honking horns and angry voices. The driver throws up his hands in disgust and slaps the steering wheel.

"Fuck this," Brody says, opening the door. "I'm going to grab the subway. Meet you at the union." He slams the door and runs across the street, disappearing down the steps to the subway.

"Your friend, he is in a hurry," the driver says. He's black but has some kind of West Indian accent. "Some music, yes?" He turns on the radio to some blaring reggae sound.

We finally break free and in a succession of turns, back streets, alleys, we pull up in front of the union. I pay the driver and get out. "Say hi to Bob Marley."

Inside, the union is busy. New York is the largest local in the country governing everything musical in New York City and surrounding areas. The Philharmonic, Ballet, the pit bands of Broadway shows, recording, clubs—if you work as a musician in New York City, you have to come here, and today, it seems like half the musicians in New York have decided to visit.

Nearby Roseland Ballroom was once used as a cattle call for casual gigs, weddings, parties, fashion shows, anything put together for a one time event. Out of work musicians crowded the ballroom while contractors on stage behind microphones would read off what was going.

"I need a tenor saxophone for the Bronx Friday night," the voice would say. Several tenor players would rush the stage, have a quick interview, get the details or be introduced to the leader and a deal was made. It was like longshoremen showing up for day labor. The glamour of the music business.

I push my way through to the information desk and grab one of the directories attached to a chain. The listings are alphabetical or by instrument. I flip through the Bs quickly and find nothing. In the trombone section, there are three Beckwoods: James, William, and Joe "Killer Joe" Beckwood. No Al.

I get one of the girls' attention finally and point to the directory. "Hi, I'm trying to get Al Beckwood, trombonist and bassist. He's not in here. Can you tell me if he's still a member?"

She nods hits a few keys on her computer screen. "Membership lapsed a year ago."

"Do you have a number for him?"

She looks at me briefly and pauses. "You a member of 802?"

"No, 47 in Los Angeles." I take out my wallet and show her my union card.

She glances as the screen again and writes a number on a post-it note. "That's all we have."

"Thanks," I say. "I'll make sure he pays up his dues."

She rolls her eyes.

I move away toward the door and look at the number, double checking my notebook, but it's the same number I'd called several times without any luck. At least I know he's in, or was in New York. I flip open my phone and try it anyway. It rings several times and just when I'm about to hang up, a woman's voice answers in a frail soft tone.

"Hello."

"Hello, is Al Beckwood there, please?"

"Who is this?"

"I'm returning his call. We have a mutual friend by the name of Calvin Hughes."

"Al's asleep," she says. "He's very sick."

"I'm sorry to hear that. Are you Mrs. Beckwood? It's very important. Could you tell him I called and let me give you my number. I'm in New York for a few days."

"It's nobody," I hear her say as she half muffles the phone. She says something else, then I hear a man's voice. "I'm awake woman. Who is it?"

"Says he's Calvin Hughes."

"No, I'm Evan Horne, a friend of Calvin Hughes."

"Just a minute," she says and lays down the phone with a clunk.

A few moments pass then the man picks up the phone. "Hello? Who is this?"

"Al Beckwood? It's Evan Horne. You left a message for me about Calvin Hughes. I tried to call you back and now I'm in New York and—"

"I been sick."

"Is it possible we could get together? I need to talk to you about Calvin."

He pauses, coughs a couple of times. "I'm tired, having this nasty chemotherapy. You have to come here if you want to talk."

"Where is here?"

I grab a pen from the desk and write down the address. "When, Mr. Beckwood? When is a good time for you?"

"Ain't none anymore."

Chapter Twelve

It's nearly a half hour before Cameron Brody shows up. He's all smiles, a nylon computer bag slung over his shoulder. "Got it," he says, patting the bag. "Sorry it took so long. I had to boot up and load my disks at the store, just to make sure things were working right. How'd you do?"

"I found him."

"Al Beckwood?"

"Yes." I tell him about the phone call as we walk slowly away from the Musicians Union building. "It's not good. He's on chemotherapy."

"Oh shit," Brody says.

"Exactly. I need to go over there now."

Brody nods, looks away, thinking the same thing I imagine. Barging in on somebody in that condition, practically unannounced, isn't cool. But, Beckwood did call me. "You want to come with me?"

"Definitely, man. I…Jesus Christ, that's him."

I turn toward where Brody is looking. He's already hurrying over to a tall, heavyset, light skinned black man in a Mets baseball cap, dark coveralls, and boots.

"Otis, Otis James," Brody calls to him.

The man turns at the sound of his name and faces Brody, looking for a moment like he's about to run. His face tenses as Brody gets closer. "What about it?" he says, as if Brody might be a process server or a cop.

Brody sets his computer bag down and digs in his pocket, hands the man his card and starts talking rapidly. James looks at the card, listens, doubt on his face but gradually, he breaks into a smile. I get there in time to hear him say, "You not jiving me? Cause if you are…"

"No, no," Brody says excitedly. "I've been looking for you. I have the check."

"What's going on?" I ask.

Otis James looks at me. "Who are you?"

"This is my friend, Evan Horne," Brody says quickly. "He'll tell you. He's a piano player too."

"Wait a minute, man," James says, backing up a step, looking confused, holding his hands out, glancing from Brody to me and back. "Tell me this again."

Brody looks around. Some of the people walking by are giving us looks, slowing to see what's going on. "Look, let's go over there," he says, and points to a coffee place across the street. "I'll buy you a cup of coffee and explain the whole thing."

Otis James doesn't look convinced, but I guess decides he has nothing to lose and we don't look like cops, we haven't flashed any badges.

"Hey, don't forget this." I grab the computer bag and hand it to Brody.

He takes it. "Yeah, I'm always doing that."

We cross the street and go inside. It's noisy and crowded with impatient business types after their midmorning lattes. Many of them have briefcases or laptops and a few people are sitting at tables, computers open, sipping coffee. I tell Brody to find a table. I get in line for three coffees while Brody and Otis James push through to the back.

The young guy at the counter seems relieved when I finally reach him and order three regular coffees, not some decaf soy milk latte with light foam. I pay for the coffee, grab some sugar packets, cream containers, stir sticks, and join Brody and Otis James, who sit facing each other. I slide into the booth next to

Brody. He has some legal papers on the table, pointing out several places for James to sign he's marked with an X.

Otis James looks bewildered by the whole thing. He doesn't touch the coffee I sit in front of him, his eyes jumping from Brody to the paper and back again. "What am I signing for?" he asks.

Brody grins. "For this." He takes out a certified check and pushes it across to James. The big man looks at it, shakes his head. "Two thousand seven hundred and forty seven dollars," he mutters to himself then looks up at Brody.

"Your song, 'Riverwalk Stomp,' was recorded by several groups and you're due royalties in this amount. We've been looking for you a long time, man."

"I just can't believe it," James says, shaking his head. "I dropped out of things for a long time, had some hard times, you know. Shit, man, I work at Macy's now." He keeps staring at the check. "Somebody told me they heard one of my songs on the radio, and I should check it out. That's why I was at the union. But, but damn…" His voice trails off as he looks at the check again.

Brody hands him a pen. "Just sign and it's yours free and clear."

James takes the pen and signs carefully and then a receipt for the check. He folds it neatly and puts it in his coveralls pocket, looking at us both. His face finally relaxes and breaks into a broad grin.

"Damn, feel like I just won the lottery." He folds his hands in front of him on the table and shakes his head back and forth. He looks at me then holds out his beefy hand. "Sorry, man. Otis James."

I shake with him. "My pleasure."

He studies the coffee a moment, then adds cream and sugar, stirring it continuously for a minute.

"You play piano too?"

"Yeah. Jazz mostly."

"Uh huh," James says. "He's good too isn't he?" He looks at Brody for confirmation.

"Amazing," Brody says. "He just recorded with Roy Haynes last Friday."

"Yeah, I bet he's one slick mother fucker with them deep chords." He smiles at us both then glances at his watch, and drinks off half of the coffee. "Well, fellas, I gotta go." He shakes hands again and puts his other hand on top of Brody's. "Thank you, man. Thank you."

Brody looks embarrassed. "Hey, it's my job. One of the best parts is catching up with guys like you."

"If you ever need anything, you call me okay? This money is going to help me get back to Georgia. I'm tired of this city." He takes Brody's pen and writes a number on the back of the receipt.

We watch him get up and almost strut toward the door. We see him pass by a window. He points his finger and smiles big.

"Man," Brody says. "Otis James. First, I get to go to a Roy Haynes recording session, and today I finally catch up with Otis James. He's been one of my pet projects, one of those cold case files, you know."

"He wrote a lot of songs?"

Brody smiles. "You've heard of Muddy Waters, John Lee Hooker, Howlin' Wolf, guys like that?"

"Sure."

"Well James was almost in the same league. Lot of groups recorded his songs, but 'Riverwalk Stomp' really took off."

"You made his day you know."

"Yeah I did, didn't I." He looks away, shaking his head. "Once in awhile it's all worth it."

I glance at my watch. "Come on, let's get lids for these coffees and we'll take them with us. I want to get up to Beckwood's place."

"Where is he?"

"Amsterdam Avenue and 112th Street."

Brody nods. "Seventh Avenue subway. It'll be faster than a taxi."

"Lead the way."

◇◇◇

We walk about half a block from the subway up 112th Street, toward the river. The building is old and run down. Probably a rent control place, I think, as we ring the buzzer.

"Yes," a woman's voice answers.

"It's Evan Horne. I talked to you earlier."

"Third floor," she says, and buzzes us in.

We jog up the three flights and find her waiting in the doorway. She sees Brody and looks at me. "You didn't say you were bringing anybody." She seems wary, frail, light skinned in a floral print dress and house slippers. Her hair almost white.

"I know, I'm sorry. This is my friend, Cameron Brody."

Brody steps forward and offers his hand, turns on the charm with a big smile. "So nice to meet you."

She smiles then. "I'm Mavis Beckwood," she says, and invites us in. The living room is small but comfortably furnished with old pieces probably gathered over the years. She nods toward a large, overstuffed sofa. "Let me see if Al is awake." She walks down the hall.

I turn to Brody. "Why don't you keep her company while I talk to Beckwood, see what kind of shape he's in."

"Got it," Brody says as Mavis Beckwood comes back.

"Just you," she says, pointing to me and takes me back down the hall. "Here he is, honey," and motions me into the small bedroom.

It has the smell of sickness and medicine and Al Beckwood looks weak and tired lying in the bed, his head propped upon several pillows, a grayish tinge to his dark skin. His cloudy eyes shift from the screen of a small television on a table near the bed. tuned to a soap opera. I sit down in a chair near the bed.

"You can shut that off." He turns and gazes at me for a long moment.

"I'm sorry to disturb you," I say as I click off the television and glance around the room. There's a tall dresser, night tables by the bed, and a book case crammed with LPs, books, and a few framed pictures.

He continues to look at me, as if he's trying to recognize something. "So you were a friend of Cal's?"

I shift in the chair. "Cal was my father," I begin. "I just found out recently."

"Yeah," he says, seemingly not surprised. He coughs and points to a glass of water on the night stand. "Can you hand me that, please?"

I hand him the water and let him drink, then set the glass back down. "This chemo is kicking my ass," he says. "How's your mother?"

The question takes me by surprise but then I remember it was Beckwood who sent the cards, kept at least some contact with my mother.

"She's fine," I say. "Living near Boston. I guess you know she remarried."

Beckwood nods. "That's good. And you want to know about your daddy, don't you."

"Yes, Mr. Beckwood, I really do."

"Well first thing is you got to stop calling me Mr. Beckwood. It's Al."

I smile at him. "Okay, Al it is."

He settles back against the pillows and looks toward the window where the sun is streaming in, but the view is the side of another building. "How much did your mother tell you?"

"As much as she knew," I say. "How she and Cal met in Kansas City. Were you in that band?"

Beckwood nods and smiles, remembering. "Yeah we had some good times. So many bands then, so much work, but Cal wanted to go to New York. We were all set to go, leave the band and take off on our own, but then he met your mother."

"You play too, right?" Beckwood turns his head toward me again.

I nod. "I studied with Cal some these past few years. We became good...friends. I didn't know he was—"

"No way you could have," Beckwood says.

I search my mind, trying to remember some clue, some incident, some slip of the tongue during those many visits with Cal that would have tipped me off, but there was nothing. "No, I guess not. What happened when you went to New York?"

"That was the first time, before he met your mother. We hung on trying to stay in the city, picking up gigs here and there, then we got in subbing with Miles' band. Me not so much. Hell, Miles had J.J. Johnson, Kai Winding, and some young white college kid, Mike Zwerin, but there were so many guys coming and going. It was like a different band every week. John Lewis or Al Haig on piano made most of the rehearsals, but sometimes they had other gigs or were out of town, so Cal made a few sessions."

Beckwood pauses, shaking his head. "Man, that was some band. Miles and Gil Evans and Gerry Mulligan writing charts but everybody brought in things. We just knew something was going to come out of that thing."

I listen, letting Beckwood take himself and me back to those days in 1949. "When I went through Cal's things, I found some music, lead sheets, something he'd written out, a couple of those tunes. 'Boplicity' was one."

"Yeah, Cal loved that one. Said it was something like he could have wrote." Beckwood laughs. "That's what he called the band. Boplicity. Birth of the Cool was later, just the record company's name anyway. When they played that one gig at the Royal Roost, it was just the Miles Davis Organization."

I remember the few live tracks on the CD, the announcer introducing them, "The Miles Davis Organization."

"Could Cal have written 'Boplicity'?"

Beckwood shakes his head again and looks at me. "You know who wrote that don't you?"

"Cleo Henry, right? That's what it says in the notes."

"Yeah, but do you know who Cleo Henry was?"

I shake my head.

"Wasn't nobody. Cleo Henry was Miles' mother's name."

"But why did Cal have the lead sheet? There were a couple of others too."

"He wrote out all the tunes to practice, hoping John Lewis would drop out, and he sat up late every night writing stuff of his own. Everybody was bringing in things to try, but Miles and Gil and Mulligan were the main writers."

Beckwood turns toward the window again. "Cal took it hard when the band played the Royal Roost."

"Did he go down there?"

"Yeah, we both did but Cal didn't stay long. Soon as they played 'Boplicity,' he left."

I think for a minute, giving Beckwood another drink when he looks toward the glass. "My mother said after she met him, Cal wanted to go back to New York, that he'd missed his chance once and didn't want to have it happen again."

"Yeah, that's right. Even though he made a lot of the rehearsals, he had to gig. He took something out of town with some singer, Philly I think. When he came back, they'd already recorded and didn't use none of Cal's tunes either. Man, he went into such a depression. It was terrible. Started really juicin'."

"Are you sure of all of this?" Finding that music, I was so sure Cal had written one of the tunes at least, and I wanted it to be true so badly.

Beckwood turns his head toward me again. "I'm sure about how down Cal was. You don't think I'd make this up do you?"

"Well, no, I just, I don't know, I'm just disappointed."

Beckwood's eyes close then as he drifts off. I turn and see Mavis Beckwood standing in the doorway watching. She moves over to the bed. Al's eyes flutter open. She leans down and he whispers something to her. She nods, straightens up and looks at me.

"Al say he's tired. You come back tomorrow."

"Of course." I get to my feet and follow her back to the living room where Cameron has the new laptop open and he's tapping on the keys.

"Hey," he says. "How's it going? I've been showing Mavis how to send e-mails."

She smiles sheepishly. "I'm learning," she says.

"We have to go," I say. "Al's asleep. I don't want to press him."

"Sure," Cameron says, closing the case and putting the computer back in the bag. He stands up and smiles at Mavis.

"You come back tomorrow, okay?" she says.

"Yes we will. I'll call first. Tell Al I said thanks for seeing me on such short notice."

She shrugs. "He don't get many visitors. I think he liked it, telling you stories about the old days, didn't he."

She goes with us to the door. "He told me to look for the tapes too."

"Tapes? What tapes?" Cameron and I both look at her.

"Tomorrow," she says. She gives us a little smile and closes the door behind us.

◇◇◇

"What tapes do you think she was talking about," Brody says. We'd taken the subway back to midtown and found a deli and were now waiting for our sandwiches.

"I don't know. Maybe something he and Cal did together?"

"Or maybe Beckwood or Cal taped some of those rehearsals with Miles?"

I hadn't thought of that but, that would be a coup. "I guess we'll find out soon enough."

"Number twenty-four," the guy behind the counter yells.

We hand him our tickets and get two thick corned beef sandwiches with a fat dill pickle on the side that takes up most of a paper plate in a basket tray. We add two draft beers in plastic cups, and carry everything to a small table near the window. Outside, the traffic sounds filter in, a crush of people walk by.

"Wow," Brody says, taking a big bite of his sandwich. "Can't get this in San Francisco." He wolfs down half of his sandwich, then leans back and dabs mustard off his lower lip, catches me looking at him. "Hey, what can I say. All this adventure makes me hungry."

I marvel at how Cameron Brody and I have hit it off in just a few days. I nod at him and dig in into my sandwich. "Something I've been wondering," I say between bites. "How'd you happen to be at the party I played on top of the mountain. You know, the amp mogul."

Brody shrugs. "Barry's? I met him through some music contacts, did a little research for him once. Why?"

"Just curious. You seem to get around."

"Comes with the territory. Since I've had this job with ASCAP, I've met a lot of music people."

We both stop then, listening as a cell phone rings. "I think it's you," I say.

Brody digs out his phone and flips it open. "Cameron Brody." He listens for a minute, nods and says. "I can't believe it. Uh huh. Sure. About an hour then." He glances at his watch, and closes the phone.

"What?"

"That was the cops. They found my computer, want me to come down and identify it."

At the precinct station, Brody identifies himself to the desk sergeant and he directs us upstairs to the squad room. Some of the detectives are on phones, others are lounging at their desks, sipping coffee, talking. One points us to a corner desk when Brody tells him why we're there.

The detective is a big beefy guy in a crew cut, short sleeve white shirt and loosened tie. "Mr. Brody?" he half gets out of his chair and shakes hands and glances at me. "Detective Charles."

"Yeah, somebody called, said you'd found my computer."

"Right, that would be me." Charles shuffles through some papers on his desk and comes up with the report Brody had given the uniformed cop. "Not going to make you happy though." He reaches under his desk and brings up the laptop. The case is gone. He sets it on the desk and wedges the lid open with a letter opener.

The screen is smashed, some of the keys are broken or missing altogether, as if it had been pounded with a hammer. Brody isn't fazed. "Do you have a small screwdriver around?"

Detective Charles looks puzzled, then opens his top desk drawer and rummages around, finally coming up with a short screwdriver, a little bigger than one used for glasses, and hands it to Brody.

He turns the computer over, unscrews four tiny screws and lifts the keyboard entirely off the casing. Inside, it's a maze of soldered boards, colored wires and a small rectangular metal box. He pulls on it, disconnecting it from the computer's innards.

"They missed this," Brody says, holding it up triumphantly. "The hard drive." He shakes his head and smiles. "Whoever did this didn't know what he was doing."

Detective Charles leans back and regards Brody. "What was so important somebody would steal and smash your computer?"

Brody shrugs. "You got me. It's mostly data base stuff, names, royalty records. I work for ASCAP."

"I know," Charles says. "I read the report."

"Where did you find it?"

"I didn't," Charles says. "Some homeless guy found it in a dumpster not far from here. Turned it in, thought there might be a reward."

Brody nods. "I don't suppose he saw who dropped it in the dumpster."

"No, unfortunately. At least he didn't tell us. So, I guess case closed," Charles shrugs.

"I sure would like to know who it was."

"So would we," Charles adds. He closes the file and looks up. "Nothing else we can do."

"Well thanks anyway. Any chance I can find the homeless guy, maybe give him something for his trouble."

"He hangs out around 10th Street. Shopping cart full of junk, wears a Jets football jacket most of the time. Calls himself Boomer." Charles motions to the smashed computer. "You want to take that with you. We have no way of disposing of it."

Brody rolls his eyes, looks at me and grabs the computer. Outside we stand in front of the station. "What do you make of all that?"

"Weird," Brody says. "Goes to all that trouble, doesn't take the hard drive."

"Can you really recover all the info?"

"I don't know, maybe. Let's go see if we can find Boomer. Maybe he can tell us something."

We start walking toward 10th Street, looking down alleyways, side streets for a guy in a Jets jacket. At a bank, Brody pulls up. "Hang on, I want to get some cash."

He slides his ATM card in the machine. I step to the side and open my cell phone and call Andie. No answer, just her voice mail. I leave a message for her to call me and then try Dana at the house. No answer there either.

"All set," Brody says, and we continue walking.

Off 10th Street, we see an old guy squatting down, leaning against the building, a shopping cart piled with junk next to him. He's smoking a cigarette, a green and white Jets jacket zipped up to his neck.

"Boomer?" Brody calls to him. Boomer looks up, squints at us through a haze of smoke and eyes the computer under Brody's arm.

"Who wants to know?"

"My name is Cameron Brody and I just wanted to thank you for finding my computer." He squats down next to Boomer.

"I didn't break it," Boomer says.

"I know," Brody says. "Did you see who did?"

Boomer nods but doesn't offer anything more.

"Could you show us where you found it?"

Boomer silently nods again and stubs out his cigarette on the pavement. He looks at me. "He a cop?"

"No," Brody says and smiles. "Just a friend." He reaches in his pocket and pulls out a hundred dollar bill and hands it to Boomer. "I just wanted to thank you for finding it."

Boomer's hand snakes out of his jacket and pockets the bill as he rises to his feet, his eyes wide.

"This way," he says, looking at the broken computer again. "You need that?"

"All yours," Brody says.

Boomer takes the computer and carefully wedges it among the other stuff in his overflowing cart and then starts walking ahead of us, pushing the shopping cart, the wheels noisily banging on the pavement. We go down 10th and follow Boomer as he turns into a small alleyway at the back of some stores. At the end is a large dumpster, covered in graffiti. Boomer parks his cart next to it and opens the lid. "Right in there."

Brody glances in, then lets Boomer shut the lid. "Did you see who it was?"

Boomer nods. "Kinda skinny white guy, dressed okay, nice leather jacket. He had a jack handle. He was really mad. Opened it and smashed the glass, pounded on the keys, then threw it in there."

"Did he see you?"

"No, I don't think so. I was back there, behind the Chinese restaurant." He points back down the alley. "I waited till he left before I got it out."

Brody looks at me and I just shrug.

"Well, Boomer, thanks for turning it in. I appreciate it."

Brody turns to go. "You take care now, Boomer, okay?"

Boomer nods and starts off, pushing his cart. At the end of the alley, he turns and waves to us, then disappears around the corner.

"So what do you make of that? Any idea who it could be?"

"None," Brody says. "None at all."

Back at the apartment, I call Mavis Beckwood to check in and see how Al is doing.

"Not good," she says. "He took a bad turn. He's back in the hospital."

"Oh I'm sorry, Mavis. It wasn't because of our visit was it?"

"No, no," she says quickly. "Seeing you and talking about the old days was good. It's just this damn cancer."

"Is there anything I can do?" I don't have the heart to ask her about the tapes she mentioned, but she beats me to it.

"Al said no matter what he wants you to have these tapes. You call me in the morning and we'll see what's what."

"I will, Mavis. You hang in there."

"I've been doing that for a long time, baby."

Brody has been listening and looks up from his computer, open on the coffee table in front of him. "Al?"

"Yeah, he's back in the hospital. Mavis wants me to call in the morning."

Brody nods and shrugs. "Nothing we can do." He frowns at the laptop screen, his finger moving on the cursor button. "I've gone over everything and I can't see anything worth knocking me on the head and stealing the computer for."

I sit down next to him and look at the screen. "What is this?"

"It's the master list, names of artists with ASCAP accounts who are owed royalties." He scrolls up and down the list. The amounts range from a few hundred dollars to several thousand.

"Wait," I say. "Back up there a minute. Isn't that—"

"Sonofabitch," Brody says. "Otis James."

Besides James' name, and several others, there is an asterisk. I point to it. "What's that mean?"

"Just my own code. Those are accounts I've been working on personally that haven't been cleared yet." Brody sits back and gazes at the list on the screen. "You know what I'm thinking? Somebody wanted to find Otis James as much as I did but for different reasons."

"That's a stretch isn't it? How would they know you had this information?"

Brody considers. "I don't know. I'm not exactly in the witness protection program. Lot of people know what I do."

"Who knew you were coming to New York?"

Brody shrugs. "The office of course, some other contacts."

"Okay, but the money owed James, it was a lot to him but not enough to warrant a mugging and stealing your computer. And then smashing it up and dumping it too."

"Unless…" Brody trails off and thinks for a moment. "Somebody who thinks James shouldn't get the money, somebody with a grudge of some kind, somebody who thought he was owed money."

We puzzle it over for awhile but don't come up with anything useful. "There are a lot of uncredited song writers, aren't there?"

"Sure," Brody says. "That tune 'Walkin.' It was credited for awhile and assumed to have been written by Miles, but it was a guy named Richard Carpenter. You know how many people recorded 'Walkin'?"

I didn't have to answer. "Walkin'" had become a jazz staple, recorded by probably scores of musicians since it first turned up in the fifties. I remember then what Al Beckwood had told me about "Boplicity." "What happens when another name is used other than the actual composer? Beckwood told me 'Boplicity' was done by Miles and Gil Evans, but on the record it says Cleo Henry. Miles' mother."

"Get out!" Brody laughs. "That's the first time I heard that."

"It's like a writer using a pen name. The account would officially, legally, be Gil Evans and Miles Davis."

Brody studies me. "You're really hoping something like that happened aren't you, that your dad wrote even one of those tunes and didn't get credit."

I look at Brody and nod, suddenly realizing just how much I do want that to be true. "Yeah, I guess I am."

Brody shakes his head. "Don't get your hopes up. If that were true, it would have come out a long time ago."

Brody is right. If the rehearsals were as haphazard and varied as Beckwood says, anything could have happened. I watch as he taps a few keys, the screen goes black, and he closes the lid.

"So, any plans for tonight?"

"Hadn't thought about it really."

Brody rubs his head. "I'm going to take a nap. Maybe later we can grab some dinner, go hear some music, catch a movie?"

"Sounds good. You go ahead. I'm going to take a walk. Be back in a couple of hours."

Chapter Thirteen

Mavis Beckwood calls early while I'm out getting coffee for Brody and myself. I'd tossed and turned on the couch most of the night, my mind reeling with everything I'd taken in during the past couple of days. I'd doze off, then wake up suddenly, remembering something.

"You better come now, darlin'," Mavis says. "Al ain't doin' too good." There's nothing but resignation in her tone, like she's given up.

"Are you sure? I don't want to disturb his rest."

"He'll have plenty of time to rest." There was a catch in her voice. "He told me to be sure and call you."

"All right, Mavis. I'll be right over."

I cram lids on the coffees and walk quickly back to Brody's place. He's already up and dressed.

"C'mon," I say. "Mavis just called, wants me there as soon as I can. You can occupy her while I talk to Al again."

"Got it."

New York Memorial Hospital is teeming with activity as we get out of a taxi and rush inside. We find Mavis on the fifth floor, sitting, her hands folded in her lap, staring straight ahead in a chair in the waiting room. Brody and I sit down on either side of her.

"You okay, Mavis?"

She looks up and smiles. "Thank you for coming," she says, shaking her head. "He ain't going to make it this time, but it's all right. I know that." She points down the hall. "You go on in. He's in 514."

Brody takes her hand. "Let's you and me take a walk, okay Mavis?" She nods and gets up, letting him take her hand, as I go down the hall to Al Beckwood's room.

There's a curtain drawn across the center of the room, separating Beckwood from another patient. His eyes are closed, his breathing seems shallow, and he's hooked up to various monitors, IV drips, and oxygen. I pull up a chair near the bed and lightly touch his arm.

"Al, it's Evan Horne."

He opens his eyes slowly and focuses on me, grimacing as he starts to cough. "That button on the side," he says. "Raise the bed."

I find the button and press it. The bed whirs as the upper half slowly inclines till he nods. "That's good."

"How you doing, Al?"

He tries to smile. "I been better."

"Can I do anything?"

He shakes his head. "I told Mavis she's got to let me go. I can't do this no more."

"Is there any family you want called, or anything?"

"No, it's just Mavis and me. Got some relatives in California. Mavis called her sister…" His voice trails off. He grips my hand as a shudder of pain runs through his body for a few seconds "Damn." He groans and then relaxes his grip. "That was a big one."

"Al—"

"No, I gotta tell you something first. Maybeline Jones. You have to go talk to her if you want to know more about your Daddy."

"Who?"

"She was a singer at one time. She knew Cal, they lived together for awhile. She can tell you a lot more if you want to know." He turns his head toward the tray table alongside the bed. "I told Mavis to write it down for you."

I look at the scrap of paper. There's an address and phone number with a New York area code.

"That's her sister's place. If Maybeline isn't there, her sister will know where she is. You go see her."

"I will. Thanks, Al. I really appreciate this."

He waves his hand aside. "Mavis has the tapes. Cal used to bring this old tape recorder to some of the rehearsals and listen to them later. He left them with me when he went to California. Better you have them now."

He coughs again, grimacing as the cough wracks his body.

"Al, let me get the nurse."

"No," he says. "Get Mavis."

I stand up, placing his hand down on the bed, but he reaches over and touches my arm. "You see Maybeline."

"I will. Thank you, Al."

I go out, back down the hallway to find Mavis and Brody sitting in the chairs again.

"Al wants to see you, Mavis."

She nods and gets up. "Can you stay awhile?"

"Sure, long as you want."

I drop in a chair next to Brody and we watch her walk away. Brody looks at me.

"He's in a lot of pain." I sigh, wishing it didn't have to be this way but there's nothing any of us can do. "He gave me the name of a singer, Maybeline Jones. Said she lived with Cal for some time. The tapes are from the band sessions. Cal made some recordings."

"Wow." Brody leans forward. "Can you imagine what those would be worth to a collector or maybe some jazz collection? Hell, man, the Institute of Jazz is over at Rutgers. I wonder if anybody knows about them."

"Maybe. Depends on what's on them, what the quality is like."

"Lot can be done now days. They can be transferred to CDs, cleaned up. You never know."

I thought about that. Hearing Cal playing with Miles Davis. The casualness and looseness of a rehearsal, snatches of conversation among the musicians, Miles himself talking. But it was Cal I wanted to hear. Cal's voice.

Mavis comes back in a few minutes. "I told the nurse I want to talk with Al's doctor. Al just wants the pain to stop and…go. You think that's right?" She suddenly looks like a little girl, asking for approval.

I look at Mavis, not knowing what to say. "Oh, Mavis, that's for you and Al to decide. See what the doctor says."

She nods and sits down again. Amazingly, a doctor appears in less than five minutes. I don't like doctors, hospitals, clinics. I don't even like to visit hospitals. I had enough of them after my accident with surgery, rehab, follow-up visits. But this doctor is okay.

A tall Asian man, he's dressed casually in running shoes, cotton pants, and has a white coat over a golf shirt. He doesn't look any older than me. The stethoscope hanging around his neck sways as he approaches.

"Mrs. Beckwood. You wanted to see me?" He leans over her and smiles.

Mavis gets up and walks with him. They talk for a couple of minutes. He nods and I catch, "That's probably best." He puts his hand on her shoulder. Mavis glances at me, then goes off toward Al's room.

The doctor turns toward me. "I'm Doctor Chang. Mrs. Beckwood said you're a close friend of the family. There's really nothing more we can do. The cancer has spread too much."

"What did you tell her?"

"The best we can do is a morphine drip to ease the pain and let him go. That's what I'd do if it was my own father."

"How long does he have?"

Doctor Chang shakes his head. "I'll be surprised if he lasts the day."

I nod. "I'm sorry," he says. He walks over to the nurse station to begin writing up the necessary instructions. I walk back to

Al's room and peek in. Mavis is sitting on the chair, holding Al's hand. I back out before she can see me and go back to where Brody is waiting.

"You can go," I say. "I'm going to stick around for Mavis."

Brody nods. "This sucks, man."

"Yeah it does."

"Okay I'll see you back at the apartment. Call me if you need anything," Brody says.

After Brody leaves, I tell the desk nurse I'm going outside for awhile, and to tell Mavis I'll be back. I take the elevator down to the main floor and go out in the parking lot, light a cigarette and dial the number Al gave me for Maybeline Jones. A woman answers on the second ring.

"Hello, is this Maybeline Jones?"

"No, she's not here anymore."

"Oh, do you know how I can get in touch with her?"

"Not unless you go to California. She lives out there now. Can I ask your name?"

"Evan Horne. I was a friend of someone she knew. Calvin Hughes. A friend of Calvin's gave me this number. His name is Al Beckwood."

There's a pause, then, "Well I don't know you. I'll call her and give her the message and she can call you if she wants."

"Fair enough." I give her my number. "It's very important. Are you her sister?"

"Yes I am."

"Okay. Well thank you. I'd really appreciate it if you contact her as soon as possible."

"I'll try," she says, then hangs up.

I walk around a while longer, having another cigarette, then go back in the hospital. Mavis isn't in the waiting room, but I find her still sitting with Al. She sees me and comes over to the door.

"I'm going to stay with Al, darlin'. Thank you for staying."

"I'll be here or outside, Mavis."

She nods and squeezes my hand, then goes back to Al's bedside.

A half hour later my cell phone rings. I press the answer button.

"Hello."

"Is this Evan Horne?"

"Yes. Maybeline Jones?"

"Yes. How can I help you? My sister said you called. You know Calvin Hughes?"

"Yes, well it's more than that. Al Beckwood gave me your number—your sister's number." I pause for a moment. "I thought you'd want to know. Calvin died recently."

Her turn to pause. "Oh my. I didn't know. You said Evan is your name?"

"Yes. I've just recently found out Calvin was my father."

"Honey, I know who you are. Where are you?"

"I'm in New York now, but I live near San Francisco. I was hoping we could meet, talk."

She sighs. "I know you have lots of questions. Calvin and I, we lived together for a few years."

"Yes I know. Can we meet?"

"Sure. You call me when you get back out here." She gives me a number I recognize as the San Fernando Valley.

"Cal was living in Hollywood when he died. Did you know that?"

I hear her sigh into the phone. "No I didn't. I wish I had. I have some pictures of Calvin you'd like to see."

"That would be great. I'll be back in L.A. in a couple of days, maybe sooner."

"Honey, didn't nobody tell you?"

"No, nobody told me anything."

Al Beckwood died four hours later.

I'd talked Mavis into a short walk outside, to get some air and away from the hospital for a few minutes. Al had been out for over an hour, sinking deeper into oblivion, the morphine drip doing its thing.

When we get out of the elevator, Doctor Chang is waiting, nodding somberly. "He's gone," is all he says.

Mavis nods and squeezes my hand. She'd said her goodbyes already. I take her over to a chair and let her sit down while I walk with the doctor.

"There was nothing more we could do," he says. "She understands that, doesn't she?"

"I'm sure she does."

"I understand he was a musician. Are you a musician too?"

"Yes, piano. Al played trombone. He played in Miles Davis' band for awhile. *The Birth of the Cool*," I add, not really knowing why. To give Al Beckwood his due? "He was a friend of my father's."

The doctor stops and looks at me. "Really? I have some jazz records. *Kind of Blue* is one of my favorites. Is your father still alive?"

I pause for a moment, knowing it's always going to be this way now. "No, he died just last week."

"I'm sorry for your loss." He glances at his watch. "I have to go. If you, Mrs. Beckwood need some help with the arrangements, let me know."

"Thanks."

I go over and sit down with Mavis, and take her hand. "Are you okay?"

She nods and looks at me. There's a peacefulness to her face now. "I know he's better off now."

"Mavis, what about funeral arrangements, do you—"

"No, darlin'. I already called my sister. She's coming out. We'll be fine."

"You know you can call me."

She nods again, gets up and goes to the nurses' station, says something and comes back with a small box. "I almost forgot." She hands me the box. "These are the tapes. They're so old I don't know if they even play now, but Al wanted you to have them."

I take the box from her. "Thank you, Mavis. Thank you so much."

She kisses me on the cheek. "I want to be with Al awhile." She turns and walks back down the hall.

I get a taxi back to Brody's apartment, but just as I step out, my phone rings.

"Evan Horne. Roy Haynes."

"Hey, what's up."

"You still in New York?"

"Yes."

"Cool. We're going to mix your two tracks tomorrow morning. You want to come down and sit in on it? From what I've heard, they sound good."

"Same studio?"

"Yeah. Ten o'clock okay?"

"No problem."

There's a brief pause. "You okay, man? You sound kind of down."

"Thanks, I'm fine."

"Well this will make you feel even finer. See you in the morning."

I hang up and go inside, the box of tapes under my arm. Brody is stretched out on the couch, watching the news, his computer and a legal pad on the coffee table. He sits up when I come in.

"He's gone?"

"About an hour ago."

Brody shakes his head. "Man, cancer is such a fucking drag." He glances at the box. "Are those the tapes?"

"Yeah, Mavis brought them to the hospital."

He gets a knife from the kitchen and slits open the box. Inside are three reel to reel, three-quarter inch tapes. Brody picks one up. "You just don't see these anymore. We'll have to find a machine to play these. If they're any good, we can transfer them to CD."

I sit down and light a cigarette. "Maybe the engineer at the studio can help. Roy Haynes just called. They're mixing tomorrow morning. He wants me to come by and hear the tracks we did."

Brody says, "Cool. I can't wait to hear these." He puts the tape back in the box.

"I got in touch with Maybeline Jones too. She's the one that lived with Calvin for awhile. She's in L.A. and is willing to talk to me."

Brody nods and smiles. "Looks like you're going to get some answers now."

"I hope so. I'll try to get a flight out tomorrow night. Nothing more for me to do in New York."

"Guess not. I've got to stay around a few more days for some ASCAP business, but let's get together when I get back."

"Sure. I'm going to L.A. first and see Maybeline, then head back to San Francisco. Have to see if I can change my flight without a big hassle."

"Maybe Roy Haynes' manager can help. What's his name?"

"Larry Klein. Good idea."

Brody yawns. "Well, I'm beat, I've been on the computer and phone all afternoon. I think I'm going to just hang here tonight. You got any plans?"

"No, I'll just check in with Mavis, try to call Andie and Dana, the girl who's renting Cal's house." I was starting to wonder why I couldn't get Dana. I'd called several times.

"How's that working out?"

"Far as I know, okay. Some developer is trying to force me to sell it though, but I think Dana can handle him."

Brody nods and heads for the bedroom.

I sit for awhile after Brody goes to bed, just thinking about everything, trying to sort through all the things that have happened in a few short days. I glance down at Brody's legal pad. He's written some names and addresses down and also some doodles, probably while he talked on the phone. Near the bottom he's printed several words in big letters.

Simplicity, complicity, multiplicity, duplicity—Boplicity!!!

I grab some dinner at a small cafe with outside tables and watch the Village throng of strollers, eating, sipping some red wine. One of the biggest cities in the world and I've never felt more alone. I wonder how Mavis will make it through the night. I order some coffee and call Dana.

"Evan, how are you?"

"Doing okay, how about you?"

"Still struggling with this thesis. Are you almost finished in New York?"

"Yeah, but little change in plans. I have some business in L.A. so I'll be stopping over there for a couple of days."

"Great, I'll get to see you then."

"Yes. How's everything going with the house? No more hassles from Brent Sergent I hope." She pauses a minute.

"No. He called once but I told him what you said." There's a brief pause, then, "Evan, are you sure you don't want to consider his offer. I mean it is a lot of money. I hope you're not worried about me. I can always get another place."

"No, it isn't that, Dana. I just don't like his approach and I still haven't decided what to do about the house. But don't worry, you'll have plenty of notice if I change my mind."

"Okay," she says, but doesn't sound very convincing. "What about the search for Cal? Anything new?"

"Well a lot has been happening, but I'll tell you all about it when I see you."

"Oh, you're a terrible tease, Evan Horne. I can't wait to hear."

"You will, don't worry. I'll call you when I get in."

"Yes, please. I want to know when you're coming so I can have the house all neat and tidy."

"I'm sure you will. Talk to you soon."

"Bye."

Andie is home too. "Hi, babe, how goes it?" I say.

"Very lonely without you here. How's it going?"

"I caught up with Al Beckwood but he died this afternoon. He was in last stages of cancer."

"Oh, Evan, I'm sorry. Did you get to talk to him?"

"Yes, quite a bit actually and he put me on to someone else. An old girlfriend of Cal's who lives in Los Angeles. I'm going to see her in the next day or two if I can get a flight out of here. I'm about done with New York."

She sighs audibly. "Well at least you'll be that much closer. Then home I hope."

"Yes, then home."

"Thank God. I'm sick of sitting here alone. I'm itching to get back to work now. Just waiting for the doctor's clearance. Imagine that, a clearance to sit at a fucking desk. Not field work but at least I'll be in the loop again."

I hesitate a moment. "Anything on that file?"

I hear Andie's breathing for a moment, then, "I thought we were through with that."

"We are, I just...oh, forget it."

"I'm trying to."

"Well just take it easy, girl. It'll be soon enough."

"What are you doing right now?"

"Sitting outside at a restaurant in the village, watching people walk by."

"Plenty of girls to check out I imagine."

"Hordes of them but they're all with guys."

"Yeah, right."

"I'll call you as soon as I get a flight."

"I can't wait."

◇◇◇

"Wow, haven't seen one of these in a long time. Where did you get them?" Buzz Harris, the engineer asks me as he opens the box and looks at the tapes Mavis Beckwood gave me.

I'd arrived early for the mixing session for just this reason. "I just came into them recently. You know what kind of machine I'd need to play them."

"Yeah, a reel to reel. Friend of mine has one. An old Akai but a mother to haul around. Long way from these iPods and MP3 players." He rubs his finger over the end of the tape. "How old are these?"

"Late 1949, early 1950. Can they be transferred to CD?"

"Sure can. Remember those tapes of Bird that guy Dean Benedetti made on one of those old wire recorders? They're all on CD now." He looks around as Roy Haynes walks in, dapper as usual in a cashmere sweater, slacks, and loafers.

"Transfer what?" Haynes asks, looking at the tapes.

"Yeah," Buzz says. "What's on them?"

I feel their eyes on me. "Miles. *Birth of the Cool* band. Somebody made these during rehearsals."

"Are you serious?" Haynes picks up one of the tapes.

"Well that's what's supposed to be on them."

"You know these could be worth some money," Haynes and Buzz say almost simultaneously.

I shrug. "I suppose so."

Larry Klein walks in the booth then. "Hey, what's going on? Did somebody say money?"

"Evan found some tapes of Miles band rehearsing *Birth of the Cool*," Haynes says.

"What?" Klein's mouth drops open.

They all gather around the box, looking at the large plastic reels.

"Dude, we have to hear these," Buzz says. "I'll call my friend, see if he'll come over and bring his recorder."

"Okay," Haynes says. "Call him, but we got business to take care of." He puts his hand on my shoulder and takes me out in the studio. "How'd you get these?"

I tell him about Al Beckwood, the rehearsals, and Calvin. "I just recently found out he was my father. He made a few of the rehearsals, but he wasn't on record."

Haynes nods. "And you wish he was, don't you. He play piano too?"

"Yes. Calvin Hughes."

Haynes looks away, shaking his head. "Don't recognize the name, but hell, that don't mean anything. I was around then too, but Max Roach had that gig." He looks back at me. "Is your father still alive?"

"No, he died a couple of weeks ago."

"Oh, I'm sorry. That's why you sounded down on the phone."

"Yeah, I guess. Thanks. I only found out a couple of days ago from my mother. I've been trying to track down some of his friends. Al Beckwood was one and he had these tapes. But when I went through Cal's things, I found some lead sheets of 'Boplicity' and a couple of others."

"Roy, we're ready." Buzz's voice comes over the studio speaker.

"Come on, we'll talk more later."

We go back in the booth as Buzz cues up the first tune. Larry Klein sits in a chair near the front of the control board, watching Buzz's hands on the slide controls as the first notes of "I Hear a Rhapsody" come through the monitor speakers. On a screen in front of Buzz, an LCD screen flashes squiggly lines. It looks almost like a heart monitor.

"Jesus," Larry Klein says, swiveling in his chair and looking from me to Roy. "That's a hot track."

Haynes, smiling, nodding his head. "Buzz, you're a magician."

We listen to the whole track. Haynes' stick on the cymbal is so clear and definite, the cymbal beat so varied, and Ron Carter's buzz tone bass underlying it all. The track ends and Buzz leans back and looks at Haynes.

"Don't do anything," Haynes says. He looks at me, raising his eyebrows.

I'm just awed at the sound. "Is that me?" I can't think when I sounded better, but with Ron Carter and Roy Haynes behind me how could I not.

"Okay, save that one, Buzz. Let's hear the ballad."

Larry Klein shakes his head. "You fooled me. I really thought it was going to be 'All Blues.'"

Buzz cues up the ballad, "Goodbye Porkpie Hat," and except for a couple of places where he nudges up Carter's bass, we all agree it's a good take. Haynes brushes are silky smooth on the snare drum.

"That's it," Haynes says.

Buzz nods and fills in a form with the titles and personnel and the time of each track, and it's all saved on the hard drive. Haynes gives me a hug. "You sound great, man. I have to call Fletcher Paige and thank him for turning me on to you."

"Say hi for me."

"You got it." He glances at his watch. "I got a meeting pretty soon, but I'll call you and we'll talk some more, okay?" He glances again at the box of tapes. "Let me know how those are. Maybe we can do something with them." He looks at Larry. "Are we cool with Evan's bread?"

Klein reaches in his coat pocket and takes out a check and a release form for me to sign.

"Thanks. Any chance I could rearrange my ticket? I need to stop in L.A. before I go home."

Klein shrugs and looks a Haynes. "Might be a cancellation fee."

"Give him what he wants," he says to Klein.

"I'll pay the difference," I say.

"No problem. When do you want to leave?"

"Well tonight if possible."

Klein nods and takes out his cell phone. "Let me see what I can do."

"Later," Haynes says and follows Klein into the studio and heads for the exit.

Buzz leans back. "You want to grab some coffee or something? My friend said he'd be over soon."

"Okay. I'll be downstairs."

I go out back down to the street and light a cigarette, my heart still not slowing. Two tracks on a Roy Haynes CD and Beckwood's tapes about to be revealed. I can't decide which feels better, and I can hardly wait to meet Maybeline Jones.

I walk around the block looking for coffee, finally getting a Styrofoam cup from a hole in the wall place next to an electronics store.

"It ain't Starbucks, but it's fresh," the guy behind the counter says.

I add cream and sugar, press a lid on top and take a sip. "It's good too."

When I go back upstairs, Buzz and his friend have a reel to reel recorder set up and plugged in.

"Hey," Buzz says. "We got it happening in a minute. This is Joey, sound guy for Madison Square Garden."

"Hi," I say. Joey is a tall slim guy in jeans and a Eric Clapton tee shirt. He nods and continues threading the tape through the heads of the recorder, finally looping one end over the right reel.

"Okay, you ready?" He switches on the recorder and I hold my breath.

There's a lot of background noise, papers being rattled, muted conversations we only get snatches of and some bumping sounds.

"Setting the microphone up," Joey says.

Then the piano, some chords, runs, like somebody warming up. Somebody laughs and we hear a few notes from a couple of the horns. Who was there that day? Gil Evans, Gerry Mulligan, Max Roach? My mind reels through the personnel. If that's Cal at the piano, then John Lewis is doing something else.

Finally a raspy voice says, "Let's play it down."

"Wow, is that Miles?" Buzz says.

"Don't sound like him," Joey says.

"Maybe it's Gil Evans."

"No, man, Miles was the leader."

There's a shaky start and stop sequence as Miles says something else that's hard to hear, then an almost complete play through of "Boplicity." Miles stops things and we hear him say, "Cal, hold that chord there, at the end, longer."

Cal's voice then, sounding younger but no doubt it's Cal. "Sorry, I got it now."

"Don't be sorry, motherfucker, just play it." Then Miles and some others laughing.

They start again and go through the whole tune. I strain, listening. The quality is not balanced or clean but we can hear the whole band. The rest of the tape is similar. Lots of noise, short conversations, remarks, clearly the sound of a bottle opening as the rehearsal continues. We listen to the whole tape. It stops in the middle of one tune and the tape runs through the recorder then flapping as it spins off the empty reel.

I watch Joey and Buzz look at each other. "I could clean this up a bit," Buzz says.

"Yeah, it's recorded at fifteen so we can fix it a little." They continue talking as if I'm not there. Two recording guys immersed in technical jargon about tape speeds, static noise, blank spots. Finally, they look at me.

"Can you transfer those to a CD?"

Joey nods. "Sure, not a problem. I'm on a deadline for another project though. Can you leave them with me?"

I feel only the slightest hesitation to let the tapes out of my sight. "I'm going back to California tonight. Let me pay you for your time."

Joey glances at Buzz. "Two bills okay?"

"I'll have to get some cash. I'll leave it with Buzz and enough extra for shipping. Can you Fed-Ex it to me?"

"Sure. I'll do it here. Save me lugging this big thing around."

Buzz says, "It's cool, man. I'll lock up the tapes here."

"Great." I write down my Monte Rio address and cell phone number and give it to Joey. "I really appreciate this, guys."

"How do you want me to label the CD?" Buzz says.

"Miles and Cal—Boplicity."

Chapter Fourteen

I get to the airport two hours before my flight, hoping it's not crowded and I can have a couple of seats to myself. It's not a red eye but my own are gritty at six in the morning. I'm ready to nap at 37,000 feet.

Larry Klein had arranged for a stopover in Los Angeles and had even waived the rebooking charge. It wasn't much anyway, but it's a nice gesture and makes me think even more highly of Roy Haynes.

"The way you played, Roy said anything you want," Klein said when he'd called me with the flight information.

Now that I'm here, I'm almost sorry to be leaving New York, but at the same time I'm excited about meeting Maybeline Jones, and finally getting some real first hand information about Cal's earlier life. The tapes are very much on my mind too. I want to sit down with headphones and listen to them over and over. The little bit I'd heard made me long for everything, and, in a couple of days, I'll have them in CD form.

I have a last cigarette outside the terminal, watching people being dropped off for flights, saying their goodbyes, and head inside to run the security gamut, but again it's fairly painless. Maybe it's the time of morning, but I'm through and walking toward my gate in fifteen minutes.

I grab coffee at the nearest snack bar, then spend a few minutes browsing around a gift shop, skimming magazines, thumbing through the latest best-selling books. I finally take a seat in the boarding area, anxious to get on the plane. From the size of the crowd, it's not going to be too bad and I've got a window seat. I'm already yawning when they finally make the boarding call. I find my seat, stow my bag in the overhead compartment, and wait to see the draw on any companions. There are several close calls as people check their seat numbers and glance at me, but in the end I have a row to myself. I buckle up, put my head back and wait for the plane to taxi out and prepare for takeoff.

There's an hour spent serving a light snack and drinks, then the cabin lights dim and a movie comes up. I lean back, close my eyes, and I'm asleep in minutes.

The descent of the plane is all that awakens me. I sit up and look at Los Angeles spread out below. I just have time to get to the restroom, splash some cold water on my face, and get back to my seat as the pilot makes the landing announcement. I feel groggy and stiff walking through the terminal and almost nod off standing in line at the car rental desk.

I turn on my cell and call Danny Cooper. He answers curtly. "This is Cooper."

"This is Horne. Roger that."

He laughs. "Hey where are you?"

"Waiting in line at Hertz at LAX."

"Save some money. I'm on lunch down on Lincoln. Want me to pick you up?"

"No, stay there. I need a car for a couple of days. Have another doughnut. I'll be there in half an hour. Norm's?"

"How did you know?" He laughs again.

"Where else? See ya."

I finally get a car and snake through the airport traffic, heading for Lincoln Boulevard, down past Marina del Rey, Venice, and finally, a right on Pico to Norm's coffee shop. I pull in and find Coop staring out the window at me.

I barely get to this booth when his cell phone rings. "This is Cooper," he says into the phone, holding up a finger. "Got it. Be right there." He looks at me and shrugs. "Sorry. I have a situation as we say. I gotta go."

"No problem. How about dinner. I have lots to tell you."

He gets up, adjusts his coat, his gun flashing briefly. "Sounds good. I'm off at six."

"Okay. Call me when you're free and we'll figure out a place."

I wave off the waitress, saying I've changed my mind and get back in my car and head for Hollywood, deciding to go straight to the house, but I can't resist a coffee place on Franklin. I pull in quickly and go inside, then stop suddenly.

Tucked away at a corner table, a couple catches my eye. Dana is sitting, her back to me. The guy facing her is Brent Sergent. He has his hand on hers across the table, his eyes traveling around the room as he talks, and eventually, lock on mine. He jerks his hand away from Dana and sits back in his chair, shaking his head.

I watch Dana look at him, then turn. Her eyes meet mine, then she drops her head again. I walk over and stand by their table.

"Well, well," I say, looking from one to the other. I glare at Sergent. "Don't you have someplace you have to be?"

He gets up, grabs his briefcase, glances at Dana. "I'll call you," he says to her. He carefully avoids me, skirting around another table and makes for the exit.

"Yeah, do that," I say, watching him go. I turn back to l look at Dana. "You want to tell me what's going on?"

"I...I didn't know when you were coming," she says, her voice almost a whisper.

"I can see that."

"Evan, it's not what it looks like."

"Oh, what does it look like?"

"Please let me explain."

"Yeah, sure. No, you know what? Don't bother." I shove a chair aside and walk quickly away. Pushing through the door I get outside but Dana follows me.

"Evan, please."

I stop and turn around. "For what, Dana? I get the picture."

"Just give me five minutes. Please."

"This should be good. Okay five minutes."

"I'll be right back," she says. "I left my purse inside."

I find a vacant table, light a cigarette and wait. She comes back in less than two, carrying a coffee for me and sits down. I sit down, get a cigarette going and look at her. "How long have you known Sergent?"

She sighs. "Since college. We were in a couple of classes together, but that time he came to the house, it was the first time I'd seen him since."

"So you're just renewing your old acquaintance?" I make no attempt to keep the sarcasm out of my voice, and I see it pains Dana to hear it.

She leans forward. "I know this looks bad, Evan, but please, I can explain everything."

I look away, take a deep drag on my cigarette and sip some coffee. "Yeah, sure. Everybody can always explain everything. Dana, I trusted you. At least I thought I could. Is Sergent paying you to hustle me? You have some kind of commission deal going."

She shakes her head. "No, it's not like that."

"What is it like then?" I wanted to believe her. I wanted to believe my instinct about her had been right when I'd heard her talk about Cal, rented her the house, but seeing her with Sergent now changes everything.

She runs her hands through her hair, winding up, considering what she's going to say. "Brent saw me once, with Cal. He was up there scouting properties in the neighborhood, said he was working for this big developer, and anything I could tell him would be helpful. I didn't see any harm in that. When I asked Cal about it, he just laughed. 'They've been sniffing around here for years, but where would I go if I did sell, he said.'"

"Brent called a couple of weeks later but by that time, Cal was gone and I'd met you. That's when he came to the house and talked to you. He said there would be a finder's fee if I could talk you into selling, but by then, I was..."

Her voice trails off and she looks at me. "I know it's crazy and I have no right, but that little time we spent together, well, you know what I'm talking about. I was uncomfortable talking with Brent after that. He called several times, pushing me to persuade you to sell. I met him today to tell him I don't want anymore to do with it. He even threatened to tell you I worked for him. He thinks you and I had something going on. That's all that happened, Evan. Really."

I'm quiet for a few moments, thinking, turning things over in my mind. I drink off half the coffee, feeling Dana's eyes on me. When I turn to look at her again, I see her eyes pooling.

"I don't know, Dana. I guess I'm feeling pretty sensitive about trust after what I've learned in the past few days."

"Please believe me, Evan. If you want I'll move out today, and you can find another tenant. I don't want you to think I'm involved in any conspiracy with Brent. He gives me the creeps now."

What choice do I have? I don't have time to make new arrangements, decide what to do with Milton. There's no place in my life now for a dog, and so far no harm done. I still own the house and after all, Brent Sergent can't force me to sell.

"I want to believe you, Dana, and I don't want you to move out either, but if I find out you have anything more to do with Brent Sergent other than hanging up on him if he calls, I'll close the house down. I don't want to do that but I will. I want to be clear about that."

She nods and wipes her eyes with a napkin. "Thank you. I'm so sorry I did anything for you to doubt me, and don't worry, I don't want anything more to do with him anyway."

She doesn't say why, but at this point I don't care. "Okay, fair enough. Let's just forget it. It's over and we'll move on for now."

She manages a smile and nods again. "Why did you come to L.A."

"To meet with a woman who knew Cal pretty well. I went up to my folks when I was in New York, and my mother finally told me everything. Cal is my father and she was, is, Jean Lane."

I catch her up quickly and drop her at the house, hoping I'm not making a mistake.

She gets out of the car then leans back in the window. "Are you sure we're okay?"

I nod. "Yeah, we're okay." She turns away, obviously not sure. I watch her walk up the steep flight of steps, then turn and wave at me. For all I know, Brent Sergent is waiting around the corner, watching the house. I make a U-turn and go back to Beachwood Drive, turning left instead of back into Hollywood.

Driving up a few blocks, I turn around, go back and park a half a block or so from the house. I sit for half an hour, feeling sillier with every passing minute.

Dana's confusion and remorse do seem genuine, so why am I still wary, checking on her? Why can't I trust anybody anymore? Dana, my long time friend—so I thought—Ace Buffington, who sold me out to drug dealers in Amsterdam, even Andie. I realize suddenly what I'm feeling is probably only the beginning of a long road back to normalcy in my dealing with people close to me. My mother's revelations have seen to that.

I glance at my watch and start the car. I have to go with it until something else proves me wrong. Turning around, I head back to Beachwood Drive, drop down to Franklin, and make for the Hollywood Freeway. Driving through the Cahuenga Pass, I dial Maybeline Jones.

"Where are you, baby?" she says.

"On the freeway heading toward the Valley. Just got in a couple of hours ago."

"Don't think I'm weird but can we meet someplace public? On Ventura Boulevard, Coffee Plus. You get one of the outside patio tables, okay?"

"I think I know the place. How will I know you?"

"Oh, I'll know you, sugar. You just look for the best looking, sixty-one year old black woman you've ever seen."

I laugh and close the phone. I like her already. The traffic is heavy at the Ventura Interchange. I go a couple of exits and turn left toward Ventura Boulevard. Coffee Plus is down a couple of blocks connected to a huge bookstore.

I park, get a large coffee, and go through the glass doors to the patio tables and wait. Fifteen minutes later, I see a tall black woman in a floral print dress and big sunglasses. I start to wave, but she spots me and comes over. She doesn't say anything at first, just drops her bag and cell phone on the table, sits down and looks at me.

"I'd know you anywhere," she says. "I'm Maybeline."

I take her hand. "Nice to finally meet you." She's slim with caramel colored skin. Nails, jewelry, everything happening, but all very tasteful. She may be sixty one but she looks much younger.

She smiles. "It's living good, baby. That's the secret," she says, as if answering my thoughts.

"I'll try to remember that." There's a long moment of silence as neither of us seems to know where to start. I'm sitting here across from a woman who probably knew Cal as well as my mother did, maybe better. I have so many questions spinning through my mind. so much to cover.

She looks in my eyes and smiles warmly. "You're hurting aren't you baby. Well, I'm not surprised. I never thought we'd meet."

"It's kind of a shock to find out you're not who you thought you were at this late date."

She nods. "That used to worry Cal so much, wondering how you were doing, what you were doing."

I feel a flash of anger. "Why didn't he try to find out?" It comes out more harshly than I intend. "I mean he could have tried to make contact couldn't he?"

She looks away for a moment. "Oh he wanted to, but the longer he let it go, the harder it was." She reaches over and touches my hand. "He was afraid, baby, afraid you wouldn't want to see him."

"Hey, I didn't even know he existed. When I met him, spent time with him, I still had no idea who he was. Why didn't he tell me then?" I look away for a moment. "I'm sorry. I don't mean to go off on you."

She looks surprised. "What, just come right out and say, oh by the way, I'm your father? No, baby. That wouldn't have been

Cal's way. He was just glad you'd found him, even if it was by accident."

"How do you know that?"

She leans back in her chair. "We had one phone conversation after you started taking lessons with him. I hadn't seen or heard from him in ages but I knew his voice right away, like it had been only days instead of years. I don't even know how he got my number and didn't ask either. He just said, 'I found him, Maybeline, but he doesn't know.'"

She shrugs. "We talked for almost an hour. I told him he should tell you but he was afraid that would drive you away or you wouldn't believe him. I think eventually he would have."

I shake my head. "Maybe not." I tell her about the note he left, the long buried secret, the chase he'd sent me on with nothing to go on but an old photo and a name.

Maybeline nods, watching me. "He wanted your mother to be the one to tell you. Remember, baby, he loved your mother."

"Why didn't you see him after that call?"

"He didn't want it. He said our time had long passed and I could tell he wasn't well. He was right. I had my life, he had his. It was better to keep those memories."

"That's what I want to hear about."

"I know, and I'm going to tell you."

"How did you meet?" I light a cigarette. "You want some coffee or something?"

"No, I'm fine. We were in New York. I was a singer back then. Not as good as I thought, but a singer." She laughs. "I was auditioning at a small club and Cal was the piano player. He was so sweet, helping me with my music. I really didn't know what I was doing. I just wanted to be Ella or Sarah so bad."

Her face darkens as she remembers. "The club owner was a mean guy, sitting there with a big cigar in his mouth, a few tables in front of the stage with another guy who I guess was the manager. I barely got through the first chorus of 'All of Me,' when he turned to the other guy and said, 'Jackie, tell that singer bye.' I wasn't sure I'd heard right, but Cal did.

"He stopped playing and walked over and said, 'Jackie, you can tell this piano player bye too.' He gathered up my music and took my hand and said, 'Come on. You don't want to work here.'"

I smile, thinking it's exactly the kind of thing I would have done.

"Just like that, he gave up his gig. I was just in shock at the whole thing. Nobody had ever done anything like that for me. He took me next door to a diner and bought me lunch. We ate lunch and talked and talked and talked. He told me, warned me about what I was in for if I wanted to be a singer, but he was honest too. Told me I wasn't good enough yet for New York. Made me cry. Cal could do that sometimes. He'd just say right out what other people only thought."

The story makes me smile again. How many times had I been told that? How many times had it got me in trouble?

"He offered to work with me, get my music together and we did, whenever he could. I went to his gigs, listened to him play, saw the burn in his eyes and right then I knew, I was wasting my time. I was never going to be good enough. When I told him that, he just nodded and said, 'I know that, but you had to find out for yourself.'"

She puts her head back and laughs. "Didn't change a thing about the way I felt about him though. I was already in love."

She looks at her watch. "I got so much to tell you, but I have work to do too. How about you come over to my place later tonight, about 8:30. I have a business dinner but I should be back by then."

I can't keep the disappointment off my face, but she pats my hand. "Don't worry baby." She opens her purse and takes out a business card and pen and writes her address on the back. "I'm not far from here," she says handing me the card. May Jones, it says on the card. Realtor–Broker.

She smiles as I look at the card. "Nobody is going to buy a house from someone named Maybeline." She stands up, grabs her purse and phone. "I'm glad you called me. I'll see you tonight."

I watch her go and sit for a long time, smoking, finishing my coffee, oblivious to the shreds of conversation around me as people come and go. When I look up, most the tables have emptied, a bus boy is clearing tables, getting things ready for the after work crowd.

I go out to the car and call Coop. With a few hours to kill I don't want to go back to Hollywood.

"Where are you?" Coop asks.

"In the Valley on Ventura. Want to have an early dinner?"

"I'm already there. Had to see a witness in Encino. There's a deli around Havenhurst that used to be famous. You know it?"

"Yeah, I think so. "

"Okay, about twenty minutes?"

"See you there."

I cruise down Ventura looking for the deli, finally spot it and pull in the parking lot in back. Coop is already there in a booth, frowning, flipping through the ten page menu.

"How can they have so many things?" he says as I slide in a booth opposite him.

I'm too tired to struggle through it. There's a picture of a huge pastrami sandwich on the inside page with Still The Best printed above it. I order that, potato salad, and an iced tea. Coop does the same.

Coop leans back and looks at me. "You look like you just came back from the Twilight Zone."

"I feel like it." I can picture Rod Serling looking at the camera saying. "Meet Evan Horne, jazz pianist, erstwhile detective, whose journey takes him to a place where time is another dimension…"

"It's been a strange few days, Coop." I catch him up on all that's happened. He listens quietly, sipping his iced tea, his expression hardly changing as I tell him about my mother, Al Beckwood, the tapes, Maybeline Jones. I stop as the waiter brings our sandwiches. Coop barely looks at his.

"Jesus, I can't imagine what that must feel like. You probably haven't really gotten used to the idea yet yourself. I mean, finding out Cal was your father, all that stuff. Are you sure you want to talk with this Maybeline Jones?"

"What do you mean?"

"Well, if she tells all, really opens up there might be some stuff you don't, maybe should be…" He waves his sandwich in the air as he searches for the right words. "Left alone, you know? Oh I guess I should shut up. I don't know what I'm talking about. I can't imagine finding out something like this." He takes a bite of his sandwich.

I have to smile but I know what Coop is getting at. For whatever reason, Cal left my mother pregnant and then—did he abandon us, or did she simply choose not to follow? I need to know everything, good, bad, or indifferent. I want all the blanks filled in and Maybeline can provide a lot of answers.

"I know it's not going to be all good, Coop, but I just have to find out whatever I can. A week ago, I spread this man's ashes in Santa Monica Bay. I want to know who he was."

We eat in silence for awhile. Then Coop changes the subject. "What about the house? Did that guy come around while you were gone?"

I tell Coop about finding Brent Sergent with Dana and her story about Sergent.

"Do you believe her?"

"I don't know. I guess. I just don't feel like dealing with it now. The house is in no danger. He's just looking for a commission, using Dana to get it. She seemed genuinely remorseful. She really is sorry for getting involved or she's a damn good actress."

Coop nods. "Well all you can do is keep a close watch." He sips his iced tea.

"What about the music scene? You mentioned a recording session in New York."

I tell him about the session and how it went. "Roy Haynes is amazing, Coop, and this recording will get me out there again in a big way."

Coop grins. "I don't know Roy Haynes from Roy Rogers but I'll take your word for it. Those other tapes worry me though.

And this Cameron Brody guy. How much do you know about him?"

"Not a lot but he seems to be an okay guy. I was with him when he tracked down this singer who was owed royalties. He did that on his own." I hesitate for a moment and then decide to tell Coop about the mugging and theft of Cameron's computer.

Coop frowns. "Excuse my suspicious cop mind, but that doesn't sound like some random incident."

"No I don't think so either, but he couldn't figure it out."

Coop checks his watch. "I'd like to hear more about this. What about the tapes, Cal, your dad was playing on. Even I know Miles Davis. Who else knows about them?"

"Besides Cameron? The engineer at the studio, his friend who is transferring them to CD for me." I look at Coop. He seems troubled. "What?"

"Oh nothing. I was just thinking about some other tapes you got involved in and what happened."

"These tapes are different, Coop. These are just for me. Nobody else."

Chapter Fifteen

Maybeline Jones lives in a small condo complex in Encino. The units are built around a tree-lined cul de sac, on a narrow road that winds up just off Ventura Boulevard. I pull into one of the guest parking spaces and get out of the car. It's so quiet I have to strain to hear the traffic. Hard to believe the noise and crowding on Ventura are just down the hill. I ring her bell just after eight thirty.

She comes to the door a little breathless, clutching her shoes in her hand.

"Hi, I'm running a little late. That dinner went longer than I thought. Come on in and make yourself at home."

I follow her in. Just off the entry way, it's all soft lighting, tastefully decorated, and the stereo set to a jazz station with Keith Jarrett moaning his way through "Too Young to Go Steady."

"Nice," I say, looking around at the comfortable furniture, full bookshelves and, a fireplace. I feel Maybeline watching me.

"There's some beer and white wine. Help yourself. I'm just going to run upstairs and change."

"Okay." I wander into the pristine kitchen and grab a bottle of pale ale out of the fridge. There's an array of countertop appliances, but it looks like they're hardly used.

In the living room dining area, there are some art deco poster prints and one section of wall space reserved for framed photos. I look closely at one black and white of Maybeline in an evening gown, standing in front of a microphone, the blurry faces of a bassist and drummer behind her. Next to it is another of her and a young Cal I recognize from the photos my mother showed me. Cal is seated at a piano, Maybeline next to him.

I'm still staring at it when she comes back downstairs in a loose, floor length gown. "Your Daddy was a handsome man."

"How old was he here?"

"Oh, maybe late twenties, early thirties. We hadn't been together long when that was taken."

I see the obvious facial characteristics we share, and feel the jolt of a sudden memory when I was introduced to a friend of my mother's. The woman had looked at me and said jokingly, "This is Richard's son? He doesn't look anything like him?" I try to picture my mother's face then but I can't. How many times had that happened?

Maybeline motions me over to the couch. "Sit down, baby. You okay with that beer?"

"Yeah, I'm fine."

She settles herself on the other end of the couch. "Well, here we are." She looks at me, her expression more serious now. "I've been thinking about this since you called me from New York. I knew I'd meet you one day. I just can't believe nobody told you about Cal."

"Neither can I. My mother said she thought she was doing the right thing, always meant to tell me but…" I shrug. "It caught me totally by surprise."

"I bet it did, and she probably did think she was doing right by not telling you, protecting you maybe."

"From what?"

"Oh everything that happened. She might have been afraid Cal would come into your life and then leave again. I'm sorry, baby, but Cal was no saint."

"No, I guess he wasn't."

"He had his own way but he was a good man. There are plenty like him. Suddenly a young father, a career before him, trying to make choices. Only with Cal it wasn't just a career, it was an obsession. And he was so talented."

"Tell me about the Miles' band. Were you with him then?"

She sighs. "Yes. That was so hard on him. He was so excited about it and then so disappointed and frustrated. You know John Lewis was the pianist and this was before the Modern Jazz Quartet days."

"Yes, but I heard there were a lot of musicians in and out of that band."

Maybeline nods. "Yes. Cal knew John and another pianist, Al Haig who sometimes made the rehearsals, so he subbed a lot. It looked like for awhile that John wouldn't make it, so Cal got his hopes up."

"Did you know he taped some of the rehearsals?"

"Oh God, yes. He played them all the time. He would stay up late, scribbling music, hoping Miles would want to use one of his tunes. Gerry Mulligan came by once to talk to Cal about it. He was doing a lot of the writing. So did Gil Evans. They were like a little club and Cal was almost a full member. He'd be so disappointed when he'd get the call from Miles or Gil Evans that they didn't need him that week. It was like a roller coaster."

I try to process all this as Maybeline talks. Gerry Mulligan, Gil Evans dropping by, talking music with Cal, getting calls to rehearse or stay home that day. Cal had never mentioned a word of this phase of his life. I tell Maybeline about the music sheets I found at Cal's. "One of them was 'Boplicity.'"

Maybeline smiles. "That was his favorite. He could sing all the parts, played it over and over, made notes about it."

"Do you think he wrote it? The credit is to Cleo Henry. I found out 'Cleo' was Miles' mother."

"I don't know. Really I don't. He wrote down so many things and always took them to the rehearsals." She turns and looks at me. "Sometimes people want something so badly, they convince themselves it's actually happening. Sometimes I think that's the way it was with Cal, but the longer the rehearsals went on, the less Cal was used, and when they finally got the Royal Roost gig and recorded, well, Cal just about fell apart."

So near yet so far, I think. Getting so close and then having it dissolve, just pulled out from under you. "Al Beckwood told me Cal went to the first night, then left right after the band played 'Boplicity.'"

"He was gone for two days, just disappeared. He came home finally, looking like a skid row bum. Slept for a day and a half. I was working then in an office, just trying to keep things together. I came home that second day and found him sitting in a chair just staring out the window. Nothing I said could console him. He knew it was over and there was nothing he could do about it. I didn't know what to do, so I just left him alone."

It must have been like thinking you'd won the lottery, then finding you were one number off. Cal had probably already visualized playing with Miles, seeing his name on the record, anticipating the future—then nothing.

"How long was he like that?"

"It was weeks before he came out of it. He was drinking so much it scared me. He gradually got himself together though. It was all I could bear to see his sad face, the disappointment. He just looked at me and said, 'Well, baby what's my next move?' I told him, 'Cal you were good enough to play with Miles. You can play with anybody, have your own band.' He just nodded and smiled but he really didn't believe it."

"How long were you with him?"

"Almost four years, then we kind of drifted apart. He was never the same. He worked on and off with different groups, and if he was home he'd just pace around, like he was waiting for something."

"What?"

She shrugs. "Maybe you. He kept talking about contacting your mother, but like I said, he was afraid you might not want to see him or she wouldn't let him see you. He'd had enough disappointment already. I understood, but I told him you do what you have to do."

"How did it end?"

"I came home one day and found his stuff gone. He left a note, saying he had to get away for awhile, that he'd taken a gig on the road. A month later, he sent me a letter, saying it was best for both of us if he just stayed away. I knew he wasn't coming back, so I gave up the apartment and moved in with my sister."

"That was the last you heard from him, the letter?"

"No, once in awhile he'd call, just wanting to talk, but we never got back together. It had all changed." She stands up. "Excuse me for a minute."

I open the sliding door to the patio and go outside to smoke. There's a small table and two chairs. Maybeline joins me a few minutes later, bringing me another beer and continues as if she hadn't left the room.

"I know one thing. He was always wondering about you. That was a time he called me, after you two had met and you started studying with him. He wanted to tell you then but again, he just didn't know how. You never guessed huh?"

"No, never. I felt some kind of connection with him but thought it was just about music. I wish I had spent more time with him now."

"And I wish I had known he was right here in L.A."

"We both missed out."

"I followed that case in the news, about that crazy killer of those musicians, and you helping the FBI. I wondered then if he told you."

"Yeah I was in way over my head." I laugh. "Cal called me Sherlock. I spent a lot more time with him then. He knew all about what I was doing and came to the recording session when I made my first CD as a leader, even brought his dog Milton."

She laughs. "Cal had a dog?"

"Yes, an old Basset Hound."

"Never would have believed it. What happened to the dog?"

I tell her about Dana, renting her the house and having her take care of Milton. "Listen, I don't know what I'm going to do about the house yet, but if I decide to sell it, could you handle the deal."

"Where is it?"

"In the Hollywood Hills. Just a little cottage really but I've got some developer after me to sell. They want to build something on the property, condos maybe."

Maybeline leans forward. "You're sitting on some valuable land there. Sure I will. You just let me know."

"Thanks, I appreciate it." I stand up. "Well, I've taken up enough of your time. Can I call you again? I'd like it if we could stay in touch."

Maybeline stands up and gives me a hug. "Oh, anytime, honey. I'm always here. If you think of anything else, you just let me know."

"Thanks." I look at her. "This was very valuable to me. You can't know how much."

She doesn't say anything, just walks with me to the door. "Wait a minute. I have something for you."

She runs back upstairs for a moment then comes back with a manila envelope. "I want you to have this."

I look inside. It's a black and white photo. Cal is seated at a grand piano and leaning against it, smiling at Cal, is Miles Davis. Just out of focus in the background is a baritone saxophonist that can only be Gerry Mulligan.

"Are you sure?"

"Yes, baby," Maybeline says. "You need to have this. It's the happiest your daddy ever was."

Driving back to Hollywood, my mind is spinning with all the things Maybeline told me about Cal. I'd never know it all but I had a better picture now. Between my mother's memories, Maybeline's, my own brief experiences with Cal, I had a good idea what his life had been like, what he had felt, enjoyed and yes, regretted. There was still that gap between when he had left Maybeline and when I first met him. How hard had it been for him to spend time with me, teach me, not tell me he was my father? I couldn't begin to imagine.

I exit the freeway and drive up to the house. There's one light on in the living room, a pillow and a blanket on the couch, and a note from Dana on the back of an envelope.

> *Evan,*
> *I couldn't stay up any longer. I hope you're not mad. Wake me if you want to talk.*
> *D*

I take another look at the photo Maybeline gave me. She was right. Cal did look happy. Subbing with Miles' band, the leader himself smiling at him. How could he not be happy?

I put it aside and stretch out on the couch, drifting off almost as soon as my head hits the pillow. When I open my eyes again, the sun is filtering through the window, and I hear Dana rustling around in the kitchen. I sit up, the blanket still half over me as she walks in.

"I didn't wake you did I?" She hands me a mug of coffee.

"No," I say taking the coffee from her. "Thanks." I take a sip and look around. She's put up some posters, added new curtains, and rearranged the furniture. The other addition was a small desk where her computer, a stack of papers, and books with post-it notes sticking between some of the pages sit. "Place looks good." I hear water slurping in the kitchen and look at Dana. "Milton?"

She nods. "Almost time for his walk." As if he knows we're talking about him, Milton lumbers out and comes over, gives a low moan and offers his head for me to scratch. He makes some other low sound then turns and looks expectantly at Dana.

"Come on, you," she says to Milton. "I'll be back soon. I left some towels out for you."

"Thanks. Take your time. I'm still not quite awake yet."

She snaps on the leash and goes out. I get up, stretch and head for the shower, standing under the hot water for ten minutes or so. I get dressed, pour another cup of coffee and wander around, thinking this place has never been so clean and neat.

On Dana's desk, I glance at the papers and notes on her thesis. She wasn't making that up. I turn on my cell phone and call the airlines. Plenty of flights to San Francisco so I pick one for late afternoon, and call Andie.

"Hey, girl."

"Please tell me you're coming home."

"Yes. United at four twenty if all goes well. Listen, I want to go straight to Monte Rio so pack a bag. I have something coming I need to be there for."

"Okay, sounds good," Andie says. "I'm ready for some time away from the city. What is it that's coming?"

"Some tapes I got in New York. I'll tell you all about them when I see you."

"I can't wait to see you," she says. "Where did you stay last night?"

"At the house, on the couch. Very chaste and proper."

"You had better be. I think your little tenant has a thing for you."

I hesitate only a second, but Andie catches it. "Something go wrong."

"Nothing really. Just kind of a misunderstanding. I'll tell you about that too. We'll have plenty of time to talk on the ride down to Monte Rio."

The door opens as Dana and Milton come in.

"I want every detail," Andie says.

"Yes, ma'am. See you this afternoon."

"Bye, baby."

I end the call as Dana unsnaps Milton's leash. He flops on the floor, resting his head on his oversized paws.

"You're leaving today?"

"Yes. Couple of things I need to be in Monte Rio for."

Dana nods, looks down. "I was hoping maybe we could…"

"Have lunch? We can do that."

She breaks into a big smile that makes me wonder just how much I am like Cal.

Dana follows me to the car rental, then we go over the hill to a Mexican restaurant in North Hollywood. I try to keep things light but Dana keeps edging back to the embarrassment of me catching her with Brent Sergent.

"Look, Dana, it's okay. Long as you're being straight with me, I don't have a problem. Sergent is a hard sell guy and I can see how you got caught up in it, especially since you knew him before."

"Are you really sure?" She looks so serious. "Everything was going so well and I messed it up. God, I can't believe myself."

I smile and touch her arm. "Don't be so hard on yourself. You didn't mess anything up."

She looks away, then back at me. "Do you know how many times I've gone over that night we went to the record store, the coffee shop. I think that was when it happened."

I sit up straighter. "When what happened?"

"You."

I start to speak but she cuts me off.

"No, don't, let me finish. I know it's silly and you're already very involved with Andie. For all I know, you might be getting married."

For some reason that makes me laugh. "No, we're not getting married."

"Well anyway, I know you're taken at least for now, so I'm trying to be brave about this and just let you know how I feel." She puts her hands over her face. "There. I've made a fool of myself."

"Dana, listen to me. Yes I am very involved with Andie, although neither of us knows where it's going, but that's where I am now. I'm flattered with what you're telling me and if I was not with Andie, well, who knows."

"Thank you for that," she says.

I glance at my watch. "Hey, time to go."

We're both quiet on the short drive to Burbank Airport. Dana drops me off at departures. She gets out of the car and gives me a quick hug and kiss on the cheek. "Take care," she says.

"You too." I walk toward the entrance, then turn back to wave, but she's already gone.

An hour later, I'm still waiting for my flight. It's been delayed twice so far. I go back outside and sit down with the other smokers, about to call Andie when my phone rings.

"Where are you?" Coop asks. His voice is tight, rushed.

"Burbank, the airport. I'm headed back. Just waiting for my flight. It's been—" I

"It's Dana." I hear him make a big sigh. "I'm sorry, Evan. It's not good."

"What do you mean? We just had lunch. She dropped me at the airport an hour ago."

"That guy Sergent was waiting for her at the house. They got into a scuffle and she went down those steps. Evan? You there?"

"Yeah, I…is she okay?"

"Look, the locals need to talk to you since she was staying at your house. I'll radio a black and white to pick you up. Go outside and wait. Evan? You hear me?"

"Yeah, I'm already outside, at departures. Coop, is she okay?" But he's already gone.

I pace around, scanning the rush of cars pulling up, people unloading bags, saying their goodbyes. Ten minutes later I catch sight of police cruiser, red light flashing, cutting off two cars and pulling to the curb. A tall young uniformed cop in a crew cut and aviator sunglasses opens the door and looks over the roof, sees me coming toward him.

"Evan Horne?"

"Yeah." I get in front with him and he roars off. No siren but he keeps the red light flashing and we make it to Hollywood in record time. There's a fire truck, a paramedic unit and three other black and whites blocking the street in front of the house. But it's the black coroner van I focus on. A small crowd of onlookers stands across the street, pointing, talking. Two cops are talking to a woman off to the side, writing in their notebooks.

Brent Sergent is sitting on the curb, his head in his hands, two plain clothes cops looming over him.

Coop spots me and comes over as I start for the coroner van and two men in jumpsuits loading a gurney with a zipped up body bag. Coop blocks me, leads me away. I try to pull away, wanting to get at Sergent, but Coop pushes me back against one of the police cruisers. "Okay, settle down. There's nothing you can do."

The van's doors slam shut and it drives off. I look again at Sergent. His face is smudged. He looks up and his eyes meet mine for a moment, then he turns away. Coop still has his hand on my arm. "Get him out of here," he yells to the two cops hovering over Sergent.

They nod and put him in a car and drive off. Coop turns back to me. "Got a cigarette?" I dig for my pack and offer one to Coop. "I don't smoke," he says. I get mine going, take a deep drag, and he lets go of my arm. I feel numb.

"What happened?"

"See the woman talking to those two cops? She was apparently a witness. Just walking by and saw the whole thing."

"He wasn't supposed to be here, Coop."

Coop sighs. "Well, he was and evidently it was, and from what she says, it was an accident. They were arguing. Dana pushed him away, he pushed back and…"

I look up the steep flight of steps, imagining Dana tumbling down, Cal's built-in stair master. There's blood on the bottom step and the curb. "I just can't believe it. Is he going to be charged?"

Coop shrugs. "Involuntary manslaughter. Who knows. The woman who saw it was pretty definite. Says Sergent even grabbed for Dana as she started to fall, kept saying, 'No, no, no.'"

I can't get the picture out of my mind. "She was a good girl, Coop."

"Sure she was." He puts both hands on my shoulders. "Look at me. There was nothing you could have done about this, nothing for you to feel responsible for. You only knew her a few days. She just got mixed up with the wrong guy."

I know Coop is right. I just can't let go to the idea that if I'd sold the house to Sergent, Dana would still be alive.

"Has anybody contacted her aunt? She lives around here someplace."

Coop sighs and looks away. "There was no aunt, at least not according to the witness. Dana was renting a room down the street. Her family is in Iowa somewhere. They're running it down now."

"She's, was, a student at UCLA." I shrug. "At least I think she was."

Coop nods. "I'll let them know. Come on, let's get out of here."

In the car, I call Andie and tell her I'll be on a later flight without much of an explanation.

"What's wrong?"

"Not now, Andie. I can't. I'll call you when I know a flight time." I end the call before she can press more.

Coop drives me to the Hollywood police station. There's not much for me to tell them other than I had rented the house to Dana and met Brent Sergent twice. I do make sure the detective knows she and Sergent had known each other before, and he had been told not to come around again. I leave my address and phone and he tells me I may be contacted later if there are charges against Sergent.

At Burbank again, it's nearly seven when Coop drops me off, I suddenly remember Milton. "Oh shit, the dog. Can you—"

"Sure," Coop says.

I give him the keys. "Just till I figure out what to do next. Lock up the house for me."

At San Francisco Airport, Andie is waiting in the loading zone, standing by her car, scanning the faces of arriving passengers. She catches sight of me, waves, and jogs over with only a slight limp, I notice. She throws her arms around me, then leans back.

"If you don't kiss me, I'm going to be pissed." I feel her melt into me for a long deep kiss.

"Excuse me, miss. Is that your car?"

A security guard is tapping her on the shoulder. We break off and Andie looks at the guard. "Relax, we're going." The guard shakes her head and walks away as we go to the car. "You want to drive," Andie says.

"Yeah." I throw my bag in the back seat and get in and pull away.

"Life is good," Andie says, looking at me as we exit the airport and head up I-380. She curls up against the door, half facing me. I feel her looking.

"What?"

"Nothing. Just looking. It's been a long week." She has that smile on her face that I know means so much more. We're mired in slow crawling traffic along 19th Avenue.

I pull over to the curb and turn off the engine. I look at Andie, see the alarm on her face. "What is it?"

"Dana is dead."

She puts her hand to her mouth. "No. What happened?"

We sit there for fifteen minutes while I tell her everything. She takes my hand and holds it in both of hers, listening quietly. When I finish, she leans over, puts her arms around me and whispers in my ear.

"Cooper is right, baby. There was nothing you could have done. You're not responsible." She leans back, looks in my eyes. "You have to believe that, Evan."

I nod and look away. "I know, I just—"

"Come on, let's go home. Let me drive."

Neither of us says anything until we reach the Golden Gate Bridge. "So what's going to be waiting in Monte Rio?"

"A FedEx package I hope, of some tapes and CD copies." I tell her about Al Beckwood, the rehearsal tapes that Cal made. "They've been sitting around since 1949," I say. "Nobody knows about them."

"And Cal is on them."

"Yeah, he subbed with the band and apparently recorded some of the sessions."

"Wouldn't they be valuable?"

"Well yeah, but not commercially. I heard one and the quality is not so good, but they mean a lot to me, to hear Cal I mean. I might turn them over to some jazz archives somewhere."

Andie nods. "God, that must have been such a shock to hear all that history from your mother, finding out she'd been married a second time." She puts her hand on my arm. "I just can't imagine what that must feel to find out something like that. And you never suspected?"

"Not really." But even as I answer her more shards of memory fall into place. Nothing that made me suspect Richard Horne wasn't my father, but that something just wasn't right about our relationship. Processing the news seems to have opened some small doors and windows in my mind. I'd looked in but hadn't really seen.

As we near the north side of the bridge, I say, "Pull off here. I always wanted to see the city from here."

We get out of the car and start to walk along the narrow wall. "I'll be right back."

I head for the men's room and go inside. I splash cold water on the face, lean on the sink and look in the mirror, taking some deep breaths, trying to shake the numbness.

I find Andie, looking at the Bay, the city in the distance, just past Alcatraz Island. I light a cigarette and sit down on the wall next to Andie. She holds onto my arm with both hands. "You okay?"

I feel the gushing wind come off the bay and buffet us as the sun sets.

"I have an entire history now I didn't have a week ago. It's like it happened to somebody else."

Andie is quiet, leaning on my shoulder for a moment. "You're not going to go Oprah on me are you?"

"No." I laugh. "It's just hard to come to terms with it. It's like a part of me that was missing has been returned, but I never knew it had been lost."

We sit for a few more minutes then get up and go back to the car. I drive this time and pull back on 101 heading north to Santa Rosa. We have dinner at one of those family style restaurants just past Santa Rosa. Back on the road, Andie dozes and I'm alone with my thoughts trying to push the image of Dana tumbling down those steps from my mind.

Reluctant as I am to let go, from what Maybeline told me my doubts have increased that Cal composed "Boplicity" or any of the other tunes on *Birth of the Cool.* Having thought about it more, it sounds like Cal had been so obsessed, he'd convinced himself. Maybe he'd kept the lead sheet I'd found in his house simply as a souvenir of the rehearsals, a lost opportunity. Maybe I would never know for sure.

I have decided to have Cameron Brody do some more checking with his contacts. It was pretty well known that Miles had a rather cavalier attitude about giving credit. The best evidence for that was the feud between him and Bill Evans on "Blue and Green" from the *Kind of Blue* recording ten years after *Birth of the Cool.* But I don't know how far I can pursue it or where it will go.

Andie wakes up when I exit on River Road. "Sorry, babe," she says, sitting up and rubbing her eyes. "What are you going to do about the house now?"

I shrug. "I honestly don't know. Turn it over to a management company, sell it. With Dana gone, I…"

"Please, Evan, don't be mad," Andie says. "I know I acted like a jealous bitch, but something about that whole thing was not right. I just had a feeling about it."

I shrug. "I believed her. She seemed genuinely remorseful about the whole thing."

Andie shakes her head. "Sometimes you're just too trusting, Evan." She leans her head back on the seat and stares out the window.

She dozes off and I'm alone with my thoughts again as I roll down River Road to Guerneville. As I pass Main Street Station, I glance in the window and see a solo guitarist on stage. It's dark as I cross over the bridge and turn onto Bohemian Avenue and park. It feels good to be home.

I reach over and shake Andie. "Hey you, we're here."

She looks up, blinks and rubs her eyes and slides across to kiss me. "C'mon, baby its been a long time."

There's a delivery slip stuck to the front door from FedEx, saying they will try again tomorrow.

"Your tapes?" Andie asks.

"I hope so."

But by noon the next day, there's nothing. I decide to check my mail box and tell Andie to sign for the package if it shows up while I'm gone. I drive down to the post office just off Northwood Golf Course. A few bills, some junk mail, and a yellow slip for something bigger I present to the clerk. She hands me a flat priority mail envelope.

"Thanks," I say, and take everything out to the car. I don't recognize the return address on the packet. Ripping it open, I pull out a file folder and stare for a moment. Inside is Cal's FBI file. No note, nor explanation. There are five pages of info, signatures, and dates. Wendell Cook, who had been the agent in charge, Ted Rollins, and Andie had all signed off. But on one page, several lines are blacked out with a marker pen.

I scan it quickly, see nothing I don't already know. No mention of Jean Lane. Simply "subject married, subsequent divorce two years later." I close the file and put it back in the envelope and light a cigarette, gazing at the huge redwood trees that ring the nine hole golf course.

Where did this come from? Who sent it? It's a photo copy so the original is still somewhere in the FBI files. Who besides Andie knew about the file? Anyone who worked on the case of course, but after? More recently? The only name I can come up with is Ted Rollins.

I drive back to the house and find Andie on the deck, her legs stretched out, her skirt up around her legs, getting some sun.

"Nothing from FedEx?"

"No, not a word," she says. "Any good mail?"

"Yeah, couple of things." I drop everything on the dining table and grab the phone. "I'm going to call them."

I read off the number on the delivery slip to whoever answers the phone.

"Oh, yeah," a woman says. "Driver couldn't find your house."

"Really. I'm using the delivery slip he left yesterday to call you."

"Different driver today, hon. He got lost I guess."

"So what about my package? How could he not find it. I've seen your TV ads of you delivering to tree houses in the jungle."

"Settle down," she says. "We'll get your package. Give me the names of major cross streets nearest to you."

I sigh. "This is Monte Rio. There are no major cross streets." I give her directions from the 116 highway and the movie theater. "Tell him to turn left, cross over the bridge, and take the second left. That's Bohemian Avenue."

"Got it," she says.

"How long do you think it will take?"

"Not sure. I'll try to get him on the radio. We're just a sub contractor for FedEx."

"I'll be waiting."

I hang up and go out to join Andie on the deck. I drop the priority envelope on her lap, and lean against the railing. "Take a look at that."

She sits up, glances at me and pulls the file folder out. I watch her face as she opens the folder. She flips through the pages and stops on the one with the blacked out lines. "Oh shit," she says. She flips back to the front, then looks at the envelope, checking the return address.

"Who sent this?"

"I thought maybe you'd know," I say.

She shakes her head then slaps her hand on the envelope. "That sonofabitch."

"Who?"

"Rollins, who else?"

"What's it mean, Andie? Those blacked out lines, and why would he send it to me?"

She gets up and walks around the deck, rubbing her head. "To make me look bad of course. I asked him about it several times. He knew I was going to show it to you if we found it."

"What about the blacked out lines?"

She looks again, shaking her head. "I don't know, I don't know. It's been a long time since I've seen it, but I know I didn't black anything out." She raises her eyes to mine. "Evan, I don't know what to tell you."

"I don't know either, Andie."

She flips through the pages again, then sets the file down on the small table between us. It lies there, neither of us wanting to touch it. "Don't you believe me?"

First Dana, now Andie. "I want to believe you. You can't know how much, but I'm not doing very well on trust at the moment, not after this week. I've been lied to for years, my whole life. How do you think it feels to find out you're not who you thought you were. There's a big piece of my life missing. I'm just now finding out how much, and now this fucking file." I turn to look at Andie. How much do I know about her? Who is she?

Andrea Lawrence, Special Agent, FBI. Why was the file missing and now suddenly found? What was blacked out? What was so important? And if Ted Rollins sent it, why was he trying to drive a wedge between Andie and me?

I take both her hands in mine and look in her eyes. "Just tell me, Andie. Were you seeing Rollins while I was gone?"

Chapter Sixteen

Before Andie can answer, there's a loud knock on the door. I jog downstairs two at a time and open the door. A young guy in shorts, denim shirt, and a FedEx baseball cap is looking up at the glassed in second story.

"Cool place," he says. "Evan Horne?"

"Yes. You finally found it, huh?"

He shrugs and hands me a flat, heavy cardboard envelope. "Tricky area, man."

I take the package from him and sign for it. He turns to go but I stop him. "Wait." I open it, find two CDs shrink wrapped in generic jewel cases, which are thinner than commercial ones, and both in separate zip-loc plastic bag. Buzz wasn't taking any chances. Each has a typed label I can read through the bags. Just like I had requested: Miles and Cal–Boplicity. There was also one of Buzz's business cards from Avatar Studios. "There's only this one package?"

"That's it," the driver says, looking at his watch, anxious to get going.

"Okay, thanks."

I shut the door and walk slowly back up the stairs. Andie is waiting at the top.

"That your CDs?"

"Yeah but the tapes aren't here." For the moment, the file is forgotten.

I brush past her and grab the phone to call Buzz in New York. It rings several times then a young girl's voice. "Studios."

"Is Buzz around? It's Evan Horne."

"Hang on," she says.

"Evan? What's up man?" In the background I hear some loud rock music.

"Hi Buzz. I got the CDs but where are the tapes?"

"Hang on a sec." I hear the music go down then he's back on. "That guy who was with you at the session, Cameron something? He took them. Said he'd hand-carry them to you in case the package got lost."

"When did he pick them up?"

"Yesterday. Said he was flying back to California today sometime."

"Okay, thanks, Buzz. Did the CDs come out okay."

"Yeah. We cleaned them up some. Still not great quality but they are playable."

"Well, tell your friend Joey thanks too."

"Will do. Hey, I finished the mix on your two tracks with Roy. Want a copy?"

"Definitely."

"Okay, I'll burn a CD and mail it out today."

"Thanks, Buzz. I appreciate it."

I hang up, thinking about Cameron Brody with my tapes. Maybe it was a smart move. Things get lost in the mail, even with UPS or FedEx. I stand for a moment thinking about it.

Andie moves nearby, waiting. "Is everything all right?"

I sigh. "Yeah, I think so. They were supposed to send the tapes and the CD copies together, but that guy I told you about, Cameron Brody, he has the tapes."

"At least you know they're safe then." When I don't answer, she looks at me. "Aren't they?"

I don't want to answer. "I'm going for a walk," I say. Andie doesn't move as I jog down the stairs. When I round the corner, heading toward the bridge, I look up and see her on the deck, head down, looking through the file again.

I walk halfway across the Monte Rio Bridge and lean on the concrete railing, looking down at the dark water flowing past toward the ocean, trying to be okay with Cameron Brody taking the tapes with him. I know what he was thinking, but he should have called me first, talked about it. He knows how important they are to me. I would have probably agreed it was better to not send them in the same package with the CDs, but again, it's not knowing they're safe, on the way, tucked into his computer bag.

I light a cigarette and stare across the water, my mind drifting back to Andie. Just when everything is starting to come together there's that damn file. What was blacked out and who did it? I didn't really think Andie had anything to do with it, and if it is from Rollins, it would be like him to pull something like this. But what could be so important? As Andie said, vetting Cal was a routine matter. He had no actual participation in the Gillian Payne case.

I look across the river. I can just make out the hotel Ace Buffington had stayed in when I'd come back from Amsterdam, remembering the last time I saw him, the ugly confrontation. My good friend, Ace, who'd sold me out to make his own escape. Can I trust anybody anymore, ever?

I'm sure Andie didn't know about the file being mailed or else she's missed her calling and should be in Hollywood, starring in independent films. But there's that tiny, nagging doubt. I have to know.

I turn and start walking back over the bridge, but I'm not ready to go home yet. I turn the corner and go in the Pink Elephant Bar. It's almost empty except for two guys at one end of the bar having a draft beer. A woman bartender is talking with the two guys. She looks up, sees me and comes down. I take a stool at the other end and order a beer. I'm about halfway through my glass, when Andie walks in.

"Evan!"

I turn and see her walking, toward me, my cell phone in her hand. She stops, a little out of breath.

"What's the matter?"

"Cameron Brody. You left your cell phone. He just called."
She bends over her hands on her knees. "God I'm out of shape.
I walked across the bridge looking for you. He has the tapes with
him. It's okay." She hands me my phone. "Call him back. He's
waiting for his flight now."

I grab the phone from her, go outside, pull out the small
antenna, moving around trying to get a signal and dial.

"Cameron?"

"Hey, man. Sorry to freak you out about the tapes. Just
seemed better to keep them separate from the CDs, right."

I sigh with relief. "Yeah, just wish you had told me. I got the
CDs today."

"Good. Hang on a second. They're making some announcement about my flight."

I look at Andie. She's come outside with me. I give her the
okay sign.

"Evan? Flight's been delayed two hours or more."

"Okay. Call me when you get in."

"Will do. If it's too late, I'll call you in the morning. I have to
swing by my folks' place, check on things. They're out of town."

"I'll be waiting." I press the end button and put the phone
in my pocket. "He's got them, but his flight is delayed. Probably
won't see him till tomorrow."

She nods, looks at me. "Evan, I just can't remember, about
the file I mean. I can't remember anything being blacked out
and I certainly didn't do it. It has to be Rollins. He's just fucking with us."

"What about Rollins? Why would he do this?"

"Nothing. He came around, called a few times using the
shooting as an excuse to check on me, but nothing happened,
Evan. Nothing. Not then or while you were in Amsterdam. I
wouldn't do anything to jeopardize our relationship, and Rollins
would be the last guy. This is just his way of getting back. He's
been jealous of you from the beginning."

I look at Andie. I don't think I've ever seen her look so ear-
nest. "I believe you."

She looks up at me. "Do you? Do you really?"

"Yes." I pull her to me. She slumps against me, her head on my chest.

"Thank God," she says. "Let's go home."

I go back inside the bar and pay for my beer, then we walk back to the house.

Later, we drive into Guerneville, get a pizza to go at Mainstreet Station and have dinner on the deck in the last light of day. I feel the tension seeping out of my body. When it gets too cool for the deck, we go inside. I light the wood stove and tell Andie to hand me the file. I feed the pages into the fire one by one. Andie watches me, holding onto my arm.

"I'm going to take a long hot bath," she says. "You can join me if you want." She flicks her eyelashes in exaggerated flirtatiousness.

"I just might after I listen to these CDs."

"Take your time," she says and heads for the bedroom.

I go up to the loft with the CDs, plug in the head phones and sit back to listen. Buzz was right. They are clearer. Still not studio quality, but at over fifty years old, they are amazing. I turn up the volume and listen. It's all there.

I hear Miles' voice. "Hey, Cal, you taping this shit?" There's some shuffling of paper, horns tuning up, then the band runs down "Move," a fast, "I Got Rhythm" changes tune. They go over it a couple of times, then try John Carisi's "Israel." There's starting and stopping several times as details of chords or notes are worked out under Miles' directions.

"All right," he says, "let's try the one Cal likes." There's a pause, then they go into "Boplicity." I listen to the music, the snatches of conversation, imagining myself sitting next to Cal at the piano. The sound stops midway through another tune and I load the second CD. It's not as long as the first but I hear Miles say something to Gil Evans who must have come in late.

"Gil, listen to this chord on the bridge." Then to Cal, "play that minor seventh, Cal."

I listen to what seems the end. Miles Davis, Gil Evans, Gerry Mulligan, Max Roach on drums, and Calvin Hughes, my father on piano.

I listen for another thirty seconds or so, but that must be it. I turn off the player and sit for a minute in the dark, letting the sensation of all this wash over me, then I go down stairs to the bathroom and peek in.

Andie, her head back against the edge of the tub looks up at me. "Come on, baby, the water is still warm."

I wake up early and slip out of bed. Andie mumbles something and turns over, falling back to sleep immediately. I make some coffee and take it out of the deck. The morning is crisp and clear, the night moisture still on the trees as I dial Cameron Brody's cell phone number. No answer. I listen to it switch over to voice mail and leave a message for him to call me as soon as he can.

Okay, relax, I think. He's probably turned it off, still asleep, charging the phone. Something. But by the time Andie gets up there's still no word.

"He probably got in late, still asleep," she says, echoing my thoughts, but it's nearly noon before he calls.

"Evan?" Just the way he says my name tells me something is wrong.

"What is it?" There's a long pause before he answers.

"Oh shit, man."

"What?"

"They got my phone, my computer. The tapes were in the computer bag."

"Are you serious? Who?"

"I sat it down for a minute to pay for some coffee, turned around and it was gone." I flash back on him doing the same thing when we ran into Otis James in New York.

I grip the phone tighter and sigh. "Where are you now?"

"I'm at my folks place in Tiburon." He gives me directions I scribble down quickly. "I'll be there as soon as I can."

"I'm sorry, Evan."
"Yeah, so am I."

It takes us over an hour to get through San Rafael where the traffic is backed up for the Richmond Bridge. We finally break through, faster now, through Corte Madera and the turnoff on 131 to Tiburon. Following Cameron's directions we climb up the hill into an estate area of multimillion dollar homes. There are speed bumps, no trespassing notices, and alarm company signs in practically every yard as I look for the house number.

"Jesus," Andie says, looking at the houses. "Who is this guy?"

I find the corner house and park in front. We open a huge wooden gate and walk up to the front door and ring the bell. Andie looks around, peering in the window. "I don't see anybody," she says.

We walk around the side of the house, down some steps, past a garage. Perched on the slope in back is a small guest house or studio of some kind. From where we're standing, we can see both the city and the Golden Gate Bridge partially shrouded in fog.

"In there," I say, pointing to the guest house. We drop down another level to a flagstone sidewalk. Cameron must have seen us coming because he's standing in the door way.

He sticks out his hand. We shake and I introduce him to Andie. He nods at her, shaking his head. "I feel so stupid. Come on in."

He looks like he hasn't had much sleep, as he flops down on a couch under a window that duplicates the view of San Francisco and the bridge.

"So what happened?"

He shrugs. "I don't know, man. It happened so fast, no more than a few seconds."

Andie stands looking at him. "Somebody from the flight?"

"I don't know."

"Has to be, unless you were farther in the terminal."

"That's right," Brody says, "but I'd cleared the gate. I was almost to the street. I stopped for coffee, set the bag down for a second." He shrugs. "When I turned around it was gone."

"Well, could be anybody then. Laptop theft is common these days," Andie says. She looks at me, sees my growing disappointment. "I'm sorry, Evan. He won't see it again."

She turns to Cameron, all business now. "What else was in the case?"

"Laptop, my phone, some papers, business cards...the tapes."

"What numbers are on the cards?"

"Home, cell number, ASCAP office, and this one."

"Who lives here?"

"My parents," Brody says. "I crash here sometimes, but I have an apartment in Berkeley. Just got tired of living at home."

Andie looks out the window again. "Why? Jesus, what a view?"

I look at Andie. "Got any ideas?"

"No. He didn't see who did it. If it had been in arrivals, we could check the passenger list, but—" She pauses a moment. "Maybe it was someone on the flight. Maybe they followed you off the plane, waited for the right moment and—"

"Can you do that," I ask Andie, "check the passenger list?"

Cameron buries his face in his hands. "I can't believe I did that."

"Not your fault," I say, but I know I'm not convincing. The three of us don't speak for several moments, then the phone rings on the desk and breaks the silence.

Cameron lets it ring several times before picking it up. "Yeah?" He sits up straighter, looking at us, his eyes wide. "Who is this?"

Andie looks at the phone, presses the speaker button and motions to Cameron.

"I said, are you missing something," the high pitched, flat, monotone voice says, like something computer generated.

"Yes," Cameron says.

"What are you missing?"

"My laptop computer."

Andie circles her hand in the air, signaling Cameron to keep him talking.

"What else are you missing?" Each word is deliberate, slow, measured.

"Some papers, business cards, tapes," Cameron says.

"What is on the tapes?"

"Music."

"Do you want them back?"

"Yes, yes of course. What do you want?"

"I will call again." Then he hangs up.

Cameron replaces the phone. "What the fuck was that?"

Andie sits down, looks at Cameron. "It's somebody who knows you, knows what you do. What's on the laptop?"

"But the voice?"

Andie says, "Anybody can buy a device like that at Radio Shack. That or it's some computer generated software hooked up to his phone. What's on the laptop?"

Cameron shrugs. "Database, ASCAP files, accounts, personal stuff, phone numbers, you know." Andie frowns at him, not understanding ASCAP. Cameron gives her a quick sketch of ASCAP and what he does.

"Tell her about the guy that stole your computer in New York."

Cameron looks at me. "You think it's the same guy?"

"What guy in New York?" Andie asks.

Cameron tells her about the theft, the mugging, getting the laptop back from the police, talking to the homeless guy Boomer who saw the thief smash the computer and throw it in the dumpster.

"Okay," Andie says. "Slow down, tell me again." She makes him tell the whole story again, step by step, then she looks at me. "You weren't with him?"

"No," I say, "just when we went to the police and talked to the homeless guy."

Andie gets up and paces around for a couple of minutes, then stops and turns back to me. "He doesn't want your tapes, they were just there."

Cameron and I both look at her, not understanding.

"He's going to call back and demand money."

While we sit and wait, Andie gets Cameron's ticket and calls the airlines and asks for the supervisor. "This is FBI Special Agent Andrea Lawrence, San Francisco Bureau." She recites her identification number. "We're investigating the movements of a subject on the Homeland Security No Fly List. I need the manifest for your Flight 216, New York to San Francisco."

She listens for a moment. "I know the flight arrived last night." She puts her hand over the phone and looks around. "Do you have a fax?" she asks Cameron.

He nods. "In the main house." He writes the number down for her and she repeats it, relaying it to the airline supervisor."

"Yes, as soon as possible," she says into the phone. "Thanks, we appreciate your cooperation." She hangs up and looks at Cameron. "I want to see if you recognize any of the names."

"Andie, don't you need some authorization for this?" I ask.

She just waves me off. "Don't worry about it." She holds out her hand. "The key. Where is the fax?"

Cameron takes out a ring of keys and shows her the one for the house. "The fax is in the study on the second floor, but there's an alarm, just inside the door." He scribbles down the code and hands her the key.

"Are your parents coming back anytime soon?"

"No, they're in Europe."

Andie nods. "Evan, you stay here. If our guy calls back, come get me." She heads for the door and we watch her walk back up to the house and go inside.

"Man, she doesn't mess around, does she?" Cameron says.

"You have no idea."

Twenty minutes later, she's back with several pages of fax copy. "Nice house," she says. She hands the fax pages to Cameron. "Take a look."

Cameron sits down and starts going over the manifest. I glance over his shoulder. There are 287 names.

"Let's go outside for a minute," Andie says to me.

We go outside and stand, looking toward the Bay. "Andie, it isn't worth it. What happens if the bureau gets word of this?"

She shrugs. "I get a reprimand, my hand slapped. If they do I tell them I had to act fast on a tip. I'll think of something."

"Yeah, right, Rollins would love that."

She turns and looks right at me, her eyes blazing. "Fuck Rollins. The only time I want to see his face again is if it's on a milk carton."

We turn as Cameron taps on the window and motions us inside. We go back in. He's circled one of the names and points to it. "This one I know."

Andie and I both look. "Edward Solano? Who is he?" Andie asks. The name means nothing to either of us.

"Yeah. Slow Hands Eddie. Played in a few bad rock bands in the eighties but wrote a lot of songs, although authorship was never confirmed. He sent a bunch of letters to ASCAP complaining about it and was finally turned down. Case was pending for a long time."

"So now he wants his money. Do you remember how much he supposedly had coming?"

Cameron shrugs. "Not for sure but I know it wasn't that much. Few thousand maybe. All the info is on my laptop."

"This guy is squirrelly. He's going to call back with a precise amount I bet," Andie says. She looks at me. "Would he have any idea of what's on your tapes or what they would be worth?"

"I don't see how. Nobody knew they even existed till a week ago."

"Well let's hope he doesn't check them out," Andie says.

"Or just throw them away," Cameron says. "You're right. This guy is on a mission. His letters to ASCAP got pretty ugly."

We wait another half hour, talking over possibilities and then the phone rings again. Cameron answers, keeping it on the speaker. "Hello?"

Again, it's the computerized voice. "You owe me $14,564." Andie motions Cameron again to keep him talking "If you had done your job, you could have just written a check. Now you will bring cash."

"Who is this?" Cameron asks again. "How do I know you have this money coming? I have to check with the office to verify the account."

"No, no office. You just bring me the money."

"I can't do that," Cameron says. "I have to know who you are." As he talks, Cameron scribbles a question for Andie. Do I tell him I know? She shakes her head.

"You know who I am. You know I've been cheated. I'm tired of waiting. I just want what's mine."

Andie nods at Cameron. "All right, I'll check with the office. I need some time."

"You have until tomorrow morning at nine o'clock. I will call again."

Before Cameron can answer, the line goes dead and he switches off the speaker.

"Now what?" Cameron says.

"He's worried about a trace," Andie says, "but there's no way we can do that, not from here."

Cameron looks at us both. "I can get the money."

I pace around thinking. Andie jeopardizing her job, Cameron having to account to ASCAP, it's too much to risk. "Forget it," I say. "It's not worth it. You can write off the laptop. I have the CDs. That's enough." But they both overrule me.

"No," Cameron says. "This was my fault. I have to make good."

Andie says, "I told you not to worry about the bureau. They won't even know, but there's something else we have to think about."

"What?" Cameron says.

"When he calls back he's going to want you to meet him someplace—alone, probably someplace bad, or possibly a very public place, which for us would be better."

I look at Andie. "What are you thinking?"

"Don't fight me on this, Evan. I can't let Cameron meet this guy alone. It's too dangerous."

"Andie—"

She holds up her hand. "That's it. It's not going down any other way. Let's wait and see what he says. If he wants to meet somewhere public, that's the best case scenario, and he might. I don't think he's experienced in this. I can stake it out. He doesn't know me and we don't know if he's seen you."

Looking at Cameron, I can see his mind reeling. He's never been here, but I have. I just listen, knowing there's no stopping Andie now. She wants to make up for the doubt I had about her over Rollins, the file. This is her way.

She grabs her purse. "You stay here, Cameron, just in case he calls sooner." Then she turns to me. "Evan, I need you to take me home."

I nod. I know what that means. She wants her gun.

Driving back into the city, we don't say much. Andie, I know is working things out in her head. We stop at a coffee shop for dinner and she makes me run through the whole story from finding Cameron on his front step when I came back from Boston, going with him to the police precinct to get the computer, talking with the homeless guy, who was the one witness, the whole thing. She just nods, not interrupting me. When our order comes, she digs in without looking up for several minutes, then smiles at me.

"You know, it feels good to be involved with something," she says, "even unofficially."

Despite my misgivings, I feel the rush of adrenaline. I know exactly what she means. "If something goes wrong it will be official," I say watching her. But she ignores my comment. She's pumped, excited, calling on her instincts.

"I'll deal with that when it happens. One more thing, You didn't have the tapes yet did you, when Cameron was mugged?"

"No, that was after."

"Okay." She finishes eating and signals the waitress for more coffee. "It's not likely he knows anything about them, right?"

"If he's who Cameron thinks he is, no. Sounds like a rock and roller. Even if he played them, and that's very unlikely, I doubt if he'd know what they were."

"Why unlikely?"

"He'd need an old style reel-to-reel tape recorder to play them. It's all digital now, CD players, cassette, downloading from computers."

Andie nods, as if confirming her own thoughts. "You ready to get out of here?"

"Yeah, sure." I stand up and grab the check.

She touches my arm. "Relax, Evan. I know what I'm doing."

At Andie's apartment, there's a note taped to her door. She grabs it, shows it to me. It's from Ted Rollins, wanting her to call. He's underlined urgent.

We go inside. She picks up the phone and dials. "Rollins? It's Andie." I watch her roll her eyes and hold the phone away from her ear a few inches. I can hear Rollins' voice angrily booming through the phone.

"Look, Ted, settle down. I was just following up on something I'd heard about." More static from Rollins, then. "Yes I'm home now. I was down at the river with Evan." She sighs with exasperation. "I know I'm still on medical leave. That doesn't mean I can't go out or make a couple of calls. No, you don't have to remind me. Goodbye."

She slams down the phone and looks at me. "The airline guy called the bureau for confirmation on my I.D." She shrugs. "It got back to Rollins. I'm a bad girl."

"Is he going to push it?"

"No, I don't think so."

"Andie—"

"Don't. Let me handle this. We're going to get your tapes back." She goes to her desk and opens her laptop. "I need some time, okay? Watch a movie or something."

I don't argue. I turn on the TV and find an old movie. *The Friends of Eddie Coyle*, with Robert Mitchum and Peter Boyle. One of the characters is an FBI agent, pressuring Mitchum for information on bank robberies in exchange for a lighter sentence. In the end, it doesn't work, everything goes all wrong for Mitchum and he's killed. Not very reassuring.

As the credits roll, my cell phone rings. It's Cameron.

Andie looks up from her computer as I answer. I listen for a minute as he tells me Solano called back. "He wants me to be at a Borders Book store in San Rafael at ten thirty tomorrow morning."

Andie gets up and walks over. "Wait, tell Andie." I hand her the phone.

"Cameron? Tell me exactly what he said." She listens for a couple of minutes, nods then, "Okay, I'll be there but don't under any circumstances acknowledge me, understand?" She listens again. "Okay, here's Evan."

She hands me the phone. "He wants to talk to you again."

"Evan? Is this going to work?"

"Let's hope so. See you tomorrow." I end the call and look at Andie. She punches the air with her fist. "Yes, yes, yes," she says. "This is perfect. A very public place, lots of people. We let him make the contact with Cameron and we've got him."

"If he brings the computer," I say.

"Oh, he'll bring it. He wants his money."

"I'm going too, right?"

She smiles. "Of course. You're going to be my date."

I go through the motions of trying to talk her out of it, get her to turn it over to the bureau, let them handle it, but it's no go. Andie wants this bust herself, and I realize it's not all to get my tapes back. She can prove she's ready for field work again if she pulls it off.

I try to play devil's advocate, suggesting a number of things that could go wrong, Cameron could panic, give it away, the guy could freak out. We don't know if he's coming armed. The list is long but Andie doesn't buy any of it.

She listens, nods, but in the end, nothing changes. "It's very sweet of you to worry so much, but I know we can make this work. I know no matter what you say, you want those tapes back. Evan, that's your real father playing on those tapes."

She has me there and she knows it.

Chapter Seventeen

We pull into the Borders parking lot in San Rafael just after nine thirty. The cavernous book store anchors the sprawling strip mall, and there are the usual other smaller shops—a deli, a mattress store, and a tiny cafe that advertises internet connections. The parking lot is about half full of cars, early shoppers getting a jump on things.

Andie is dressed casually in jeans, sweatshirt, running shoes, and sun glasses. Just another young woman dragging her boyfriend out for some early browsing. The difference with Andie is she has a gun tucked in her shoulder bag.

There are several tables in front, an extension of the coffee bar just inside the double glass doors. Given the number of cars in the lot, it's less crowded than I imagined. "Go look at some books," Andie says. "I want to see if there's a rear entrance."

"Yes, ma'am," I say, giving her a mock salute. I wander through the bargain tables where best sellers from three months ago are going for $6.95. Even Stephen King and John Grisham are there. In the mystery section, I skim titles, picking up a book now and then, pausing at a display of a new novel by Michael Connelly, one of Cal's favorites. I also periodically check the entrance for any sign of Cameron Brody, then gradually work my way back to the coffee area. There are only a few people sipping morning lattes and poring over magazines and newspapers, but business is picking up fast.

I spot Andie surveying the area, taking the measure of the place where Cameron is supposed to meet our guy. I circle around Andie and make for the information booth near the center of the store just as Cameron Brody comes through the double glass doors, a small manila envelope in his hand.

He flicks a glance at me for just a moment, then continues on toward the coffee area. I catch Andie's eye, nod toward Cameron. She nods back and I go outside for a cigarette, standing off to the side, behind a pillar by a large concrete barrel filled with sand. I glance at my watch. Just after ten. The parking lot is fast filling up now. I scan the cars, the people coming toward the store, looking for somebody with a laptop case slung over his shoulder. All I want now is for this to be over.

Despite Andie's assurances and enthusiasm, there are too many variables, too many things that can go wrong. The whole thing is crazy but we're here now and committed. Tapes or not, I almost hope the guy doesn't show up.

I put my cigarette out and turn to go back inside when somebody tugs on my arm.

I turn and see Ted Rollins, wearing his usual smirk. "Morning," he says, enjoying the surprise on my face.

"What are you doing here, Rollins?"

"I followed you here and I know Andie is inside. What's she doing?"

"Looking for a book I imagine."

"Cut the bullshit, Horne. I know she's up to something. She's already in trouble for that airline manifest stunt yesterday. Don't make it worse."

"I don't know what you're talking about."

"Good, then let's go inside and say hello."

He puts his hand on my elbow, as if he's going to escort me inside. I pull away from him. "I don't need any help," I say.

At the double glass door entrance, two young moms, pushing baby strollers the size of golf carts, are just coming out. I duck around them, leaving Rollins blocked long enough for me to get ahead of him. I duck down an aisle and circle around past the coffee bar. Cameron is seated at one table, looking around, trying I know, to be casual, but he's not making it. His eyes are darting everywhere and there's a light sheen of sweat on his forehead.

Andie is at an adjacent table, her back to me, a coffee in front of her, flipping through a magazine but not really looking at the pages. Rollins comes up, walking fast, looking up and down aisles, searching for Andie.

Cameron looks at me in panic, realizing this is not the plan. I'm not supposed to be there. I point to Andie, hoping he'll get the message I want her attention. He freezes for a moment, confused, then turns and taps on her shoulder. She turns, glances at him, then over his shoulder at me and glares. I point behind me with my thumb.

She turns and looks. Rollins is coming back fast, almost to the coffee bar area now, scanning the tables. Andie sees him at the same time he sees her. She gets up quickly, leaving her table at the very moment a short wiry guy with graying hair sits down with Cameron.

Rollins veers off to intercept Andie. He catches her by the arm and spins her around. The other people in the area look up at the disturbance, including the guy at Cameron's table. He looks at Cameron, confused, then gets up and bolts for the exit.

Rollins sees him and starts toward Cameron's table but Andie, furious, sticks out her foot and trips Rollins. He goes sprawling into a table of two women, who scream as coffee cups go flying and the table tips over. Rollins lands in a heap, coffee on his suit, trying to scramble to his feet, apologizing to the women, his eyes on our guy all at the same time.

By then, Eddie Solano is long gone.

"You fucking idiot," Andie says to Rollins. "That guy wasn't a terrorist. He was meeting with him." She points to Cameron Brody.

After Rollins' spill, the manager showed up, apologized to the women and demanded an explanation. Rollins had flashed his

I.D, said everything was under control, and we all went outside to the parking lot.

Rollins glares at Andie. "I know something was going down here and I want to know right now what it is."

Andie walks a few paces away then back. "I don't have to explain anything to you. What the hell were you doing following me anyway?"

A few people walking by glance at the four of us but keep going, walking slowly to their cars. So close I think, but now Rollins has blown the whole thing.

"You told the airlines supervisor he was on the no fly list. What do you think you're doing without authorization? I would have brought in backup and handled the whole thing."

"The guy was on the same flight." She points again to Cameron. "He picked up his laptop by mistake. We were just meeting here to get it back."

"Oh please," Rollins says. He turns, his feet planted, hands on his hips, coffee stains on his shirt and tie. "I need to see some identification," he says to Cameron.

"No," Andie says. She pushes Rollins away, out of earshot, and they walk between a row of parked cars.

"Now what?" Cameron says. "I don't care about the computer, but your tapes, man. Is she going to get in trouble for this?"

"She can handle him," I say. We watch as Rollins and Andie have stopped and Andie is shaking her finger in his face.

"He didn't have the computer," Cameron says, "unless it was in his car."

"I know. I think he wanted to check things out first. Andie could have taken him quietly right there in the coffee area if Rollins hadn't shown up. He followed us here."

I see Rollins saying something to Andie, then stomp off toward his car and get in. He rolls down the window, gives Andie a parting shot, and drives off, tires screeching. She watches him go and stalks back toward us, her eyes flashing.

"God, he's an asshole," Andie says. "He was sniffing around for a bust." She sighs and leans against a car and crosses her arms over her chest. "He's going to file a report on all this."

"I'm sorry," Cameron says. "This was all my fault."

"Forget it," Andie says. "He's bluffing. I told him he'd have to explain causing an incident and Borders was going to file a complaint. Besides, I'm in good standing. I got shot in the line of duty." She looks at me. "I also called him on mailing the file." Andie smiles as she says it. "You should have seen the look on his face."

Shocked because she knew or because he didn't know what she was talking about? I can't decide which it is.

"What file?" Cameron asks, but Andie doesn't answer him.

"Did you recognize the guy?" she asks Cameron.

"No," Cameron says. "But that must have been him. He just came in and sat down."

"Did he say anything?"

"He started to then, when he saw that guy crashing into the table, he jumped up and left. He didn't have the computer with him either. We've scared him off entirely but maybe he'll call back."

"Yeah," Andie says. "It's not over, but if he does call, it's going to be different now."

"Hey wait, guys," I say. "Let's let it go. It's too complicated now. Andie, you're going to get yourself suspended."

Andie looks at me, still angry about Rollins' intervention. "You know what? I don't really care. I'm so sick of working with jerks like Rollins."

"Andie, you don't mean that."

She lets her head fall forward. "Maybe," she says quietly. "Dammit, we almost had him. Did you have the money?" she asks Cameron.

"Yes," Cameron says. He takes the envelope out of his jacket pocket.

"Okay, here's what we do," she says. "It'll take Rollins time to stir up things, if he actually does. Let's wait and see if the guy calls back again. Then we'll go from there."

They both look at me. There's no stopping Andie, I can see that. She hates to fail and she's determined not to now. I shrug. "It's your call. I just hope you know what you're doing."

"I always know what I'm doing." She starts off back to the store. "I'll be right back," she calls over her shoulder.

"Man, she is something."

"You have no idea," I say.

"What was the file she was talking about?"

"It's a long story. Nothing to do with this. I'll tell you some-time maybe." I light a cigarette, looking around the parking lot. People are coming and going, totally unaware two FBI agents had clashed over an extortionist.

Andie comes back then. "I smoothed things over with the manager so he won't report anything. Let's go."

We all drive back to Tiburon and wait in the guest house, admiring the view, making small talk, trying not to check our watches every five minutes.

Now, I almost hope we don't get a call, tapes or not. Andie can finesse her way out of any trouble Rollins can cause her. No harm done so far. But half an hour later he does call, just after noon. This time the voice is not synthesized.

"I told you to come alone," the caller says. There's an edge to his voice now, a desperate note we can all hear. "Those were cops in Borders weren't they?"

"It was all a mistake," Cameron says.

"Yes, your mistake. Now we do it differently, and this is your last chance. If I don't get my money, you can forget your computer and I'll destroy those tapes. I don't care what's on them, understand?"

Andie listens and nods at Cameron.

"Yes, I understand."

"Good. Tonight then, at Hunters Point. Ten o'clock. Building C-128, by the water." Then he hangs up before Cameron can acknowledge.

Andie and Cameron both glance at each other. He hits the hang up button and we listen to the drone of a dial tone for a moment through the speaker.

I look at both of them. "What? What's Hunter's Point?"

"Worst possible place," Cameron says. "The old Navy Shipyard, right on the Bay. Mostly deserted now except for some artists who have leased a few buildings and made them into studios. It's very exposed, bad, dangerous area, especially at night. Lot of gang activity nearby."

"He's right," Andie says. "I've heard about it." Andie grabs her cell phone. "I'm going for a walk," she says. "I need to think about this. Have you got a map of the city?"

Cameron nods. "I think so." He shuffles through some papers and magazines on a book shelf and comes up with one from a car rental company.

"Good," Andie says, then she leaves.

I suggest to Cameron we go get some coffee. We get in my car and start down the hill. I see Andie walking, head down in measured steps. I pull alongside her and stop. "Hey, we're going for some coffee. Want me to bring you back something?"

She stops and looks up. "No, I'm fine. I'll get something later."

I drive on, watching Andie in the rearview mirror till she's out of sight. We find a coffee place Cameron knows near the waterfront and sit at the outside tables. We order coffee and some sweet rolls, listening to the water lap against the landing pier.

"She got shot?"

"She did, in a bank robbery that went wrong."

"Jesus," Cameron says. "She is tough."

"So tell me about Hunter's Point."

"There was a big write-up about it a few months ago." He goes on for several minutes telling me about the shipyard and its landlord, the U.S. Navy. There are about three or four hundred artists—painters, sculptors, some musicians—that have rented some of the old buildings and turned them into studios. Once a year they have a big art festival that draws thousands and that's where a lot of the artists make their money and connections for galleries around the city.

In addition, the San Francisco Police Department's crime lab occupies some buildings, as well as the SWAT team headquarters. There's also a railroad museum.

"The Navy has been required to clean it up before it can be transferred to the city so they have to tear up sewer lines, storm drains, and test for contamination. The yard had been used as a repair facility and decontamination of ships exposed to atomic weapons, so everybody leasing space is going to have to move out. The shipyard was deactivated in the mid seventies. A lot of testing has been done since then and only low levels of radioactive materials have been found. Once it's cleaned up, the city is taking over and planning on turning it into commercial and retail space, parks, housing, but that will take years."

"So at night, it's deserted huh?"

"Pretty much, and I imagine a very spooky place," Cameron says. "I have an artist friend who was there for awhile. I went during the day to visit him. It's weird. All the old navy signs are still on the buildings. It's like a ghost town, going back in time. The artists who rent are not supposed to sleep over there but it's not very well enforced."

"This guy must know it or he would never have decided to meet there."

"I was thinking the same thing," Cameron says. "He even gave me a building number. He either has friends there or has spent some time."

I look out over the water. The ferry from San Francisco is just pulling in. "So, open, deserted for the most part, abandoned buildings. Not a great place to meet some guy to exchange money for a laptop computer."

"No," Cameron says. "I don't think we should do it. Fuck man, I don't want to go down there at night."

"Let's wait and see what Andie says."

We drive back to the house and find Andie waiting, studying the map. She has it folded open to show the area around Hunter's Point.

"What's this?" she asks Cameron, pointing to a square with a star alongside it just outside the navy yard.

"Restaurant. Been there forever. Pretty famous at one time, but I don't remember the name."

Andie nods and paces around for a couple of minutes. She turns and looks at us, her face set and determined.

"Okay, here's what we're going to do."

Chapter Eighteen

I'm still not used to the change in weather that happens so suddenly in San Francisco. Driving down 101 from Tiburon, it's cool but clear, a three quarter moon competing with freeway and car lights. But as we come out of the Waldo tunnel, down the incline, the Golden Gate Bridge is shrouded in a bank of fog, and the temperature has dropped twenty degrees.

Andie and I are in her Ford; Cameron Brody's BMW is just ahead of us as we cross the bridge and pull into one of the toll booth lanes. I pay the five dollars and follow Cameron as we head into the city. We stay on the two-lane divided road then drop down to Bay Street and turn on to the Embarcadero, past the Ferry Building, and continue on, skirting AT&T Park, the Giants baseball stadium. Cameron turns left on Third Street and I follow. He knows the way but Andie keeps checking the map.

At Evans Avenue, we turn left and pass through an older area of boarded up shops, buildings under construction, deserted office buildings and the occasional neon of a convenience store lighting the dark street. At the end of Evans, we make a little jog left near the entrance to the navy yard. Cameron pulls over by the curb. I park behind him and watch as he gets out and walks back to our car.

"I don't think there's anyone in the guard shack," he says.

"Good," Andie says. If there was, she had planned to flash her FBI credentials to gain entrance. "Pull in the restaurant parking lot."

Cameron nods and goes back to his car and pulls in the lot. I park next to him. We go inside and sit at the bar, Andie between me and Cameron. We order three draft beers and look around. The walls of Dago Mary's are covered with black and white, framed photos from decades earlier. There's lots of oak paneling, ornate carving, done during the restaurant's better days, but Cameron says it's still a popular place.

Now that we're actually here, I have even more reservations about Andie's plan. She's going to ride in with Cameron on the floor by the back seat, wait for the exchange to happen, then take Solano. She'd already grilled Cameron about Hunters Point.

"If he's coming, he's probably already here. For all we know, he's friendly with somebody in there that has a studio," she says. "He wouldn't have picked this place if he didn't know it well. You," she tells me, "are going to stay here. Just in case."

"Just in case what?"

"I don't know. We'll have to play it by ear. Just keep your cell phone on. Once we have him, I'll call you."

"Be right back," Cameron says. He gets up and heads for the Men's room.

Andie watches him go. "Is he going to be okay?"

"Yeah, I think so." I look at Andie. I can see she's pumped, ready for action, dressed in dark jeans, a black sweatshirt and running shoes. "Look, Andie, maybe we should just bail on this. We don't know enough about this guy, what he's going to do. There are too many variables."

She shakes her head. "No, we're here, we're going to do it." She pats my arm. "We're going to get those tapes." She sees the doubt on my face. "Don't worry, it'll be all right."

"Somebody probably said that to General Custer too." Andie just rolls her eyes.

Cameron comes back, looking okay, not nervous, but I can imagine what's going on in his mind.

Andie studies her watch. "Okay," she says. "Let's do it."

We pay the check and go outside." Andie gets in the back seat of Cameron's BMW, and scoots down on the floor. She gives me a little wave as I shut the door. Cameron gets in, nods at me and drives off. I watch the car slowly cruise past the darkened guard shack, and bear right. I watch until the tail lights disappear, then turn back.

This is the part I hate, the waiting. I light a cigarette and pace around the parking lot. A few people come out of the restaurant going to their cars, but nobody pays any attention or even looks at me. Next to the restaurant is a small shop that's closed now. I stand close to the street, in the doorway, but no cars approach for the next twenty minutes.

What if Solano doesn't show? Maybe he decided after the fiasco at Borders, it was too risky, but Andie is probably right. He's already there, waiting. I play out all kinds of worst case scenarios in my mind and grip my cell phone tightly, willing it to ring.

The restaurant parking lot is emptying out now as they start to close up for the night. I check my watch again, then see a car coming off Evans Avenue, heading for the entrance to the Navy Yard. I move back deeper in the doorway of the shop. I don't know what kind of car Solano has, but I bet it's not a tan Ford Taurus. As it passes me, I see the driver's face clearly for a second. Ted Rollins.

Shit. How did he know? I watch him pass the guard shack, then brake and make a U-turn, and pull into the parking lot, stopping behind Andie's car. He sits for a minute, engine idling, like he can't decide what to do. The lot is almost empty now. Finally, he exits the parking lot and turns toward the Naval Yard.

I run for my car, jump in and follow Rollins, my lights off, staying back far enough to just keep his taillights in sight. He circles around several buildings, all with numbers on them, obviously not sure where he's going, but eventually, he comes out in a flat area with huge spaces between the large warehouse type buildings that are silhouetted in the moonlight. Across the bay I can see the winking lights of Oakland and the Bay Bridge looming in the distance, traffic going back and forth, the cars looking like toys.

The taillights on Rollins' car brighten as he brakes, then starts again, driving between two of the big buildings. One of them has a weak light mounted on the roof, trained on large block letters on a yellow background. C-128. Submarine Cafeteria. Damn, how did Rollins know?

I park behind another building and get out and circle behind Rollins, looking for Andie, not sure if she's still in Cameron's car or already inside the building. I watch for a minute as Rollins approaches the car and looks inside. He glances around then cautiously heads for the entrance to the building. I start to follow him when I feel a hand on my arm. I jump and turn to see Andie, gun in hand, crouching behind me.

"What are you doing here?" she whispers. "I told you to wait at the restaurant."

"Rollins is here," I say. I point to the building.

"What?"

We both look toward the building. Rollins must have heard something as he flattens himself against the wall at the other end of the building. The door opens and Cameron and Eddie Solano come walking out, heading for Cameron's car. I can't see anything clearly but Solano's hand on Cameron's arm.

Andie stands up and starts running toward them.

"FBI Special Agent," she yells.

Rollins, whirls around toward her at the same time he sees Solano and Cameron. He starts toward them, gun drawn.

"No!" Andie screams, but she's too late. Rollins is sprinting toward Eddie Solano like a defensive back closing on for an interception. Cameron crouches then drops to the ground. Solano freezes for a moment, then starts running toward the retaining wall by the water.

A few steps behind Andie, I stop, then she does too, her arm dropping, her gun to her side. We both freeze, watching helplessly as Eddie "Slow Hands" Solano, trying to dodge Rollins, trips, falls back, his arms flying out to his sides, the shoulder strap of the computer bag slipping off his arm and racing through the air toward the water.

It's as if I'm seeing everything in slow motion. Ted Rollins lurches out to grab for Solano, realizing too late he's on the edge. His knee hits the low wall, the momentum propels him forward, arms and legs flailing, as he goes over the side.

Ted Rollins, Eddie Solano, Cameron's laptop, all plunging into the water.

And inside that bag, my tapes. The only documented recording of the *Birth of the Cool* rehearsals, right along with them, splashing into San Francisco Bay.

Cameron Brody and I sit on a couple of wooden crates watching the area around Building C-128 become a scene from a television crime show. A few members of the San Francisco SWAT team pace around mumbling curses, helmets tilted back on their heads, their rifles slung over their shoulders now, awaiting orders to disperse.

What must be ten or twelve squad cars, lights still flashing, ring the area. Someone has set up a couple of klieg lights facing the retaining wall where Rollins and Solano went over the side. I can see them both huddled on the ground, blankets wrapped around them after being fished out by two uniformed officers.

Andie is standing, shifting her weight from one foot to the other, listening to a tirade from a tall heavyset man in jeans and a dark wind breaker with FBI in yellow letters on the back, glaring at her and pointing to Rollins.

"I want to know what the fuck was going down here and somebody better tell me damn quick," he says, his voice booming out over the water. "I've got a senior agent splashing around in the Bay with a has been blues singer over some goddamn laptop computer and some recording tapes fifty years old." He takes a breath and looks around at the chaos. "I've got the fucking SFPD SWAT team here, and an agent who is on medical leave, apparently responsible for the whole thing. Jesus!" He turns and walks a few paces away, then whirls on Andie again.

"God dammit, Lawrence, talk to me."

"I think that's my cue," I say to Cameron. I get up and walk over. "Excuse me," I say. "I think I can help clear this up."

Andie flashes me a look. "Stay out of this, Evan," Andie says.

"Who the fuck are you?" the big man says to me.

"Evan Horne. The tapes, are, were, mine. I simply came down here to get them back when your man Rollins showed up and interfered with the exchange."

"How do you know Special Agent Rollins?"

"Through Wendell Cook in your Los Angeles office."

"Wendell Cook?" He looks at me for a moment, his eyes squinting, then some flicker of recognition washes over his face. "Are you the guy who...the Gillian Payne case a couple of years ago—"

"That would be me."

Out of the corner of my eye I catch Andie shaking her head and sighing.

"If you call Agent Cook, I'm sure he'll vouch for me. This has just been a big misunderstanding all around."

The big man looks down, scrapes his foot on the asphalt, like he's about to step into the batters box. He nods, turns and walks away, then turns back. "Agent Lawrence, I'll want to see you in the morning, my office."

"Yes, sir," Andie says. She takes something out of her pocket and hands it to her boss. "I think this belongs to Agent Rollins." He shakes his head and walks away.

She looks at me and shakes her head. "You are something else," she says, but manages a slight smile.

"What was that?"

"Tracking device. It was under the bumper of my car. That's how he knew where we were."

"Hey," somebody yells. "It's one of the two divers that arrived earlier." He pulls himself up and over the edge on the wall, his rubber suit glistening in the moonlight, clutching Cameron's laptop bag by the strap. "Got it," he says.

He holds it up, water dripping and pooling on the asphalt around his fins, the mask pulled up on his forehead. Cameron gets up and walks over, taking it from him. He looks at me and shrugs.

We all watch as Eddie Solano is handcuffed and put in one of the police cruisers. Rollins is right behind him, escorted to a waiting FBI car.

"This isn't over, Horne," he says as he walks by. His clothes are dripping water, his hair plastered to his head. He points at Andie. "You, you're finished Lawrence," he snaps at Andie, then he's gone.

Things start breaking up then. Car doors slam, engines start, the lights are taken down as Andie, Cameron, and I walk to our cars. Cameron throws the water logged laptop in the trunk. There's nothing for any of us to say now.

"Talk to you," he says, and gets in his car and drives off. Andie and I go to her car and I wind slowly back toward the main entrance, not wanting to talk, not wanting to think. When we get to the guard shack it's manned now. They must have shaken awake whoever should have been on duty. Cameron's car is in front of us, the doors and trunk lid open. Suddenly security conscious, the guard, flashlight in hand, is going through everything.

Cameron glances toward us and puts his hands out in a helpless shrug as the guard lifts the wet laptop case out of the trunk. I roll down the window and hear the guard tell Cameron to open it and take the computer out.

"Oh for Christ's sake," Cameron says but complies with the guard's instructions. He unzips the case and pulls out the laptop, then opens the side pocket with his cell phone and the tapes. I stare in morbid fascination as Cameron holds them up. He studies them for a moment, then turns to me and yells. "Evan!"

I get out and walk to his car, Andie right beside me. "Jesus," he says. "Look."

Just like the CDs that Buzz had sent FedEx, the tapes are shrink wrapped and encased in zip lock bags. Cameron unzips one of the bags and holds the tape up to the guard's flashlight.

Then we both smile. The guard looks confused but Cameron, Andie, and I all smile.

"Yes!" Cameron says.

Thank you, Buzz. The tapes are bone dry. Not a drop of water on them.

Coda

"Sure looks different in the daytime doesn't it?" Cameron Brody says.

We're standing on the sidewalk, just outside the Hunters Point Naval Yard, looking toward the guard shack. It's manned now, and after what happened there it probably will be all the time.

"Yeah, it does." We can see past the shack at the collections of buildings, old structures that housed Navy personnel at one time. Further on, the dark water where ships once docked, and the span of the Bay Bridge, filled now with traffic on both decks.

We turn and walk back to Dago Mary's restaurant and go inside. It's crowded, but we find a table out on the patio and order the lunch special.

"Andie is meeting us here?" Cameron asks.

"Yeah, she had another meeting at the Bureau, kind of winding things up, but the review board gave her a clean pass on the bank robbery shooting. Today is more about her and Rollins and what happened here."

It's been nearly two weeks since Rollins and Eddie Solano went in the Bay along with Cameron's computer and my tapes. Things had settled down considerably since then. I was even finally getting my mind around Dana's death.

Coop had followed up with his contacts at Hollywood police. Brent Sergent confirmed he had coerced Dana to help him get me to sell Cal's house, exploiting the relationship they'd had earlier. She'd gone along with it at first, but later balked and refused to cooperate further.

"She just got caught up in things with the wrong guy," Coop said.

Her status as a UCLA grad student was genuine, and her family had come out to take her back to Iowa for the funeral. They wanted to prosecute Sergent, but Coop didn't think it would fly. Tragic, but an accident nevertheless. It would never go away completely, but I was dealing with the finality that she was just gone.

The waitress brings our order and we dig into thick hamburgers and a pile of fries. "You're right, the food is good."

Cameron nods. "Yeah imagine what this place was like sixty years ago." He looks up and waves then. "Hey, here comes the FBI."

I turn and see Andie standing at the entrance to the dining room waving back. She comes over, eyeing our plates, kisses me lightly and sits down. She's dressed smartly in a dark pants suit and white blouse.

"So, tell us. How'd it go?" I ask.

Andie puts both hands on the table and looks at us, a grin spreading over her face. "How'd it go? It went fucking great!" She looks around for the waitress. "God, I'm hungry."

She orders what we have and still grinning, looks at us. "The best part is Rollins got reamed for unauthorized use of a tracking device, and transferred. With any luck to North Dakota." She sits up straighter and beams. "I, on the other hand, have been reassigned to active duty."

"So you're a good girl again," I say.

"Well there was, shall we say, somewhat of a reprimand, but nothing serious."

"Congratulations." Cameron joins in with me.

"Thank you gentlemen." She looks at Cameron. "Eddie Solano has been arraigned too. New York waived extradition for the assault charge, so it'll all happen here."

Cameron had already made a statement to the police. He frowns. "You know," he says, "I feel kind of sorry for him in a way. He did have that money coming."

"Maybe so, but that wasn't the way to get it." Andie says. "He'll be doing some time."

I'd thought about Solano too, what the waiting had done to him, knowing his song had been recorded and unable to collect the royalties. He'd gone over the edge but in a way I could almost understand. The same could have happened to Cal but he turned the frustration in on himself.

"Hey," Andie adds, seeing Cameron's face. "It's a first offense. It might not be too hard on him."

Cameron nods and finishes his hamburger without looking up.

Andie gives me a puzzled look, but I just shrug. Things were finally almost back to normal. I'd started to get a trio together and was doing some gigs locally, hanging out at Niki's Deli in Crockett on Sundays, and enjoying the quiet of Monte Rio. I'd already had some feelers from Yoshi's, the Bay Area's premier jazz club. The release of the Roy Haynes CD should help things along nicely. I'd played and replayed my two tracks and was very satisfied with the final mix.

Cameron had done more checking for me on the *Birth of the Cool* band, but it was pretty definite that Cal had not penned any of the tunes. It was disappointing but deep down I knew it was true, and I did have the tapes. It was enough for me to know and have proof that Cal played a small role. I hadn't told Andie or Cameron about the call from Dan Morgenstern.

"The Institute of Jazz Studies is interested in the tapes and how I came into them," I tell them. "They want to add them to their collection, and have me tape the story for their oral history collection."

"Awesome," Cameron says. "Another little piece of jazz history falls into place."

"Oh, sweetie, that's wonderful," Andie says. She squeezes my hand.

"Did you hear about the Monk and Coltrane discovery?" Cameron asks.

"No. What was it?"

"Wait," Andie says. "That's Thelonious Monk and John Coltrane?"

"Exactly," Cameron says.

Andie beams and nods toward me.

"At Carnegie Hall in 1957. It was originally done as a Voice of America broadcast, but it was never aired. Somebody going through some old tapes found a box just marked. T. Monk."

"Amazing."

"So jazz things get lost too," Andie says, smiling, looking at me.

We hadn't talked about it anymore, but we both assumed Rollins had mailed me the file on Cal. His non denial when Andie had called him on it was proof enough for me. As for the blacked out lines, well, we'd never know and it didn't matter now.

I'd called my mother and had a couple of long talks to assure her I was okay with things and update her a little. She'd sounded pleased but I was still digesting everything I'd learned, not sure when I'd really have it all together, getting used to the idea that Richard Horne was not my real father. I may not ever. That seems to be more difficult than accepting Cal. I know though, that Richard is right. I may have come from a different name, a different father, but I'm still who I am, and I can live with that.

We finish lunch and walk out to the parking lot, all of us instinctively glancing again at the guard shack at the entrance to the Naval Yard one last time.

"Well, I'm outta here," Cameron says. We shake hands and he hugs Andie. "Stay in touch. Let me know where you're playing."

"Will do." He gets in his car and we watch him drive off.

"I want to spend the rest of the week in Monte Rio," I tell Andie.

"Me too," she says. "Now I can really relax. I'll be down later. Just have to do a few things at home."

◇◇◇

I sit upstairs in the loft, the headphones on, listening to the tapes one last time before I pack them up to send to the Institute of Jazz at Rutgers University. A light rain coats the redwood trees and trickles down the glass, and I can hear a steady tapping on the sky lights. Fall is definitely here now as I feel the chill in the air.

The CD copies are better quality of course, but somehow for me, not the same as the actual tapes, the raw recordings. Miles Davis, the band, and Calvin on piano. Maybe it's just watching those plastic reels slowly turn. I'd managed to borrow an old reel to reel recorder to listen to them again.

I glance out the window and see Andie's car turn into the driveway, then the front door opens and I hear her footsteps on the stairs. Milton raises his head off my foot and perks up his big floppy ears.

I switch off the recorder and walk down to the living room, thinking how I like the idea that the tapes will be at Rutgers, making Calvin Hughes at least a footnote in jazz history.

I think my father would like that.

To receive a free catalog of Poisoned Pen Press titles, please contact us in one of the following ways:

Phone: 1-800-421-3976
Facsimile: 1-480-949-1707
Email: info@poisonedpenpress.com
Website: www.poisonedpenpress.com

Poisoned Pen Press
6962 E. First Ave. Ste. 103
Scottsdale, AZ 85251